PRAISE FOR
PINNED UP

I absolutely love a book that has a perfect mixture of everything! Pinned Up was funny, sad, edgy, witty, stressful, happy, sexy, exciting, etc...I really had a great time reading it!

—Julienne from The Bookaholix Club

C. Michelle weaves in witty lines and heart stopping moments with her more than sizzling romance to bring in a novel that is completely full of entertainment. And while this book was fun and flirty, it was not without darkness, betrayal, twists, and shocking revelations.

—Jessirae from Words, Pages, and Books

So, we have a great setting, a diverse and interesting cast of characters, a bit of romance paired with a side of angst, and then come some surprising twists and turns that really bring this plot to life, providing intrigue and intensity. Overall, this is a quirky, romantic, exciting, and enjoyable read.

—Gillian from Tattooed Book Review

All in all if you don't read this book you are missing out. If the idea of having this gorgeous cover on your bookshelf doesn't persuade you then let it be known that this book had me ugly cry, twice. But I also ugly laughed and chewed my nails down to mere stumps. If that doesn't interest you nothing will.

—Jade Goodmore (Author of Forget Me Not and Winter Blues)

I will say that if you liked Beautiful Bastard, Bared to You, Pieces of Lies, Tangled and Dark Light you'll like Pinned up! Why? Because Nina reminds me of the females in each of those books. Strong, smart, independent, beautiful and feisty! I love that about a female character And oh my God that mouth of hers, I LOVE IT! She speaks her mind and has no filter!

—Akilah from the SMI Book Club

This book was funny, a lot of dark and witty humor (right up my alley), characters I absolutely loved, and a twist I wasn't expecting. I needed this book in my life. **A MUST READ** get on it when this book comes out.

—Anjuli from Chi Chi's Corner – Books & Stuff

PINNED DOWN

THE PINNED UP TRILOGY, BOOK II

PINNED DOWN

C. MICHELLE

Acknowledgements

A special thanks to my family for your support.

Thank you, Jennifer Finch for being a beta reader for me and assisting me with the editing process. Even though you were sick and I failed to give you my manuscript in a timely manner, you still came through for me. You provided your opinion of the book and also assisted with the editing process all while feeling ill. You, my dear, are a trooper and I appreciate you greatly. A million thanks!

The readers who enjoyed *Pinned Up* and asked for more Nina, Josh, and Kade...you're simply AH-MAZING!!! I wrote *Pinned Up* for fun. When I started to receive positive feedback, there were several times I became choked up from overwhelming gratitude. Having someone read my work feels like I'm providing a naked picture of myself waiting for others to point out the problem areas. How nerve wrecking is that? Despite the flaws, you still welcomed the characters and story into your heart. ***Thank you***

Now, for those who posted negative reviews of the first *Pinned Up* edition (luckily, there weren't many), I analyzed your comments, reflected on them, and learned valuable insight. I revised my book taking into account "some" of your input. I'm sure you won't be seeing this, but nonetheless, I wanted to thank you for your opinion and honesty.

Playlist of Songs

1) "Arms" by Christina Perri
2) "Have You Ever Really Loved a Woman" by Bryan Adams
3) "Come Here" by Talib Kweli and Miguel
4) "Danse" by Mia Martina
5) "Wheel in the Sky" by Journey
6) "Ribbon in the Sky" by Stevie Wonder
7) "For the Love of You" by the Isley Brothers
8) "Don't Speak" by No Doubt
9) "Wishing on a Star" by Rose Royce
10) "Tell Me This is a Dream" by the Delfonics
11) "Pass That Bottle" by the Devil's Daughters
12) "Higher" by Jhene Aiko
13) "One in a Million" by Aaliyah
14) "Vuelvo a Nacer" by Frankie Ruiz
15) "I Need Your Love" by Calvin Harris and Ellie Goulding

Dedication

To those of you struggling to accomplish your goals...
hang in there, stay strong, don't let anyone
rain on your parade...you've got this!

Table of Contents

Prologue

The eerie sound of silence is all I hear, yet chaos rapidly unfolds in front of me as the sound of gun shots surround me. Why is there no scent of gunpowder? Why has my mouth gone dry leaving nothing to spare for my parched lips and quenching thirst? Why do I feel too weak to support myself, but somehow feel a contradiction of numbness and weightlessness? My mind is definitely playing tricks on me.

Familiar, dark predatory eyes menacingly stare at me. An array of mixed emotions isn't allowing me to speak or concentrate. Due to panic, I choke on my desperate scream for help. The tension in the air feels like a thick cloud of smoke refusing to dissipate. Fight or flight...those are my only options, but my body is paralyzed, unable to make the slightest attempt to save myself or loved ones. It's too late for them. They're in gun battle and are highly outnumbered. I notice their lifeless bodies drop to the ground, first my mom then Kade. I know I should be running to their aid or searching for my man, Josh, but I can't. I remain in place...unable to move and staring at the man before me, Mateo Blanco. Vaguely, I wonder how he can still be alive. I wonder how this man, my boyfriend's father is gazing at me, savoring every second of torment that he causes me to feel. He should be dead, but he's not. Instead, he's gloriously standing before me with a demonic grin enjoying the pain he inflicts upon me. Slowly, I realize that I cannot move from the shock of seeing him alive and well.

How can this be?

"You're next, you stupid cunt." Mateo Blanco spits through gritted teeth. "I'm going to take my time with you." He says with malevolence radiating off him, but with excitement to begin the physical torture he has in stored for me.

Doesn't he know no physical pain can be greater than that of losing loved ones? Why does he hate me so much? Why does he want to cause me harm? The realization of his revenge slowly registers.

He wants to hurt my father through me.

Mateo Blanco moves towards me at a fast and determined pace with a lascivious sneer.

I need to move. I have to get away.

My body betrays me. It refuses to cooperate and remains paralyzed. Panic quickly consumes my entire being. I feel my hopes and dreams shatter. This man is here for me and has eliminated my loved ones without mercy. All that's left of me are uncontrollable tears, excruciating pain, and a broken spirit.

My eyes swell up from tears of death, tears of paralyzation, and tears of consuming rage. He nears me and clasps my face with force. The strong pressure of his hand is agonizing. He restrains himself slightly ensuring not to break my jaw...just yet. As he stands hovering over me, I notice his eyes spiraling into a malignant mind frame, more so now that he violently invades my personal space. As I stare at Mateo Blanco's face up close, I see Josh...a much older and sadistic version of Josh, but nonetheless...there's no denying this disgusting brute is my man's father.

"I'm going to have a delicious time with you. When your daddy gets the autopsy report, he'll know I fucked his little girl in every way possible before dismembering your body." He belches an evil laugh right by my ear. His hot breath smells of tobacco while his expensive, overpowering cologne intoxicates my senses. A scent that will forever be engraved in memory.

He sardonically laughs at my sheepish yet desperate attempts to escape his grasp. He adds more pressure to my face then lewdly licks my lips with his stiff tongue. A vile substance instantly rises up my throat. I try getting away from him once again to vomit the horrid liquid, but my efforts of escape are futile. He continues to clasp my face with his mighty grip. Almost immediately, I begin to choke on my own vomit.

Chapter 1 (Nina)

Missing You

"**B**aby, wake up. Come on, love. Wake up." I hazily recognize the whispered voice. My eyes sluggishly open, feeling too weak to raise my heavy lids. Gradually, he comes to view. My man. My Josh. His gorgeous hazel eyes scan my face with concern penetrated in them.

Why is he so worried?

"Baby, you were having a nightmare. Are you okay?" Josh asks cautiously.

I'm slightly confused. "I was?" I'm relieved to see him, but the anguish in my chest refuses to perish. I notice then that my face is wet and that I'm still weeping uncontrollably. It takes a moment to register my last few thoughts. Bit by bit, I recall the determination and loathing behind Mateo Blanco's eyes.

"Your dad...he was after me, but first, he hurt the people I love. He still wants to see me suffer. He won't rest until he gets me." I say in between faint sobs.

"Baby, he's dead. He'll never touch you or anyone else again. I made sure of it. As long as I'm alive, I'll never let anyone harm you." Josh cradles me tightly to his bare chest. He seals his promise with a resolute kiss on top of my head. I eagerly return his embrace. I heave a long sigh. I want to remain like this forever.

I believe him. Josh has shown me that he's a man of his word. "Thanks, babe. You make me feel so much better. I'm sorry. It's just that my nightmare felt so real. I'm glad you're here. You give me a sense of security. I feel protected when I'm with you." I smile as the side of my face is now resting on his firm, sculpted chest and our legs are entwined with each other. Right now, I only want to be held. I'm thankful Josh gives me exactly what I need...his comfort. I feel the burden of my heavy lids and quickly fall into a deep slumber once again. This time, Mateo Blanco doesn't invade my dreams.

I wake up feeling groggy. Sunlight is creeping in my room through the blinds on my window. While stretching my arms, I realize I'm alone. I get out of bed at a snail's pace due to my hangover. Last night's drinking fest was imperative. Initially, the pity party was for me to drown my sorrows while watching a movie, but once Josh arrived to my house unexpectedly, my reasons for drinking changed. I had a beer to ease my nerves as I discussed my father, Diego's confessions. Later, additional drinks were necessary as I heard Josh's own admissions to the past week's dreadful turn of events. Despite the revelation of our disturbing truths, our open communication and renewed commitment provide me with the relief I desperately crave.

I make a pit stop at the bathroom then head over to the living room and find Josh drinking a cup of coffee while standing by the window looking outside. I remain in the hallway and observe him from a short distance. His stance is tall and domineering, his shoulders broad with a narrow waist. He has a serious expression that lets me know his mind is running a mile a minute. He's wearing dark grey slacks and a black button up dress shirt with a matching tie. Josh finally senses me and turns around, locking his honey colored eyes with mine. Immediately, he gives me his lazy, boyish grin that automatically sets my soul on fire. "Hey, pretty lady...come here and give daddy some sugar." He raises his right eyebrow twice and places the coffee mug on the end table.

"Good morning, babe. You look mighty tasty. What are you up to today?" I ask as I quickly make my way into his open arms.

"Baby, it's way past noon. You've been knocked out most of the morning." He brushes a few strands of my hair away from my face. "Unfortunately, I'm waiting for my cab. I'm flying back to Arkansas right now. I have a business meeting this evening over dinner with top management from the retailer who just contracted my company. I tried rescheduling, but couldn't. I'll be returning towards the end of next week." Josh says as he holds me tighter allowing me to feel the dread that consumes him for leaving me behind.

"What? Why? I just got you back last night. I'm not ready to let you go again and for so many days." The news of his departure tugs at my heart.

"I know, baby. Trust me...leaving you is the last thing I want to do, but this meeting is very important and can't be rescheduled. I'll work my ass off the next few days to ensure I don't have any more business trips in the near future. Deal?" He lifts up my chin with his index finger and stares into my eyes, confirming the truth behind his words.

"Deal." I grudgingly agree. "You haven't even left, yet I miss you already." I whine. *Since when do I fuckin' whine? Stop acting so damn needy, Nina!* I shove a sock down my inner voice's mouth because right now, I don't give a rat's ass if I'm being clingy. I've been without Josh for too long and to be apart from him again after we just reconciled simply sucks balls...hairy, saggy balls at that. "But you're my boy toy, what will I do without you in the meantime?"

"Your boy toy?" Josh laughs. "You can play with all of me, except my heart." He glides his lips gently across my cheek. "How about you think about me? Miss me. Figure out ways to devour me when I return. I would love for you to come, but right now I need you to look after my mom and keep me posted with her recovery." He places both hands on either side of my face and gently leans his forehead against mine. "I love you, baby. Know that I'll be thinking of you every moment that I'm away. I can't wait to fuck you like crazy again."

Our private moment gets interrupted.

"What's up, you crazy love birds?" Kade yells as he barges into the house wearing sweats and a t-shirt. "Damn, it's a beautiful day! Hey, there's a cab out front. Is it yours?"

"Yeah, it's Josh's. He's leaving me." I pout. "He's going back to Arkansas today and won't be returning until next week."

"That sucks! Oh well, look at the bright side. At least you two can practice sexting and doing weird kinky shit on Skype. Besides, as hard as you two were fucking at the crack of dawn, I'm surprised you're still standing, Cheesecake." Kade laughs. "All right then, Josh...we'll see you soon." Kade heads to the kitchen allowing us some privacy to say goodbye.

Immediately, I rush his lips. I want to savor every bit of his delicious mouth as our tongues dance gracefully with each other. Reluctantly, Josh backs away from me. "I have to go, baby." His voice and stare portray sadness, but he tries to lighten the mood. "Don't worry, I'll be sure to bring back some toys for both our pleasure." He winks giving me that devilishly handsome grin that always makes my insides melt.

"Sounds good to me. You know I'm always game." I wink back. "I love you with all my heart, Tree Hugger. I miss you already" I frown.

Josh closes his eyes and allows my words to sink into his memory. "I love you with all my might, baby. I'll call you when I land." He quickly gives me a kiss and heads to the door. Before he leaves, he yells, "Kade! Be sure to take good care of my lady! I'm trusting you with her life!"

Kade rushes out of the kitchen. "What? I'm on Cheesecake duty? Fuck yeah! Don't worry, Josh...I'm gonna be the best sitter EVER!" Kade turns to me and says, "You heard that Cheesecake? I'm your sitter until further notice. You have to do everything I say or else Josh isn't gonna dick you down when he returns. Mmm hmm. I got you, Josh...don't trip."

Josh remains standing by the door, he pinches the bridge of his nose trying his best to contain the laugh that threatens to escape. Once he composes himself, he leaves with a hint of a smile. He'll be gone for what seems like forever...and ever. Instantly, I feel blue. A long sigh escapes me. *I'm so dramatic.*

Kade startles me. "Hey! Turn that frown upside down. You can't go around sulking all weekend. Would a *Sons of Anarchy* marathon make you feel better? I walked longer than I was supposed to, now my shitty wound is hurting like a bitch. How about we stay in and rest?"

I sigh. "Sounds good. I'm just going out on Sunday for a photo shoot that I completely forgot about. It's at Ocean Beach. Maybe if you're feeling better by then, you can come with me and we can have lunch at the Cliff House after the shoot." Although I'm suggesting, my plans with Kade are concrete in my mind. I cherish his presence, especially when I recall that odious day he was shot by Mateo Blanco, the root of all evil. It still breaks my heart to ponder that I was so close to losing him. After a few moments, I snap out of my reverie. "Okay, I'm gonna freshen up then we can start our drooling marathon over Jax Teller. Yum."

"Sounds like a plan. Hurry up because I'm next." Kade demands as he's walking back to the kitchen.

As I'm showering, I plan a special meal for Josh's return. I've never cooked for him and figure that day is a good day to start. He needs to acknowledge that I'm a woman with many special talents. While I'm forming the menu in my mind, a loud pounding on my bathroom door interrupts my thoughts.

"Cheesecake!" Kade yells. "How much longer? I need to use the restroom! Hurry!"

"Ugh! Why didn't you use it before I showered? I'll be out in five minutes. Wait!" I irritatingly yell back.

Just then, I hear the bathroom door open and shut.

What the hell?

I rinse off the shampoo and slightly open the shower curtain to see what's going on. "Kade? What the fuck are you doing here? Get out!" I shriek completely appalled at seeing him sitting on the toilet.

"OMG, Cheesecake. I can't. I had Indian food last night on my date with Jacob and now, it's going straight through me. I've had an upset stomach all morning!" He groans.

I shut the shower curtain. "I can't believe you're taking a sit down while I'm in the shower! This is a hostage situation!" Just as I'm speaking, I hear a fairly loud plop and smell a foul scent. "Courtesy flush, motherfucker! Courtesy flush!" I yell completely grossed out then start to gag.

"Calm. Down. Taking a dump is natural. No need for you to get into hysterics." Kade laughs. Just then, I hear him pass gas. "Daaaaamn, Cheesecake! Did you hear that asshole talk shit behind my back?" Now, he's chuckling hard.

"You're not funny! Open the window! You'd better spray or light a candle! Now, get out! I swear...you will pay for this, Kade Daly! You're gross! You completely crossed the line this time!" I yell.

I hear the toilet flush. "Okay, okay. I'm done. Sheesh! I'll have you know I've been kicked out of fancier places than this." Kade states completely unashamed as he washes his hands.

"You're so full of shit! You need to kick rocks like right now!" My voice screeches the more irritated I become.

"Full of shit? Not anymore...I feel ten pounds lighter!" He cackles as he leaves me in the bathroom with the stench of his crap combined with the scent of apple cinnamon. *Eww...*

After three hours of watching *SOA*, I decide to check on Celeste, not only to appease my man's request, but because I want to. Before I leave, I gather some essentials I feel she may need.

As I arrive to the hospital, I briefly pray that Celeste is continuing to do well. Once I reach the floor in which she has been residing in for the past few weeks, I notice two men in suits leaving Celeste's room. I speed up my pace to see who these strangers are, but they manage to enter the elevator located on the opposite end of the building before I get a chance to see their faces. I quickly barge into Celeste's sterile and private room. "Celeste! Who were those men? What did they want?" I ask forgetting my manners.

"Well, hello to you too, dear." Celeste pushes a button on the rail of her bed to sit upright. She appears tired, pale, and thinner than when I first met her, but nonetheless, her beauty doesn't fade. She's in her mid-fifties, but doesn't appear to be. Her short auburn hair, emerald eyes, and delicate features compliment her ivory complexion beautifully. She smiles at me weakly. Celeste may be slowly recuperating, but she's still in a frail state after suffering from prior medical issues and then being shot by Mateo Blanco. "They're just federal agents who are still questioning me about that dreadful day. I wonder when the questioning will stop. All these different agents keep asking me the same questions." She sighs.

I walk over to her and gently give her a hug. "Okay. I was

11

caught off guard when I saw those two strange men leaving your room."

"There's nothing to worry about." She reassures me and tries to calm my paranoia by holding my hand for comfort. "Now, tell me. How do you feel?" She asks with a warm smile on her face.

"I'm fine, but I should be asking you that. How do you feel? Any improvement? Your face has a beautiful glow to it. Do you care to tell me why?" I hint at wanting to know more about her male friend, Michael.

Celeste lightly giggles. "I'm happy. I feel relieved we can all finally live in peace. But most important, I'm glad you and my son are back together." Now, pure joy is radiating off her.

"Dang...that man doesn't waste any time!" I tease.

Celeste stares at me lovingly. "He adores you. He couldn't contain his excitement. He called me on his way to the airport. Now, you two can be happy and build a life together. And I can finally be a grandmother." She quickly adds nonchalantly.

"Wait. What? Celeste, no! We just got back together and neither of us has discussed a family. We've only been dating for a short while. Marriage is not something either one of us wants. It's too soon." I state rapidly in a panic before I begin hyperventilating.

"I'm sorry, dear. I didn't mean to startle you with my comment. I promised him I wouldn't mention it, but since I had my fingers crossed when I made the promise, I didn't think there would be any harm in bringing it up." She slightly chuckles. "But for the record, sweetie...I never mentioned marriage. That thought came on your own." She smiles with a look of triumph on her face. "Would you like to know which baby names I have picked out for my grandchildren? Just for fun?" She asks slyly.

"Celeste! Bite your tongue! Absolutely not!" I laugh. "You're freaking me out."

"Don't worry, dear." Celeste lightly taps my knee. "You'll get used to it." She winks at me.

I can't help, but be amused. "Anyway..." I drag out the word. "I brought you some reading material." I hand her three paperbacks. "I hope you enjoy them." I laugh loudly, eager to see what she thinks of my smut books.

After spending two hours in the hospital and catching up with Celeste and her friend, Michael who joined us shortly after my arrival, I return home to rest.

"Hey, Cheesecake." Kade says sleepily as he's lying on the couch. "Don't wake me if I fall asleep." Then turns around and covers his body and head with my *Twilight* fleece throw.

I change into some comfy clothes and eat the meal Kade prepared. I watch *The Real Husbands of Hollywood* quietly and do my best not to wake Kade up since I'm constantly having to cover my mouth and hold in my laugh. Once I'm finishing up, my phone rings. I get excited when I read, "My Tree Hugger" on the screen.

"Babe!" I shriek. "I've missed you so much." I blurt out.

"I've missed you too, baby." Josh says with his deep voice. "God, I wish I was by your side right now."

I smile and get up, but first grab two cucumber slices from the salad I failed to eat then head to my room.

"Good. I'm glad you miss me. Hopefully, you won't leave me again." I pout as I turn on the radio. The song, "Arms" by Christina Perri begins to play. I adjust the volume to a low setting and then I throw myself on the bed.

Ouch!

I shouldn't have done that. The gunshot wound by my shoulder and upper arm is still healing. I disregard the pain, close my eyes, and place the cucumber slices on top of my eyelids.

"I won't leave you again, baby." He promises. Now that I'm completely relaxed, I'm savoring the sound of his delicious, sexy voice.

"I went to the hospital to visit your mom. We had an interesting conversation." I laugh remembering that she already has the names of my nonexistent kids picked out.

"I know. I already spoke with her. But, what's so funny, pretty lady? Never mind, don't answer that. Why don't we talk more about you? For starters, why don't you tell me what you're wearing?" The tone in his voice becomes huskier.

I laugh as I visualize my ensemble. "A black, satin nightie with lace barely covering my breasts." I state as my breathing slightly begins to increase. "I'm also wearing a matching G-string; I wish you were here to rip it off with your teeth." I add as I picture his handsome face between my inner thighs.

"You're not lying to me...right, baby? I don't like being lied to. But please continue, what else would you like me to do to you if I was next to you?" He asks as he's breathing down the phone.

"I'd like you to be on top of me, savoring every inch of my body with your tongue as you work your way from my lips down to my warm cookie." I state as I begin to massage my heavy breasts and feel the longing of his fat dick inside me.

The picture I've conjured up for Josh makes him moan. "Mmm, baby. If I were there, I would bury my face between your legs and devour your cookie at a slow pace; making you beg for every single bite, suck, and lick. Do you want to get wet, baby?" He asks as a way of teasing me.

"Yes." I whimper.

"That's my good girl." He continues. "If I were next to you, I would relish in your sweet scent and warm, scrumptious filling. I would work my tongue slow and deep, then fast and aggressive...always giving you the unexpected, making you crave every stroke of my tongue. When your inner thighs tighten around my head, I would insert a finger and stroke your sensitive, tight pussy gently licking you to the point of insanity. Once you beg for more, I would bury another finger deep inside you and stretch you out to get you ready for my fat cock that so eagerly wants to fuck you, over and over again until your voice is dry from yelling out my name. As my dick is surrounded by your perfectly tight bottom lips, I would go in hard and deep, making you feel all the love I have for you."

I begin to pinch and twist one bare nipple. The longing between my legs becomes unbearable. "Babe, I'm gonna put you on speaker." I breathe out heavily.

Immediately, I lower my hand to move my panties aside and begin massaging my entrance.

"Are you touching yourself, baby?" He asks slowly as he swallows hard.

"Yes. I miss you. I need you. I want you to fuck me hard. I want you to bury your face between my thighs and lick me clean. I want you to only come up for air to give my tits the attention they crave. I want you to use that expert tongue of yours all over my body. I want you to show me that I'm the only woman you want." I say as I'm aggressively rubbing my clit and penetrating myself with two fingers.

"Fuck, baby! I want your tight pussy wrapped around my dick. I wanna fuck you so hard you'll be screaming my name and begging for more. I wanna grab your perfect, huge tits with my mouth and suck on them while you melt beneath me. I want—" I interrupt Josh.

I'm stroking my inside anxiously as I excitedly massage my breasts with my other hand. I'm craving his touch, his body, his scent, the taste of him. "Babe, I'm gonna cum." I struggle to say.

"Cum, baby. Imagine me inside you, holding you, caressing

you, fucking you hard. Think of your legs over my shoulders as I'm buried deep inside you. I want you. If I could be there by your side, I would be licking every drop of your savory juice." He moans out.

And with the visual he painted for me, my body tightens and a blissful explosion releases from my body. The sensation feels exquisite. I'm afraid to move in fear the tingling throughout my body will disappear. It just feels so, so good.

I hear Josh lightly chuckle. "Baby, the things you do to me! I'm in my car parked outside the restaurant with my dick as hard as a rock. How am I supposed to go back inside and finish with the meeting?"

"What? You're not in your hotel room? Why didn't you tell me? This conversation could've waited until then." I laugh.

"I called to say hi, but once I heard your sexy voice...it was a rap. I couldn't just say hi and bye...I wanted more. I can't get enough of you. You should know that by now. So tell me, what should I do to stop my dick from being at a full salute stance?" He asks trying his best to sound serious.

"Hang up. I'm going to text you something. Once you receive it, call me right back." I deviously grin.

"Okay." Josh agrees.

I send him a short ten second video that is both disturbing and comical all at once. I wait for his call. Within a minute, my phone rings. It's Josh. "Nina! What the fuck? What did you send me? My eyes! My poor fuckin' eyes! I'll never be able to erase that image from my mind! I can't believe you! Baby, you're a pervert. It makes me wonder what kind of crap you're into! And the worst part? I saw the whole fuckin' thing! Fuuuuuuck!"

I'm in hysterics. I take deep breaths and exhale. In the video, a person answers the door resembling a she-male. She...ummm...he has long hair, makeup, and only a bra to cover up her huge breasts...BUT the lower naked part shows an extremely long, floppy dick that dangles as he dances and sings a raunchy hook. I have tears in my eyes. I'm laughing so hard, I snort out loud without shame. "Babe. Wait. I can't." Speaking is a challenge since I can't stop cackling. I would've given anything to see Josh's expression when he saw the video, I'm sure it will be engraved in his memory for years to come.

"Lucy...you has son esplaining to do." Josh says.

Oh. My. God! His impression of Desi Arnaz from that old show, *I Love Lucy* is dead on...including the accent. Now, I really can't stop giggling.

"Baby, I have to go. The meeting is about to start. Erase that nasty shit from your phone." He laughs. "My little pervert, I love you so much! I'll call you later tonight."

"Bye, babe." I manage to blurt out as I'm still chuckling. Then, I hang up and immediately get out of bed to wash my hands.

I run into Kade at full speed as soon as I open my door.

"I knew you weren't wearing a fuckin' nightie! Oooh, girl, you're the one who's full of shit! I can't believe you tried seducing your man while wearing a spaghetti stained t-shirt and old raggedy sweats that you've had since high school. You should be ashamed of yourself for full blown lying! Sexy nightie...my ass! High five for showing him the video I sent you last week though. His reaction was funny as shit!" He raises his hand for me to slap it. I happily do (with my clean hand) since my little prank wouldn't have been possible without my bestie. "And to think, I was running behind you to tell you off for waking me up. Then I hear all the nasty crap you two kids were saying and I ended up getting one hell of a show. Cheesecake, you're a freak!"

"Move out of my way before I make you smell my fingers." I jokingly threaten as I laugh my ass off.

"Eww! Real mature, Valentina...real fuckin' mature. Now, I'm completely grossed out!" Kade states with pure disgust.

Good! That's what he gets!

Sunday morning, Kade and I leave the house at three in the morning for the photo shoot of a vintage style magazine. One of the scenes has the sun rising in the background so timing is imperative for the success of the shots. Next month, I'll be the magazine's featured pin-up model. My excitement was so grand, it led me to temporarily dye my hair a combination of hot pink and burgundy to spice things up for the shoot. Although it's not the dark, brown color I'm so used to, I'll admit the vibrant shade looks great against my fair complexion.

We arrive at Ocean Beach in the Sutro Historic District. It's dark and dreary, the only glow available is from a few street lights. The moon and stars aren't visible due to the thick fog that hovers along the beach front. I wonder if the sun's presence will be captured in the shots. Mother Nature besieges an obstacle upon us that is out of our control. The only sound is from waves crashing, usually I find it calming, but this morning the atmosphere feels eerie. We drive until we spot a few cars and an RV. I park next to the RV I'll be using as a dressing room to change my wardrobe, have my hair styled, and have my makeup done.

Since the shoot is located at the beach, the stylist opts for casual attire. My first ensemble consists of plaid turquoise high waisted capris, a white sweetheart top, and a black bolero with a turquoise plaid Peter Pan collar. My lips are outlined and painted to match the vibrant shade of my long locks. My dark eyes are enhanced by cat inspired eyeliner and exaggerated lashes that provide the perfect hint of sex appeal. The back of my vivacious colored hair is styled in retro glam curls while the front showcases perfectly shaped victory rolls. I take a moment to observe myself in the mirror. I resemble a flawless pin-up doll...I absolutely love it.

The photographer's equipment is set up; he's ready to begin the shoot. I walk on the beach barefoot and feel the rough grainy sand beneath my feet. The air is piercingly cold, but the wind is still as the sun's rays slowly make their appearance through patches in the morning's dense fog.

Various carefree pictures are taken with the beach and sunrise as my background. Once the photographer is satisfied with his shots, I'm directed to change into the next ensemble. When I enter the RV, the stylist already has my clothes laid out, white capris and a navy blue pilot top with white details. My hair is restyled into a retro up do with victory bangs and a white bandana holding it all together. My rockabilly makeup remains the same. I finish off my look with oversized, cat eye sunglasses. By this time, the morning fog has passed allowing the sun to shine in all its glory, but since this is San Francisco...the air maintains its crisp, cool feel.

Once we're done with the photo shoot, Kade and I head over to the Cliff House for their brunch buffet. We enter the lower level of the historic building. We're taken back by the astonishing views of Seal Rocks, Ocean Beach, and the Pacific Ocean. We enjoy our meal with champagne while listening to live harp music.

"I just love getting shit-faced drunk in a beautiful atmosphere." Kade sighs heavily as he admires our amazing view. "We're so fuckin' classy, we shit diamonds."

I laugh. "I know, right? Let's toast to being classy bitches." We clink our champagne flutes together. "I'm glad you're treating because I would never pay over a hundred bucks for brunch. It better come with a fat cock for that price!"

An evil smirk plants itself on Kade's pretty boy face as he spreads a touch of flavored butter on half a scone. "Don't trip, boo. I got you. Unfortunately for you, it does come with a fat cock, it's just not for you. Speaking of my fat cock, I'm gonna

19

fuck the makeup artist you were just working with. When she wasn't busy coloring your face, she was busy eye fucking the shit out of me. I got her number. Oh, yes...she definitely wants a taste of this K.D. She looks like she can take a dick." Kade smirks as he bites his scone.

I'm confused. "What the fuck? What about Jacob? I thought you liked him. You just said you were willing to give a serious relationship a try. What changed?"

"Oh, yeah...that ship has sailed. Don't get me wrong, I'll still date and fuck him, but that's it. I've thought about it...I'm too much of a hot commodity to settle for one person. There are too many flavors left in this world for me to sample. Why should I be in a committed relationship? I'm too young for that crap. I just wanna live a happy life and fuck all the beautiful people out there." He says with a sweet boyish smile that reaches his baby blues.

"You're such a hoe. I just can't with you." I shake my head as I take another sip of my champagne.

Kade reaches across the table to pinch my nose. "You say 'hoe' like it's a bad thing...I say 'sexually generous'...if I like it, I'm fucking it...end of story. By the way, we're either going for a walk along the beach or we're hiking the Land End trails...you decide. We need to sober up before we go home. As a bonus, we'll burn off these excess calories."

"Damn! You bug! Why must you always kill the mood by wanting to do something healthy and active? I'm tired. I don't feel like taking a walk or a hike. I hate that you can be such a health nut sometimes." I look at him with an ugly sneer.

He chuckles and almost spits out his champagne. "You should be thanking me! Because of me pushing you and your mom blessing you with amazing curves, your body looks the way it does! If it were up to you, you would just sit on your ass, watch TV, read books, fuck, and shove junk food down your throat."

I sigh dreamily as I picture doing just that. "A girl can dream."

After a short deliberation, I groan. "Fine...we'll go for a hike, but I'll be pouting throughout the whole time. Why can't I just eat whatever I want and not gain weight? I fuckin' hate exercising. It. Sucks. Balls. And so do the people who love it!"

Kade laughs. "Calm down, 'Negative Nancy.' As a matter of fact, I do suck...very well...so I've been told."

"Eww! You're such a perv! Let's go back to being classy bitches and finish up our meal so we can get that damn hike over with. I can't wait to go home and call my man." I raise my eye brows twice rapidly with excitement.

"You mean...be a dirty whore over the phone while you pet your kitty?" Kade winks at me.

"Mmm hmm. My kitty requires a lot of love and affection. " I state with absolutely no shame and a huge grin on my face. The more I think about it, the more anxious I am to return home and hear Josh's sexy voice.

Chapter 2 (Josh)

Tattoo

Who has business meetings on a Sunday? These assholes better agree to my terms and sign everything tomorrow. Although I'm excited about this new contract, the timing couldn't be worse. I need to be home, feeling my lady beneath me as I'm between her luscious thighs, but no...instead I'm with my project manager, Daniel and these boring fuckers.

After discussing my plans, timelines, and details, we're finally done with our meeting and return to the hotel. I have to keep reminding myself that I only have a few days left in this hell hole before I can go home.

Once I'm at the hotel, I stop at the front desk to see if I have any messages since my phone's battery died sometime during my meeting. The girl behind the desk hands me two from my new assistant. Before I leave, she gives me the I-wanna-devour-you-alive look. I've seen it countless times, but instead of jumping at meaningless sex like I would have in the past, I smile at her and walk away. Daniel on the other hand, decides to keep the receptionist company. I feel great about my decision. I'm never settling for rocks again now that I have a diamond in my life.

As soon as I get situated in my room, I call my diamond.

Rather than answering her phone with a simple hello, she responds with, "Babe! Oh, my goodness! I've missed you so much! Hurry up and come home to me!"

Damn. This girl makes my heart melt and knows just what to say to bring a smile to my face. "Soooo what you're saying is that you miss me so much you wanna play 'Hide the Wiener' and make me cum inside you? Is that what you're saying? Because that's what I understood."

Nina laughs. "Hell yeah! That's exactly what I'm saying!" Then, her voice portrays a hint of sadness. "Hurry, babe. Come home. I miss you."

"Believe me, baby. I'm doing my best to be with you as soon as possible. It's hard concentrating on work when you're always on my mind. I've missed you too." I confess. "Now, tell me about your day. How was the photo shoot? Please tell me you were completely covered up. I don't want any men drooling over what belongs to me."

"Of course, I was fully clothed." She sighs. "I had to conceal my gunshot wound. Then, Kade made me go on a hike with him. He sucks."

"Good. I'm glad he's taking care of you and helping you build your stamina. You'll need it when I return and fuck your brains out."

"Yes! I love it when you leave me walking like a duck the next day! It's my fave." My lady giggles and makes my dick tingle at the same time. "Babe! Before I forget...guess what I want?" She doesn't allow me the chance to respond. "You'll never guess, so I'll just tell you. I want a tattoo!" She yells out enthusiastically. "I want it around my shoulder and down to my arm, enough to cover up my wound. Kind of like where yours is placed. What do you think?"

"Sounds good. What kind of tattoo do you want?" I'm curious.

Nina thinks about it for a second. "I'm still undecided, I have yet to find a good tattoo artist. Anyway, let's go back to our rated R conversation."

Sounds good to me. I take a chance and sneak in a question I've wondered about for a while. "Okay. So what's one of your sexual fantasies? If you need time to think about it, you can always tell me later."

Too eagerly, she blurts out, "To be watched!"

I'm shocked, it takes me a moment to register her ardent response. "What? You want someone to see us having sex?" Yes, I include myself in the equation. She's never having sex with anyone else, but me. Only I get to savor and eat her cookie.

"Exactly." She takes a moment to ponder her next words. "Well, I've had that fantasy before I met you. You see…I've hid my body for so many years feeling self-conscious, that now, I just want to show it off in the intimacy of a beautiful act. It's my way of rebelling and showing others they didn't win, I finally feel confident within my own skin. But, since the thought of some woman lusting over you, fantasizing to have you in her repulses me, and you can't fathom a man yearning me…it's never going to work."

Hell no! I'm not letting anyone see my lady in all her naked brilliance. Fuck. That. Shit! I'm surprised with my reaction. I may have been a freak once upon a time, but now, my views and morals concerning my lady have become old fashioned. How did this happen? I don't know. Since when? Since I realized she holds my heart and was meant for only me. "How about you come up with another fantasy? I'm hyperventilating over here."

She giggles, but changes the subject. We only remain on the phone for an hour. Tomorrow is her first day back at work since her injury. It'll be extremely busy for her and I want her well rested.

Within the week, I throw myself into work. Occasionally, stopping to send Nina a text letting her know how much I miss her and want my dick deep inside her. We end our days with long conversations over the phone through FaceTime and Skype.

It's finally Wednesday night. I just landed at SFO airport. I managed to catch the last flight home. I was supposed to arrive tomorrow, but hauled ass to be with my lady tonight. She doesn't know. I left Daniel in charge during my absence.

As I'm driving to Nina's house, I call my mom to check up on her. Luckily, she's recuperating from her gunshot wound even though her health was already in a delicate state. Once we hang up, Mateo Blanco comes to mind. That man always crosses my thoughts when I recall being so close to losing the only two women in my life. He's done nothing but cause turmoil in our lives. My mom was sheltered and full of fear due to this heartless, vengeful man. How can it be that I carry his blood...in more ways than one? Not only does his blood run through my veins, but it's also on my hands. Without an ounce of regret, I mercilessly shot and killed him. If I had to, I'd do it again. I'm not one to take someone's life, but if my mom and the woman I love are in danger, then there's no mercy for whoever attempts to cause them harm. I turn on the radio to distract my dark thoughts. As I'm switching stations, the song, "Have You Ever Really Loved a Woman," by Bryan Adams begins to play. Right away, all negativity escapes my mind and all I can think is...*I sure have.*

Once I arrive at Nina's house, Kade answers the door. "Josh! My man! What's up? I thought you weren't gonna be here until tomorrow? Man...are you just as pussy whipped as my boo is dick whipped? I swear, you two horn dogs were meant for each other. I've heard some of your nasty conversations, both talking about tossing salads, devouring sausages, eating pink tacos...I don't know if I should be hungry, grossed out, or horny! You wanna toss her salad? Seriously? You're not in prison. Slow your roll."

"Fuckin' Kade." I'm in hysterics. "Always talking shit. She belongs to me. I'm going to claim her any way I want. Now...where is she?"

"She's in her room. She wasn't feeling well, so she took some pills. She's knocked out. I have to warn you though. We ate some Taco Bell tonight and immediately, she got a serious case of the farts...they're stinkers. I would open her bedroom's window if I were you."

"Are they silent but deadly or loud nuclear bombs?" I laugh. "Never mind...I'll take my chances." I give Kade a pat on the shoulder, head over to the end of the hall, and open Nina's bedroom door.

She's sound asleep. I take a moment to observe her, she's absolutely beautiful. Her presence is my new home. She's at peace, her facial expression is relaxed, her luscious, full lips slightly parted, and her silky, smooth skin looks radiant with the minimal light that's reflected from her window. Her dark, brown hair is in that messy bun I love to see her in. It exposes her long, delicate neck and jawline. She's perfect. Instantly, I drop my duffle bag, undress, and join her in bed.

I dab kisses on her shoulder, neck, and work my way up to her jawline. The only reaction I get from her is a subtle smile, but otherwise, she's profoundly asleep. Although I'll be stuck with blue balls for the rest of the night, I'm grateful she's by my side. I position myself beneath her with part of her upper body draped over me and shortly, I'm fast asleep right along with her.

In the morning, I wake up abruptly due to a screeching sound. "Babe! OMG! When did you get here? Why didn't you wake me? I slept so comfortable by your side, I overslept. Ugh! I didn't even welcome you home properly." My gorgeous lady pouts then smothers me with kisses along my face. "You said you weren't going to be home until next week." She gives me a final peck and begins to retreat away from me. Immediately, I bring her back down crushing her on top of me while caressing her firm, sweet ass.

"I know, but I wanted to surprise you." Nina's beauty overwhelms me. Her alluring chocolate eyes stare at me with a look of awe, excitement, and love. "I couldn't spend our first Valentine's Day apart from you. I'm here for the day. I'll be catching the red eye flight tomorrow morning back to Arkansas. I've done nothing, but miss you since I left." I bring her to me and close my eyes to inhale her sweet clean scent that has become my new found drug. I could lose myself in her exquisite fragrance forever.

"Oh, my Tree Hugger! I've missed you with all my heart!" She tightens her hold on me. "I'm so glad you're here. Happy Valentine's Day, babe!" She plants a long animated kiss on my lips then gives me a pout. "I have to go to work and I need to leave soon. I'm already running behind, I have court this morning. I'm sorry. Can I make it up to you tonight by fucking you like crazy?" She asks sweetly with a sensual and seductive gaze. Automatically, my dick thrills with lust and I become hard beneath her.

"Stay." I feebly command. I know her job is important so I don't push the issue.

"Any other day I would, babe. Unfortunately, today, I can't. I'll be in court with a twelve-year-old girl who was molested by a police officer. The victim and her parents are completely devastated. It happened after he met her through a youth program held by the police department. The purpose is great, it aids in deterring gangs and preventing crimes, but this asshole abused his position of authority, took advantage of her trust, and caused the girl harm. The guilt the parents are enduring is heartbreaking because they befriended the officer and never questioned his actions when he took special interest in her. Now, they feel as if they threw their most prized possession, their daughter into the lion's den to be served as a meal." Sadly, Nina ponders on her thoughts for a slight moment as she rests on top of me. "It's a shame that some people can be so malicious and selfish, they're completely oblivious and indifferent to the effect their cruel actions have on their victims." Nina lowers her face and lightly kisses my lips. "I'm sorry, babe, but she needs me. Today, she'll be testifying against him and I'll be right next to her supporting her through the process. After court, I have documents I need to sort through for a different case. I'll see you right after work. Okay?" She smiles at me lovingly.

Nina is a good woman. I stare at her in awe. "Okay, baby. I'll see you this afternoon."

She gives me a lingering kiss then jumps off the bed and begins frantically getting ready for work. I get up and head to Kade's room to request that he drops Nina off at work and me at my warehouse. He agrees with the condition that I drive while he continues to get some beauty sleep in the backseat.

The drive to Nina's work is peaceful with just mellow music playing in the background. Our fingers remain interlocked while I occasionally dab light kisses on the back of her hand. The feel of her smooth skin feels like silk as I gently caress it across my lips. Nina's face radiates as she beams at me amorously. "I love you so, so much. I'm glad you're here...even if it's just until tomorrow morning."

"You're my world. How could I not be here today? It's our first Valentine's Day together, baby." I remind her.

As usual, Kade interrupts, "Oh, hell no! It's too early for you two to be giving me cavities. Save your lovey dovey crap for tonight when you're alone. I know you have a lot of making up to do, but not in front of me. Josh, I know your balls must be blue as fuck, but it's not my fault Cheesecake didn't hook you up last night. Tell me the truth...was she dropping bombs? Never mind, don't answer that, just have some respect for those of us who don't give a flying fuck about this damn holiday."

I can't help, but laugh my ass off. Fuckin' Kade...always talking shit. Before I have the chance to respond, Nina reaches out to Kade from the front seat and starts slugging him. "I don't fart, you asshole! I'm a fuckin' lady! Ladies don't fart...we whisper in our panties!"

Kade is hysterically laughing as he dodges the blows Nina throws at him. "Not you! You scream in yours!" He teases her.

"Both of you! That's enough!" I yell. As I'm driving, the upper half of Nina's body is desperately trying to reach Kade and beat the shit out of him while her seatbelt is off. The last thing I need is for us to get into an accident and have something bad happen. "Nina! Sit down and buckle up." I scold her. "Kade! Shut your ass up! Leave my lady alone. She can fart all she wants to...that's how she blows me away." I turn to her and wink.

Kade immediately chimes in. "Cheesy, Josh...real fuckin' cheesy. Now, I've heard it all."

Nina continues to giggle, "Babe, you do love me! You say the most romantic things!" Now, she's wiping away the tears she has from her uncontrollable laughter. She takes a deep breath and slowly exhales. "Okay, okay...no more fart talk...it's soooo not sexy. It's I-Love-You-So-Much-Even-The-Crust-Between-Your-Eyes-Is-Sexy Day!"

"You're right, baby." I humor her.

After miraculously making it to Nina's work without any accidents, we say our goodbyes and agree to meet at my house after work. Kade then drops me off at the warehouse and I commence my day with a vast amount of tasks. The day goes by at a rapid pace. Nina wants to stay in, so I leave work early to pick up dinner, Blondie's pizza and beer.

An hour after I arrive, Nina enters carrying several items. I help her with the large square frame she's struggling with and her night bag. She carries her overfilled tote bag that reads, "I Love Jake Ryan" with the picture of some asshole and has *Sixteen Candles* printed on the bottom in smaller font. Once she places everything down on the coffee table, she jumps on me and simultaneously wraps her legs around my waist and her arms around my neck. She lands kisses anywhere she can touch. "Thank you, babe! You're the best!"

"I know." A cocky smirk comes across my face. "You're not so bad yourself. How about we get started on doing what we do best?" On reflex, I raise my right eye brow twice.

"Oh, yes...but, later. Right now, we have gifts to take care of!" She excitedly jumps off me and makes me have a seat on the couch. She grabs the large frame that has the front covered in brown kraft paper and brings it to me. "Open it." Nina nervously commands as she bites the side of her bottom lip and avoids making eye contact. Her behavior has me intrigued.

Slowly, I peel off the paper from the large square frame. I stretch my arms out holding the picture to see it in its entirety. Instantly, I'm overwhelmed with recent memories consisting of heartache, a sense of failure, but most important love...a love that has grown so rapidly in such a short amount of time. The candid black and white portrait is of Nina and me at a photo shoot by the cable car turntable at Fisherman's Warf. She's wearing a single piece white bathing suit with a red rose on the side of her hair. She's inside the cable car and is standing slightly taller than me as she caresses my face. The picture was taken when I first professed my love to her, a bitter sweet moment filled with relief at finally expressing those sacred words and agony for not hearing them in return. It was a time when Nina was broken hearted due to my mistakes. Not only is it a snapshot of my love being unveiled, but it's also a reminder of the pain I never want to cause my lady again. I love the gift.

"Thank you, baby. I'm blown away. This portrait of us is beautiful. It has an unconceivable amount of meaning, I'm glad the photographer was observant and took such a great shot. I love that the flower and your lips are the only things in color. The red is a great contrast against the black and white picture. It's perfect." I smile completely taken back and place the framed portrait to the side.

She lightly plants a kiss on my nose then positions herself on her knees right beside me. "You're welcome. I'm glad you like it. Annnnd...a million thanks for my gifts! You're so crazy, babe! I love it! Everyone at the office got a kick out of seeing me receive three books with three roses wrapped in ribbon every hour on the hour throughout the whole work day. My two dozen roses are gorgeous! I've never been given roses before...I adore them. And my books! Oh, my God! My favorite books are all signed by the authors! How did you know which books to get? And in such a short timeframe?" Nina's absolutely beaming with genuine delight. "Oh, and Alex! She's awesome! We had lunch and discussed a few things. She was a great surprise too! She's coming over in a bit."

I proudly grin. "I'm glad you like your gifts. I went through your phone, your Kindle, and your iPad to get an idea of what you would like the most...so, you're welcome. All the authors I contacted were nice and more than willing to overnight me their signed books." I ponder on her reading addiction for a few moments. "Damn, baby...your Goodreads' list of books is ridiculous! I don't think you have enough hours in this lifetime to complete your reading goals."

She looks at me in shock. Her entrancing dark eyes are literally coming out of their sockets. "Babe! You can't do that! You can't just go through my things without asking. You have to respect my privacy." She half-heartedly reprimands me for snooping through her things then slightly chuckles. "I know, I know...my list is never ending, but it's not my fault. People constantly recommend new ones, it's hard to resist a book that has such amazing reviews. Books are my crack!"

"Sorry." I shrug my shoulders and state unabashed. "If that's your addiction...I'll take it without complaints. Oh, and by the way...my name is misspelled on your bag AND that's not my picture."

Nina laughs out loud. "Silly, babe! That's Jake Ryan from the movie, *Sixteen Candles*! It's a classic. The bag was actually my mom's, but she gave it to me because I love it so much." She scrunches her face and chuckles softly. "As for Alex, she surprised me at my office and told me you had hired her to be my tattoo artist. I requested an extended lunch break. We went out to eat and I reviewed her portfolio. We discussed my ideas for tattoos and came up with a design and plan. She'll be starting my first tat today and in time, she'll finish the complete design. I told her I wanted to cover up my gunshot wound by my shoulder. Alex told me she couldn't cover the wound just yet because it's not completely healed. I'm tired of being reminded of that horrible day your father shot me. So, tonight she'll just do one art piece on my back that should only take an hour and later, she'll continue to add to it. I'm so excited! I'm going to change before she gets here. Thank you for listening and surprising me with this thoughtful gift."

"You're welcome, baby. You can trust Alex. I've known her for several years. She's an amazing artist."

Just then, the doorbell rings. Before I open the door, Nina gives me a brief kiss and rushes upstairs to change into something more loose and comfortable. I open the door and see Alex with an evil smirk planted on her face. As she enters the door, I hug my dear friend tightly. Alex is one of the few women who has my absolute respect. She's beautiful in her own way. She has a pretty face that has several piercings. Her build is on the thicker side and always covers her body with layers of clothing. I've never seen her wear makeup and she usually has her hair in a crew cut style.

I direct Alex to my bedroom to have her set up by my bedside. Nina seems nervous and excited about getting permanently inked. She's had some food, but I stop her from drinking beer. She has to remain sober until today's artwork is done. Once Alex is set up, she's ready to begin putting her creation on Nina.

Nina lies down on her side with her back facing Alex. She has her hair in a bun, is wearing a black tube top with no bra, and loose grey shorts for comfort. She's rapidly devouring a bag of Wild Berry flavored Skittles due to the thrill that's creeping up on her. I ignore Alex and focus my attention on Nina. Her face is completely animated. She's anxiously anticipating the puncturing on her delicate skin. Once Alex is done cleaning and prepping Nina's shoulder blade, I put on some music and press shuffle to hear some variance. The song, "Come Here" by Talib Kweli and Miguel begins to play, instantly Nina's stimulated facial expression softens to a sweet and calm countenance.

As I lie on the bed facing Nina, Alex warns us to be still. The last thing she wants is to make any mistakes on my lady's flawless skin. The buzzing sound of the tattoo gun blends in with the background music. "Tell me what you're getting. I'm curious." I ask as I soak in her presence to my memory.

Nina stays still as the needle pierces her delicate skin for the first time. She shuts her eyes and scrunches her face tightly. "I'm getting red roses." She answers softly.

I try to distract Nina in a poor attempt to lessen her pain. "Roses are beautiful, but why red roses?"

Her facial mien is tense, but she handles the aggravating feeling well by maintaining deep controlled breaths. "Because they symbolize love." She gradually opens her eyes and locks them with mine. "A love I never felt for myself throughout several years. I never want to be without it again. Growing up, I hated my body. I was ashamed of it and myself. In time, I learned to love me, my body, and my flaws. I'm far from perfect, but I accept me for me. Now, I'm comfortable within my own skin and I'm giving my body beautiful roses to symbolize my love. This tattoo is for me, no one else."

I grab her Skittles candy from her hand and place one piece gently in her mouth. She accepts it with a wide grin then returns to shutting her eyes tight. Although she's not complaining of pain, the effort she makes in maintaining still while experiencing an electrical pulse on and off is evident. I take a piece of candy for myself and gently slide my lips against hers in a stroking motion. I stop and plant a kiss on her soft luscious lips. Slowly, she welcomes me into her mouth. As her tongue gracefully glides with mine, I revel in its sweet taste. The rigidity on her face has softened. Despite the buzzing sound of the tattoo gun and the burning sensation she's experiencing, she manages to give herself to me.

I signal Alex to stop for a second. Briefly, I lower myself slightly. I nod to Alex so she can continue with her work. Gently, I begin kissing and caressing my lady's chest then I pinch her elongated nipples over her shirt. Knowing she wants me and is struggling to contain herself from giving in provides me a sense of satisfaction. I'm in awe that she hungers me despite the pain she's experiencing. I lower my head and release her large, creamy breast. I continue to stroke it with my lips and tongue, but once I reach her pink tender nipple, I graze it with my teeth then, I suck...hard. A moan escapes her. Her breathing escalates. As I'm sucking and biting my lady's nipple, I grab another piece of candy and place it in Nina's mouth. Immediately, she grabs ahold of my index finger with her teeth. She remains still with the exception of her tongue licking and twirling around my finger. I close my eyes and visualize her doing that to my dick. The dick that so desperately wants to be inside her, fucking her like a mad man. I need to feel her. I lower my free hand. I place it beneath her shorts and panties as I continue to provide her breasts with my mouth's undivided attention. I work my hand down to her entrance. Her opening is slick with enthusiasm, welcoming me home, anxious for me to be inside. I rub her sex as I continue to suck and bite down on her chest. After reveling in her wetness, I feel at home just by inserting a finger and gently gliding it continuously at a slow pace. *Pure ecstasy.*

"How do you feel, baby?" I look up at her exquisite face and ask with a mouthful of her delicious breast. "Is the pain tolerable? Do you want me to stop?"

Nina's eyes remain closed. She's no longer in pain...her arousal has completely taken over her mindset. "Don't you fuckin' dare." She breathes out heavily. "Don't stop, babe. Please...don't stop. I'm about to cum. Make me cum, daddy. Show me how much you love my pussy and how much you've missed me." She whimpers.

"You're always in my heart. But, this isn't YOUR pussy anymore, baby. It's MINE. All MINE." I growl as I stroke her sex, insert a second finger, and rub her clit in a continuous motion. I disregard our surrounding and the buzzing sound that's right by our side. On cue, I feel my lady's body slightly tense with amazing self-control along with a gush of her delicious nectar.

She does her best to contain her panting. "Babe, I love you so much. Words can't describe how incredible you make me feel."

"Mmm..." I moan. "Wait until I continue with you tonight."

Breathing hard, she slightly raises my head away from her breast. She observes my face for several seconds with a look of eagerness and hunger penetrated deep in her features. "Continue now." My insatiable lady demands.

I stare at her as I briefly unbuckle my belt and unzip my pants. She gives me a devious smile.

I signal Alex to stop. The buzzing sound of the tattoo gun instantly comes to a halt. I gradually slide myself upwards with my cock discreetly leaving a trail of precum on my lady's legs and inner thighs. Nina's face is now peacefully resting on my chest.

"Wait. Take this off." She attempts to yank my shirt off. In a swift motion, I remove it leaving my chest bare and ready for her master touch. Once again, I gesture Alex to continue with her art piece. She nods and focuses on her work while the buzzing sound resumes.

As soon as the needle pierces Nina's skin, she buries her face onto my chest and wraps her arm around me. Unhurriedly, her luscious lips glide across my chest as she quietly moans. Then the sucking and biting begins. "Mmm...papi...you taste so fuckin' good. I can't wait to be one with you." She sighs and steadily rakes her nails along my lower back.

Fuck me.

Without hesitation, I lower my hand, slide her loose shorts and panties aside, then position myself right at her entrance. Since her pain tolerance is high, I take a chance to turn her fantasy into a reality. I lower my head and raise hers. Like a magnetic force, our lips instantly gravitate to each other. "I need you...to remain still." I say in between kisses. "I'm going to fuck you slow and deep, baby."

She inhales deeply and gently lets out a moan into my mouth as her tongue continues to gracefully caress mine.

No need to wait. I enter her tight opening and on reflex, she carefully wraps her leg around my hip. Besides that movement, her body makes a great effort to remain motionless. The deeper I enter, the louder her moan. Now, her breathing has quickened and her self-control is rapidly slipping. "Nina, you can't move. If you move, I'll punish you. I won't move inside you at all."

"No, babe. I'll be good." She distraughtly pants. "Please...I need to feel your fat dick pounding me. I need you to fuck me...hard." My beautiful lady pleads with absolutely no shame, completely disregarding Alex, our only audience.

Her inner walls tightly grasp me inside her. I yearn to stroke her aggressively, but decide to savor this delicious instant a bit longer. I look down at her and clearly notice her desperation for more penetration. The feeling is mutual. But still, I continue to relish in this unique moment where I feel so intimate with her despite our lack of privacy...but that's what she wanted, so that's exactly what she's getting.

Slowly, I back away cautious not to move her body along with mine, her opening constricts franticly for me to remain inside. Cautiously, I penetrate myself deep inside her tight, wet, enchanting pussy once again. Nina closes her eyes and releases a loud moan. Then, she anxiously begins to suck on my chest, not once shifting her body. My slow and deliberate rhythm continues for some time. Then I feel her nails on my lower back sink into my skin and feel her pussy convulsing hard on my throbbing cock. The sensation is mind blowing. I can't contain myself any longer and join her during her release. The scent of her hair, the sweetness of her lips, and smoothness of her satin skin become instantly etched in my recollection of this evening.

I allow some time to pass before I remove myself from Nina. She doesn't want to let go and neither do I, but eventually we separate. Alex stops briefly allowing me the chance to get up. I head to the kitchen bringing back some water for my lady and return to feeding her Skittles. The music continues to play, the buzzing sound of the tattoo gun is irrelevant, and my lady's lovely face reflects complete satisfaction. She appears sedated and numb to the piercing and burning sensation on her delicate skin.

Once Alex has completed the first phase of Nina's body art, she provides Nina with an oversized mirror and quickly gathers her belongings. "Nina, check out your new tat. What do you think?"

My lady gets up from the bed and heads to the master bath to see the work of art that has been permanently penetrated onto the back of her right shoulder. Nina lets out a high shriek then rushes Alex with a big embrace. "Thanks so much, Alex. I love it!"

Alex returns the hug a bit embarrassed. "Okay, you two, it's been fun." She laughs to herself. "Nina, I'll see you soon so that I can finish your tattoo. Okay?" Alex looks at Nina with genuine admiration.

"Yes, it's a date! Oh, and I'm sorry you had to bear witness to my man fondling me inappropriately." Nina's eyes light up as she elatedly bites down on her luscious bottom lip.

"Consider it forgotten." Alex winks at Nina and leaves to spend the remainder of Valentine's Day with her partner.

I pick up Alex's things, discreetly put money into one of her bags, and walk Alex to her car. "Thank you." My face is beaming.

"You can thank me by taking me out to lunch one of these days. Don't be such a stranger. I can't believe Mr. Fucks-them-and-leaves-them is finally settling down. Wow. I'm happy to see you finally got stung by the love bug." Alex giggles and gets inside her car.

"I can't believe it either, but I wouldn't have it any other way." I walk back to my house grinning.

When I step foot inside, I get taken back by my lady's exquisite, naked curves. She's leaning to the side against the wall drinking a beer straight from the bottle, she captivatingly maintains eye contact, then seductively beckons me to her.

I don't move. Her picturesque figure has me at a standstill. Every position that I plan on fucking Nina in comes to mind. Instantly, I snap out of my trance. There's no time to waste. I need to be in her.

"Why so pensive?" She asks with a smirk on her face then takes a swig of her beer.

"Just enjoying the view."

"Is that right?" She flirtatiously asks. "Like what you see?"

"Everything. I love everything I see. Now, it's time for me to fuck and savor every bit of you. Come here. Give daddy some sugar." I demand.

"Gladly." Nina responds. She approaches me and holds me tightly...ready, desperate, excited to be with me once again. Reminding me with her kisses and touch that this is home, this is where I belong...by her side.

Chapter 3 (Kade)

Wild Beast

My eyes are closed, I'm half asleep. The sound of a tortured cat wakes me from my dream. I'm tired. I'm not ready to open my eyes just yet. I'm still incoherent and can barely make out the terrifying, yet annoying sound. It's worse than the ear-splitting buzzer from my alarm clock. Can someone please take that poor animal out of its misery and let me sleep? Vaguely, I tune in on the wailing from the cat. To my surprise, I make out words from the horrific shilling sound. Instantly, my eyes open wide.

To my surprise, I wake to see Nina sitting right by me on my bed with a cheesy smirk on her face. "Cheesecake! What the fuck? What are you doing?" I yell as I check the time from the clock on my side dresser. "It's barely five in the morning, you crazy nut!"

Nina sighs at me dreamily. "I know. I want us to go for a run before work. Josh just dropped me off. He's on his way to the airport to catch the first flight to Arkansas. Come on. Let's go. Pleeeeeease!" She begs.

It's too early to register her words. "Shhh...listen." Only silence

41

surrounds us. It slowly dawns on me the sound of the tortured cat is no longer there. Then a ludicrous thought occurs me. "Cheese-cake, while I was sleeping, were you by any chance singing?"

"I sure was!"

My jaw literally drops from shock. "I thought a cat was being tortured! You're telling me...it was just you...singing? Fuuuuuuck...you suck! I don't think you could possibly sound worse even if you tried!"

"WHAT...EVER." Nina rolls her eyes. "You're just jealous that I have mad vocal skills. You're a mean ogre."

"Mad skills? They're so mad they're pissed as fuck that they sound so horrible! Me...mean? Nope. I'm honest. Sometimes the truth is just ugly...kind of like that turd on your head."

"Shut up, hater! Hurry up and get dressed before I change my mind about running before the rooster's even up." With an exaggerated smirk she adds, "Besides, I wanna tell you all about my love day and tattoo."

"All right, all right. I see Josh is fucking some sense into you if you're willing to run this early in the morning." I stare at her with disbelief. "Wait. A tattoo? You're scared shitless of needles. I know you didn't get ink on you...quit fakin' the funk!" I chuckle loudly.

"For your information...Josh didn't just fuck some sense into me, he also fucked my fear out of me. So I did get a tat." She states proudly and after a second thought excitedly yells, "Fuck! My man's TALENTED!"

I shake my head with skepticism, but smile when I see Nina's enthusiastic facial expression. "Go make me some coffee while I get ready. I'm gonna need to be fully awake to hear all about the Tree Hugger's skills."

"Okay!" She jumps off my bed then leaves my room, but within seconds she returns, slightly raises my head, and plants a big kiss on my forehead. Then, she laughs out loud.

"You just kissed me after having Josh's dick in your mouth. Didn't you?" I scowl at her. "You better have brushed your teeth since then." Just the thought of it repulses me. "Real mature, Valentina Moretti...real fuckin' mature."

She chuckles so hard, she snorts. "That's what you get for making fun of my angelic voice!" Nina slaps my thigh hard. "Hurry up. Your coffee will be ready shortly."

"Fine...but for the record, you're a sick and twisted woman." I state gravely.

After our run, I shower and begin my day's work for my job and the projects I've been doing on the side for my own clients. Although I enjoy working for my employer as a web and graphic designer, I'm ready to venture out on my own. My list of clients has rapidly grown over the past few months. I need to stop working hard for others and making them rich. It's my turn. Focusing my undivided time, effort, and skills into my business is essential for its success. No one is going to do it for me. No one is going to come knocking on my door to tell me there are countless opportunities out there for me. I just have to go after what I want and take it. I have the experience, knowledge, and clientele. Now, it's just a matter of making things happen. Taking the initial step in achieving one's goals can be terrifying, but if I never take a chance, I'll always come out losing.

Multitasking both my jobs' responsibilities and my personal projects this morning have left me mentally drained. I've been working for six hours straight taking five minute breaks every two hours to eat my protein. Ensuring my body has all its necessary nutrients throughout the week is imperative because I like to poison it with alcohol on the weekends. Life is all about balance.

After being in front of my computer for several hours, I decide to make a chicken stir fry and take some to Celeste and Mama V. I'm sure Celeste is sick of the hospital food and Mama V usually works so much she often forgets to eat. She rarely eats what she bakes...too many carbs.

I arrive at Mama V's bakery. The first thing that catches my attention is the new young and pretty cashier behind the register.

Well, hello there...prime meat.

She looks up at me with her emerald eyes and gives me a warm smile. I return it with a seductive one of my own. Immediately, she blushes. I maintain eye contact. Seeing a woman or man become weak in the knees just from my presence alone will never get old. I love it. I love the chase. I love the hunt. I love the conquest.

Just then, Mama V steps out of the kitchen and into the store front. "Son! It's so great to see you. Why didn't you tell me you were stopping by?" She welcomes me with a grand embrace and genuine delight, then whispers in my ear, "Don't even think about it, little boy. No more fraternizing with my staff. Understand?" Then pinches the back of my arm for confirmation.

"Ouch!" I rub my arm. "I always get in trouble...even when I don't do anything wrong." I pout.

Mama V gives me "the look"...the look that is so powerful it says a million threats without a single word and holds the fear of death within its gaze. Yeah...that look.

"Fine. Sheesh! And here I came to do a good Samaritan deed by bringing you lunch."

"Thanks, son. Actually, I'm starving. Come. Let's have a seat by the window and enjoy our meal as we people watch." Mama V affectionately caresses my cheek. "I'll be right back. Let me get you some fresh treats right out of the oven."

I have a seat by the window to observe the tourist filled

street and inhale the delicious aroma of baked goods. It's a scent I've been surrounded with for over a decade, a smell that represents home, family, and love. All thanks to the beautiful woman who approaches me with a radiant smile, a large glass of milk, two cannoli, and a warm biscotti.

"You know I keep losing staff due to your Casanova ways. You need to stop leading people on." Mama V halfheartedly reprimands my whorish behavior.

"It's not my fault people don't believe me when I tell them I'm not looking for anything serious. After a few weeks, they try to sink their claws into me, wanting to be the one who makes me settle down. People are ridiculous if they think they're going to tie me down just because we fucked." The crude statement escapes my mouth too quickly for me to retract my words.

"Oops! Sorry, Mama V." I apologize with a huge grin. One would think that I could tone down my raunchiness slightly during the day or at least in front of the woman who raised me half my life...nope. Thank God she loves and accepts me for me. "Anyway, people shouldn't make irrational assumptions. I don't want a relationship. I considered it for a few days...hours actually, then realized it was just my medication talking. I'm young. I just wanna have fun. I don't lie to anyone and I'm upfront about who I am. Wild beasts aren't supposed to be tamed. We need to be free and fulfill our wild oats." I state in as much of a dignified manner as I can conjure up.

Mama V stares at me intently then bursts into laughter. She tries to speak, but can't. I notice tears begin to shed and she hurriedly wipes them away. "I can't. I just can't with you!" Then continues to laugh out loud even more.

I'm confused by her exaggerated behavior. "What's so funny?"

She continues cackling like a hyena. "You!" She takes deep breaths and begins to speak, "You...a wild beast? Honey, you're forgetting that when you're sick I'm the one who takes care of you, Mr. Please-feed-me-I'm-too-weak-to-feed-myself and Mr. Everything-aches-including-my-hair. Let's not forget how demanding and whiny you get when you're feeling under the weather. You're the biggest baby and a total nightmare!" Once again her hysterics are back. "So don't give me that nonsense about being a wild animal who can't live in the zoo! You're my delicate flower that requires fragile care!"

"Mama V! I'm a wild beast! A wild beast, mom...NOT a wild animal or a delicate flower! Get it right. I can't believe you're ridiculing my moments of weakness." I make it a point to show her my sullen expression. It only makes her chuckle harder and within moments, I join her in her laugh fest.

After having lunch and dessert with Mama V, I head over to the hospital to check on Celeste. As I'm entering the hospital, I run into Jacob, the surgical intern who I've been seeing for the past week. He invites me out to lunch tomorrow. I accept and make arrangements to pick him up at his house. Initially, I was intrigued by Jacob, but the more time I spend with him the less appealing he comes across. It's strange because when I set eyes on him, I was instantly attracted to his handsome features, chocolate skin, and faint Jamaican accent. I decide to go against my nagging feeling and go on a date with him. It's been a long minute since I've been with a man. It's time.

Celeste is asleep. I decide not to wake her. She needs to rest. I leave the food behind along with some magazines to keep her entertained once she wakes up. As I'm driving home, Nina calls to cancel our date for tonight due to work. We agree to postpone our anti-Valentine's Day bash until tomorrow night. Since the day we met, neither one of us has ever been in a serious relationship, so for Valentine's Day, we celebrate being single but in a sexy, gothic sort of way. We dress in all black, hit the sex shops, and then party our asses off at a dance club with plenty of alcohol. Although my Cheesecake is no longer single, she refuses to break our tradition. Her change of plan works for me since I still have plenty of assignments to complete.

The next morning, I head to Golden Gate Park. Although the sky rise buildings, the high energy of daily hustle, and the fast pace of every day is part of San Francisco's beauty, I also enjoy connecting with this tranquil green oasis and having my own taste of the natural world. Just for a short period, I appreciate running on trails where I'm surrounded by gardens, lakes, picnic groves, and beautiful people in tight workout clothes.

After my morning jog, I return to find Cheesecake asleep on the couch with the television still on. She dozed off watching the show *Love and Hip Hop*. I swear, her addiction to reality TV has gotten out of hand. Last week, she yelled at a man for cheating on his pregnant wife, by her reaction one would have thought babies and kittens were being slaughtered. I leave her alone and prepare for my lunch date with Jacob.

Once I arrive to Jacob's house, I text him to inform him I'm outside. For whatever reason I can't grasp, I've already lost interest in him, but decide to make the best of my Saturday afternoon. As I wait for him in my car, I'm able to appreciate the architecture of his Victorian home. I've been inside, although the outside structure is from an older era, the inside of his house has been completely renovated and showcases high end modern amenities. Jacob's parents paid for everything, his home, his medical education, and still provide him with a hefty monthly allowance. I can't comprehend such a concept since my biological mom deprived me of basic necessities. When I moved in with Mama V, she instilled good work ethics into both Cheesecake and I ensuring we both valued our hard earned money.

After waiting for quite some time, Jacob finally gets in my car. I wait for an apology. Nothing. Strike one. He simply begins to ramble about what...I have no clue. Jacob is the type of man who can be very self-centered; I doubt he's ever had to fight for anything in his life. Jacob may be easy on the eyes, but one of my pet peeves consists of inconsiderate people. I'm in a good mood and decide not to let anything ruin it. I even consider allowing him to give me some head. Just the thought of shutting him up with my dick in his mouth brings a smile to my face.

We finally arrive to the restaurant he chose. It's modern, sophisticated, and very trendy. By the time we're seated, I'm starving. We have a decent conversation over lunch, but only because I made it interesting. Jacob is quickly unveiling how egotistical, materialistic, and condescending he really is. Despite his character flaws, I refuse to end our date without first getting my dick sucked. I excuse myself to use the restroom. Once I'm exiting the bathroom, I feel a strong blow strike the pit of my stomach. The shock of seeing her again has me at a standstill. Not many things or people can leave me speechless, but at this moment I'm left dumbfounded. Standing before me is...Emme, the conniving wench who lied to Cheesecake and me, the bitch who betrayed our trust, and the evil whore who I considered a future with. It takes all my power to keep my mouth shut and not give her another tongue lashing. She's not worth my time, energy, or breath. As I begin to walk away, she grabs ahold of my arm. I stop. *What the fuck does this bitch want?*

Slowly, I turn around with absolute loathing radiating off every inch of my skin. Emme appears nervous, but with determination set in her delicate features. "Kade, we need to talk. I know it's the last thing you want to do, but I really need five minutes of your time."

I can't believe this bitch has the audacity to demand anything of me. She's fucking crazy! I bring myself closer to her and whisper, "Fuck no."

"Please." She begs. "After today, you won't have to speak to me again."

Although I don't owe her anything, curiosity gets the best of me. I sigh heavily. My annoyance is evident. "I'm going to excuse myself from my date. I'm only going to give you five minutes, not a second more. I'll meet you outside on the terrace shortly."

She nods her head in agreement and walks away. I return to my table and vaguely inform Jacob of my pending conversation on the terrace. He seems understanding and tells me to take my time since he has plenty of emails to check on his phone. I thank him for his patience and head towards the exit leading to the terrace.

I find Emme pacing back and forth at the far end in a secluded area away from the people dining outside. I make my way to her. Briefly, the good memories of us treacherously begin to invade my thoughts. Now, I'm nervous. And she definitely looks bothered. She's biting her lower lip. Her pretty face has a worried expression. *I can't comfort her. I can't comfort her. She's not who I thought she was. She's a conniving bitch. She's a conniving bitch. Just listen to her and walk away...walk away, Kade!*

Emme sees me and stops in her tracks. As soon as I approach her, I put my game face on. There's no way I can let her know how much she hurt me and that I miss her. *Fuck that shit.* "Okay, Em...time is ticking. You have five minutes." I look at my watch. "Start talking."

She looks up at me with glassy eyes and closes the distance between us. I look down at her determined not to give in to the desperate yearning I have to hold her small figure in my arms again. She exhales slowly and whispers, "You got me pregnant." Then looks down afraid to see my reaction.

What the fuck? I feel as if the wind has been knocked out of me for a second time. "You're pregnant?" I ask for confirmation.

Emme begins to gently sob and looks up at me once again. "I was." Then wipes away her tears and stares at me intensely, full of regret willing me to understand without having to utter her next words. But I stand still, waiting to register the chaotic thoughts running through my mind.

With a lifeless expression, she states, "I had an abortion last week."

What the fuck? The tension between us is profusely thick, nothing can pierce through it. This blow to my gut feels worse than the first two. Immediately, I feel myself lose control. "If you had an abortion without discussing things with me first, then why the fuck are you even telling me about the pregnancy, you stupid bitch?" Emme remains silent as she stands before me.

"Answer me! Why tell me now? What's the point?" I see red and start fantasizing of choking her until she breathes her last miserable breath.

The sadness she was displaying earlier has now transformed into anger. "Because it wasn't fair for me to be the only one who lives with the abortion on my conscience!" She yells with hate seeping from her words. She takes a deep breath then continues. "I found out the day of the 'Walk for Life' marathon. After you had that horrible confrontation with your mom, I knew you were in a vulnerable state of mind. I was afraid of how you would handle the news of my pregnancy. So, I didn't say anything. Then I decided to tell you that evening, after dinner, but that's when the shooting occurred and I didn't get a chance. When I went to visit you at the hospital to explain myself for being involved with Nina's dad, you and Nina verbally attacked me. You made it clear I repulsed you and never wanted to see me again. I couldn't bring myself to tell you I was pregnant with your baby."

I take a moment to allow her words to sink in. "How do I know you're telling me the truth? How do I know you were really pregnant? How do I know the baby was even mine?" I regret the words as soon as I say them, but hold my ground. She can't be trusted...she's a conniving, heartless liar who lacks a conscience and morality. But for whatever unfathomable reason, in the pit of my being I feel the baby was mine despite the turmoil of my feelings.

Emme looks appalled. "Why the fuck would I lie, Kade? I have nothing to gain. I already sacrificed my life to save my family from being murdered by Nina's dad, I couldn't see myself sacrificing more of myself for this baby. I need to live my life now. I'm finally free. I couldn't allow this baby to tie me down."

"I get it, but you should have told me! You should have given me the chance to step up and help you! You can't just make that type of decision on your own when it included us both! What the fuck were you thinking? I had the right to know!"

Emme laughs. "You can't seriously expect me to believe that you would've stepped up to be a father. All you do is party, worry about yourself, and fuck anything that walks! Being a parent requires a lot of sacrifice. Besides, I didn't want to be linked to you for the rest of my life. You hate me...remember?"

"No, I don't. I don't hate you." I state quietly. Her confirmation that I wouldn't be a good parent slices through my heart like a fine razor blade. "I despise you with every inch of my being." I grab her arms with more force than intended. "I had the right to know. You made the choice of killing the baby without giving me a chance. The abortion is for your conscience only. I won't carry it with me. I may fuck around and be self-absorbed, but that's because I'm single with no one depending on me! I don't know shit about kids, I've never dealt with any, but I had the right to at least try to be a father! You deal with the decision you made of killing the baby just because it would inconvenience your life, you fuckin' bitch!" I let go of her arms as if electricity just jolted from her skin. I step back and turn away from her.

"I didn't kill a baby. I aborted a fetus. It's my body, therefore my choice." She states defensively, standing by her decision.

Emme's poor attempt to minimize her actions leaves me overwhelmed with disgust and sadness. I walk away refusing to rebuttal her justification. The chapter in my life involving Emme has officially ended.

I slowly return to Jacob. My head is pounding, my heart is shattering by the second, and my thoughts have lost their clarity. I don't want to be in this place longer than necessary. I'm ready to pay the bill and leave. Jacob sees me and gives me a worried grin. I guess, I'm not as good at hiding my emotions as I thought. The waiter approaches our table shortly after I have a seat. He asks if we would be interested in dessert. Luckily, we both decline simultaneously. The waiter then places the check right in the center of the table. I take a sip of my water before paying the bill, then Jacob catches me by surprise. He grabs the bill located neatly in a leather pocket and places it directly in front of me.

Did this guy just do what I think he just did? Not today motherfucker. Not. Today.

The action makes me smile...wickedly, but nonetheless, it's still a smile. Jacob chose the worst moment to fuck with me.

"Check this out, you rich bitch...Just because your parents still spoon feed you and wipe your hairy ass, doesn't mean others are willing to do the same. I paid for our dates so far and didn't think anything of it. I was planning on paying the bill today even though YOU invited ME, but..." I take a moment to stretch my neck on both sides. "BUT...when someone EXPECTS something from me...they don't get shit! I don't owe you anything. So, before you start expecting anything from me, you need to ensure your lame ass has me interested. Go ahead and pay for your meal, I'll take care of mine, you cheap ass, sorry prick. Oh, and while you're at it, find yourself a ride home...I'm sure you can afford it." I stand up, drop a fifty dollar bill on the table to cover my meal along with a generous tip then walk out leaving Jacob with his mouth wide open from the shock of my words.

Can this day get any worse? Don't answer that, God. It's a rhetorical question, not a challenge! I drive off into the chaos of the busy streets with the thought of Emme's assurance that I would be a terrible father. Her words stung me deep, I had no choice, but to retaliate.

When I arrive home, I text Mama V to see if she'll spend the day with me tomorrow. Immediately, she agrees. There's something comforting about a mother's presence. It's just what I need.

When I enter the house, I notice Cheesecake exercising in the living room to the *Insanity* workout video. She's sweating, talking shit to the television, and struggling to keep up with the routine. "Fuck you, Shaun! You and your fine self can kiss my ass if you expect me to do more bitch ass burpees! I was only kidding when I ate that pint of Ben and Jerry's ice cream...and the large bag of Doritos...and the pizza! Shaun, you know it is physically impossible to just eat pizza without buffalo wings and beer! Come on, Shaun, let me just pay you to make all these calories go away. I have a photo shoot next week! Please, Shaun!" She begs then stops to catch her breath. With a sense of defeat and rage, she whines, "I'm saying fuckin' PLEASE! Fuck you for making me sweat like a pig! I thought we were friends, Shaun!" She grabs the towel that's beside her and throws it at the TV aiming directly at Shaun T's face.

Leave it to Cheesecake to cheer me up. "Leave my future ex-husband alone, you wench!" I yell as I throw myself on the couch.

Ouch!

"It's not his fault you don't understand the concept of a cheat meal. Your bad for not knowing when to say when." I ridicule her with my debonair smirk.

She turns around and looks at me appalled. "I do know when to say 'when'...hello? Knowing the right amount of ranch and parmesan cheese to add to my pizza requires a special kind of skill." Cheesecake says in between breaths as she drops to the ground for a push up to complete her burpee. Once she returns to her feet, her facial expression demonstrates exhaustion and pure misery as the beads of sweat clasp to her clammy skin.

"Okay. Keep telling yourself that. Finish your workout, I need some shut eye, so don't bother me." Damn, I shouldn't have said that. Now, she's going to be all over me. Regardless, I decide to walk away and head to my room.

Cheesecake doesn't miss a beat. "Hey, hey, hey!" She grabs the remote and presses pause to stop the workout video from continuing to play. She looks at me with concerned eyes. "What's wrong? Are you okay? Do you wanna talk?"

Of course she would pick up on my melancholy mood. "I'm fine. Give me some time to gather my thoughts. We'll discuss things when I wake up. What you need to do is go back to your date with my future ex-husband."

She decides to drop the issue since I have agreed to talk later. "Fine." She sighs heavily. "But I don't want to continue working out. I keep trying to make him my bitch, but the fucker has so much stamina that he makes me his bitch instead! I'm hyperventilating over here! I'm struggling to keep up!"

Cheesecake knows I have no patience for laziness. "Quit your whining! You weren't whining when you were stuffing your face, now don't start complaining when it's time for you to handle business and burn off those unnecessary calories. Man up and grow some balls! Finish your damn workout already."

She rolls her eyes. "Excuse me?" Cheesecake begins waving her index finger around as she continues to speak. "Man up? Grow some balls? Umm...no thanks, I'm happy being a lady. Balls are sensitive and shrivel up. My kitty is a beast...it can take a pounding." She smirks and chuckles showing off her beautiful smile. "Just ask my man." She adds then bursts into exaggerated laughter.

"Real classy, Valentina Moretti...real fuckin' classy." Although I'm shaking my head, I can't keep from smiling and head towards my room where my sanctuary is located.

Before I close my bedroom's door, I hear Cheesecake yell, "On a scale of one through ten, how juicy is the news you have to tell me?"

"A seven!" I yell back and close the door. Since the news is regarding Emme...not much can be expected from her. The pregnancy might be a shock, but the abortion and putting herself first...that doesn't come as a surprise. I throw myself on the bed, allowing sleep to overtake my exhausted mind while Emme and fatherhood consume my final thoughts.

I wake up in darkness. The house is strangely silent. I turn to see the clock on my nightstand and realize I've slept all afternoon through the evening. My mind is bombarded with Emme. My heart immediately aches from disappointment. Disappointment? I shake the feeling away. I need to forget about Emme, the only woman who came close to making me fall in love again...she came close, but not close enough. I need to enjoy my life as I did before she trampled all over me and left me barely standing. I jump out of bed with mere determination to erase today and the past few months spent with her out of my memory.

As I enter the living room, I notice Cheesecake FaceTiming on her iPad with Josh. When she sees me, she gives me a worried look. "Babe, I'll call you back. Kade just woke up."

"Okay. Have fun and be safe if you go out tonight." I hear Josh say to Cheesecake, then yells, "Kade! Take care of my lady. Remember...I trust you with her life."

"I know, I know. I need to babysit Cheesecake and make sure no gorillas get near her at the club. Don't worry. I've got this!" I head to the kitchen to grab something to eat and let them say their sugar coated goodbyes in private. I notice Cheesecake cooked lasagna and made a salad for dinner along with breadsticks. Awwww...she cooked my favorite comfort food. She knows me too well.

When she enters the kitchen, I stop her in her tracks. I've rarely hidden things from her, but right now I don't want to think about Emme. "We'll talk later. Tonight let's go out and have a good time. It's been weeks since we've let loose. Hurry up and get ready so that we can begin our night of Valentine's Day bashing even though V-Day was two days ago." I wink at her. "By the way, thanks for dinner."

"Okay, we'll talk when you're ready and you're welcome." She backs away and heads to her room to get ready.

An hour later, she steps into the living room as if it's her own personal runway. Cheesecake has on a black, retro inspired comic strip skater dress with Wonder Woman as its theme. It's tight at the bodice and flares out at the waist. The dress is short and exposes her long, well defined legs. She accessorized it with red peek-a-boo pumps and a matching colored rose on the right side of her reverse rolls hair style.

I whistle when I see her. "Damn, Cheesecake! You sure know how to make one hell of an entrance! Your legs look so lean and toned, I doubt I'll be able to fight off the gorillas now. They'll be on you like leeches!" I laugh. "Come on, let's have a drink or two before we leave."

"Thanks and make my drink a Beautiful, please." She says with a wicked smile.

"Since when do you drink Beautifuls?" I ask confused.

"Since I began to miss my man like crazy! He loves cognac. It's his drink of choice when he plays poker." She sighs heavily. "Oh how I love to watch him play." She states dreamily then gets out of her reverie. "Do you know how to make it or not?"

"Do you know how many bartenders I've hooked up with? Don't answer that. Just know that it's been enough for me to be considered a master mixologist." I raise my eyebrows and state proudly.

"Whore."

I laugh. "Don't be jealous."

After we've had our drinks, we get a cab and head to a lounge bar downtown in the Historic Theater District. This club plays house music and has a slide to get people below ground. I've heard of issues with people not being allowed in due to women and men ratios, but we've never had any problems. I guess when you look as good as us, exceptions are always made.

As soon as we enter, Cheesecake and I begin moving to the fast paced beat and head over to the bar swarmed with people ready to release the tension of the week and celebrate the night ahead. She hands me her phone. "Why on earth did you bring your phone?" Right away, I get irritated. I know she's not expecting to have a conversation with Josh while we're out. We haven't gone out alone in what seems like forever. Instantly, I do my best to push away the jealous ping.

Nonchalantly she yells over the loud beat of the music, "Habit." Then she leans so close to me our bodies are meshed into one and breathes into my ear, "I feel naked without it." Her clean powdery scent rapidly overwhelms my senses.

"But you don't feel naked wearing a skin tight dress letting your big ol' titties practically hang out of it?" I back away from her a bit since the crowded area doesn't allow for much room.

With a smug look, she replies, "Nope." As she exaggeratedly pops her full ruby lips. "I'll be right back. Gonna hit the ladies room before it gets too packed. Order a drink for me, kay?" She bats her lashes and gives me an innocent smile.

"Hurry up then, before I drink your drink!" I jokingly threaten. She walks away turning several heads and yells, "Please and thanks!" Then blows me a kiss and gets lost in the crowd.

After I place my order with the bartender, I feel Cheese-cake's cellphone vibrate. A text from Josh. *Mmm yesss...*

It reads:

Baby, have fun but be safe. Miss and love you.

Since I don't want him to worry, I reply on Cheesecake's behalf. *I'm sure that's what she would want me to do.*

Babe! I miss you and love you too! Here at the club. Wish I was with u instead...fucking u like crazy!

With a devious grin, I press SEND. *Aww...I'm so nice and thoughtful.*

Within seconds, the phone vibrates in my hand. It's another text from Josh. This time, it reads:

Baby, there's nothing more I want than to be between your thighs pounding you slow and deep then tasting your delicious juice as you cum inside my mouth.

My eyes pop out of their sockets, but immediately, I respond to his text.

Babe! You're making my pussy ache! I need you in me!

While laughing, I press SEND. *I swear...Cheesecake is just too lucky to have me as her best friend!*

Right away, Cheesecake...scratch that...WE get a response from OUR Tree Hugger.

Soon, baby. Real soon I'll be licking you clean.

Rapidly, I answer before Cheesecake comes back and ruins OUR conversation.

Babe, I want you to rub and stroke yourself tonight while you think of me. But first... send me a pic of that fat dick I love so much.

SEND!

I know curiosity killed the cat, but I don't give a fuck! I'm dying to know what my boo is working with.

A minute later, WE receive another text from OUR man.

I can't wait to have your lips wrapped around ALL OF ME.

With his text is a picture attached. *Oh. Shit...or should I say...Daaaamn!*

Shortly after I see the first picture, a second one appears. Repulsion immediately consumes me. *My eyes! Fuckin' shit, you asshole! Why? Why? Why would you ruin things, you sick bastard?*

The second picture is of a man probably in his eighties or nineties sun bathing at the beach wearing a loose thong that has his extremely saggy yet shriveled up balls hanging from the side of his thong. On reflex, I begin to gag. As I'm trying to compose myself, WE receive another text.

Sorry, baby. I couldn't leave you hot and bothered.
Had to make sure I put out the fire I started.
Love you and stay away from those horny motherfuckers.

Angrily, I reply to his shenanigans.

That was just wrong on so many levels! And to think...
I was going to send you some titty action!
Well, Tree Hugger...NO TITTIES FOR YOU!
I HOPE YOU'RE HAPPY!

SEND!

The nerve of him! Some people just like to cross the line!

Just then, I spot Cheesecake making her way through the crowd. I drop a bill for the bartender, put away her phone, and grab our drinks.

When she nears me, she asks with a perplexed look on her face, "What's with the pouty look? Did people fail to throw themselves at you while I was gone?"

I briefly consider her question. With smug scrutiny, I reply, "You're one lucky bitch, you know that?"

Cheesecake belches an ear-splitting laugh despite the thunderous sound of the techno beat surrounding us. "And why is that? Because I have you as a bestie? No need to tell me something I already know." She takes a few sips of her drink, continues chuckling out loud, then yells, "That's my song!" when the DJ starts playing, "Danse" by Mia Martina. "Come on...let's dance, hopefully there's room for you and your ego. Don't forget...Our anti-V-Day bash is just about us...like old times."

The next morning the annoying ringing sound of my phone wakes me. I answer it half asleep unable to open my eyes. "What?"

"What do you mean 'what?' Is that the way you should be answering your phone, little boy? Don't tell me you're still sleeping. You're supposed to be here, picking me up! I thought you wanted to have a mother/son date? Get your hung over behind up, get in the shower, and be here in the next half hour!" Mama V commands not allowing me the slightest chance to come up with an excuse for failing to pick her up on time.

Even though I'm not fully awake, her demanding ways bring a smile to my face. " Yes, ma'm! I'm on my way!"

"Good. Drive safely. See you when you get here. Love you!" She hangs up enthusiastically.

Once I'm finished getting ready, I knock on Cheesecake's door. "Hey! Hanging out with mom all day. See you tonight."

Groggily, Cheesecake responds, "Okay. Have fun. I'm gonna be a bum all day. I can't hang like I used to. I'm STILL drunk from last night!"

"Rookie!" I poke fun of her as I walk away from her door and grab a banana for breakfast on my way out. As I'm leaving the kitchen, I hear Cheesecake's door slam.

"KADE! YOU FUCKIN' ASSHOLE!" She shrieks. "I can't believe you pretended to be me so that Josh could send you a dick pic!" She comes at me with fury radiating off her every being.

Oh, shit! This can't be good.

The last time I pissed her off this bad I came home to my bed covered in pickle juice and tuna. It had sat there for several hours. When I arrived home, the stench was so bad I had to throw out my brand new mattress.

I attempt to speak, but my mouth is full of banana and I almost choke from chuckling so hard at the ridiculously distorted expression on her face. She's soooo pissed off. Her eye makeup from last night is smeared giving her raccoon eyes and her long hair has so much volume she resembles Medusa.

She rushes then jumps on me like a monkey from behind. She does her best to get me in a choke hold, but I manage to easily get her off by flipping her onto the couch. Immediately, I take off running towards the front door and head out. I take the stairs two steps at a time. Surprisingly, she doesn't follow me. As I'm about to enter my car, I hear a thud...and then another and another. I look up and see Cheesecake at the top of the stairs with an 18 pack carton of eggs throwing each one directly at me, but actually making contact with just my car. I manage to duck and get in at record time. I turn on the smooth engine of my BMW X5 and quickly evade the eggs aimed at my direction. I look at my rearview mirror and see Cheesecake exaggeratedly laughing her ass off at my expense.

Women! They're such psychos!

I arrive to Mama V's house which is actually a duplex, but she owns both sections. She purchased the second property in hopes that Cheesecake and I would move in next door one day. In the meantime, she uses the extra space as an office and workout area. As soon as I park my car, mom is exiting her house. I see her hands completely full with a picnic basket, two folding chairs, and a large overfilled tote bag. I get out and give her a hand. "What's with all the luggage?"

Mama V smiles at me and kisses one cheek while she pinches the other. "We're going to be gone all day, little boy. I'm nothing if not prepared. I'm a mom, it's in my genes to be overly equipped for anything. Don't forget to grab the small ice chest by the door. Now, hurry before we catch traffic."

Luckily, we didn't have to navigate through the city's congested traffic since it's Sunday morning and the streets are fairly desolate considering the regular week's chaos. After being on the freeway for a short period, eventually we junction onto Highway 1. Throughout the ride, Mama V discusses Dillon and their unexpected connection. I listen and don't bother cracking any of my usual jokes. As I'm focused on her words and the road ahead, I can sense Mama V's concerned stare. She knows something is bothering me, but respects me enough to give me time to approach her with my dilemma. The purpose of the road trip was to discuss Emme and the pregnancy, but now I realize those subjects aren't worth my breath. Frankly, I don't have the energy to discuss her treacherous ways. I drive with a profound numbness and lack of concentration. Vaguely, I realize we're now driving along the beautiful, picturesque coast on the two way road of twists and turns. I lower my car's windows to hear the waves crashing and allow the cool breeze to caress my face. Mama V becomes a nervous wreck due to some of the undulating turns that make the drive a hair-raising experience. The road has narrow shoulders and sharp drop-offs that make staying completely alert essential to one's safety. I hold onto Mama V's hand and give it a gentle squeeze for reassurance. There's no way I would ever jeopardize my mother's life, she may not have given birth to me, but she did give me a beautiful life. She's safe with me. Personally, I find the drive along the cliff hugging route exhilarating.

"As soon as you see a good resting place, pull over so we can have a light brunch. I brought plenty to eat, no need to waste money at some restaurant where the food isn't half as good as mine." Mama V states with a warm smile. It's her simplicity that makes her so radiant. The only makeup I've ever seen her use is a light gloss on her lips. She maintains her toned figure by constantly working out, walking, and riding her bike everywhere, she refuses to purchase a car. Growing up, Cheesecake and I only traveled by means of BART and the bus, on occasion, a taxi.

Soon I find the perfect spot. The shoulder is wide enough for me to park and the cliff has a small flat surface that accommodates our small setup. We get out, stretch our legs, and are instantly captivated by the scenery below us. Our high altitude allows us to appreciate the breathtaking beauty of the Pacific coastline. The deep blue waters crash against the rocky ground beneath us, but further away we see more subtle waves by the sandy beach. The air feels cool and crisp as the light breeze brushes against our skin.

We quickly set up our picnic area and relax. We easily tune out the road behind us since the sound of the ocean and light winds overpower the cars driving at a slow speed.

"So tell me, son. What have you and Nina been up to lately? I swear we're always playing phone tag. She's so busy with work and I...well, I've had my share of distractions lately." Mama V giggles and slightly blushes.

I begin to chant, "My mom is getting her freak on...my mom is getting her freak on."

Immediately, she halfheartedly slaps my arm to stop. "Ow! It's not my fault you're a cougar and you're schooling your new cub. I'm just singing the truth. Stop me if I lie, but aren't you doing the wild monkey dance with Dillon? I mean...we're all adults here. You can tell me the truth, Victoria Moretti."

"Son, if you don't change the subject right now, I'm not giving you any dessert. Do you understand? And don't you

EVER call me by my name again. You think because you grew a few hairs on your balls that makes you grown? Oh, I don't think so, little boy. Now tell me, what's Nina up to?"

"Mama V! That was so AWKWARD coming from you! Please don't mention my private parts again. And no, I'm not snitching on Cheesecake. I'm not a teenager anymore. Cheesecake and I...we're grown."

"Since when don't you snitch? Just a few days ago you called to tell me Nina was having phone sex with Josh."

"That wasn't snitching, mom. That was gossiping! There's a difference. It was too funny to keep to myself. Besides, Cheesecake's boring. I have nothing new to tell. We haven't experimented with drugs in years, she's still sprung on Josh, and now, she talks to Diego, her dad. See...nothing worth mentioning."

Her eyes immediately bulge out. "She talks to Diego? What? Since when? How did this happen? What did they talk about? How does she feel? Why hasn't she told me?"

"Oops." Since I opened up my big mouth as usual, I have no choice, but to spill the beans. Once I put Mama V's concerns at ease, she begins to reminisce of our past, the simpler times.

Heading home mom takes on the role of a DJ and plays all her favorite music from the Bee Gees including Andy Gibb, several Oldies, and light Rock. I make a big show of complaints, but deep down inside I love her music. When the song, "Wheel in the Sky" by Journey begins to play, she cranks up the volume and we both sing out loud. By just listening to certain music, I can clearly recall Mama V baking, singing, and dancing simultaneously completely carefree. Her music always brings fond, yet simple memories...memories that are penetrated deep in my heart.

Chapter 4 (Nina)

Jelly

Along, dreadful week has passed since I last saw my Tree Hugger. The negotiations he was working so diligently on are done. All remaining details will be finalized through his legal team. I'm just relieved to have him back again. I've done nothing, but crave him in his absence.

I leave work a bit early to get ready for tonight, but first make sure to grab the cheesecake I prepared yesterday and left in my office's fridge. I buy a few groceries then head over to my man's house. Why, oh why must he live at the very top of an extremely steep hill? Slowly, my fear of driving down these ridiculously vertical streets throughout my city has been waning...but, I mean slow-ly. I let myself in with the spare key he secretly has hidden above one of his light sconces. I decide to set the mood by lighting a few candles throughout the living room and dining area, I dim the lights, play music through his surround sound, then rush to his master bath to wash up. I send him a quick text reminding him to come to his house instead of mine. I put on my ensemble for the evening and smile deviously to myself, excited to see his expression when he sees me tonight.

I have my wine constantly in hand as I prepare dinner. The scent of the food begins to overpower that of the candles. The song, "A Ribbon in the Sky" by Stevie Wonder begins to play in the background. It's one of those songs that makes you want to sing from the top of your lungs...so I do. As I'm adding the Marsala wine to the mushrooms and shallots I'm sautéing, I sense someone's eyes fixated on me. Seductively, I flip my hair to the side and turn around. There, leaning against the wall with his arms crossed, standing in all his perfect splendor is my man...eye fucking me like crazy with his gorgeous hazel eyes.

Excitedly, I bite down on my bottom lip to contain the eagerness to jump his bones. "Hey, babe. You're home, you're finally home." As I set my wine glass down on the counter to head his way, he stops me in my tracks.

"Stop. Don't move. Stay right there." Josh commands as he stares at me, mischievously working his eyes from my face down to my toes. "It's not every day I have my woman cooking for me wearing nothing but red strappy stilettos, cheetah print silk panties, and a red apron." He grins.

The butterflies in my stomach are flapping their little wings on high speed, yet I still try to maintain my composure. "Lipstick." I swallow hard. "You forgot to mention...that I'm also wearing red lipstick."

He rewards my seduction efforts with that debonair smirk I love so much. "Well, the entire look is absolutely... mouthwatering." He affirms.

"I guess you'll just have to drool all over me then. I've waited way too long to just stand here and not touch you."

Josh walks over to me with determined strides. When we're in front of each other, he remains quiet and stares at me as he cups the side of my face with his right hand and lowers his head. He brings his mouth to mine and hungrily devours my lips. I eagerly meet his force from pure desperation of him. He removes his hand from my face; he lowers both hands to grab my ass and lifts me up. On reflex, my arms instantly wrap around his neck and my legs around his waist. He positions my back to lean against his stainless steel fridge. The coolness of the fridge shocks my bare back, but the shudder feels exquisite to my rapidly heating skin. *Oh, how I've missed him.*

Grudgingly, I remember the meal I'm preparing. "Babe, we have to stop before I burn your house down. You don't want me to burn our dinner...do you?

As he kisses my neck, he mumbles, "I want YOU to be my dinner...and dessert."

I laugh, "Me too, how about just for dessert? Deal? Dinner will be ready in less than ten minutes."

He sighs heavily onto my neck. "Fine. Deal." He reluctantly lowers me to the ground. "I'll shower in the meantime." Before he leaves, Josh slaps my ass then walks away.

The stinging from his hand on my ass cheek puts me to work on overdrive. I'm anxious to get our night started.

Once I'm done serving our plates with chicken marsala, lemon orzo, and salad, I pour more wine into my glass and quickly pour him one as well. Just as I'm about to call for him, he startles me as he wraps his arms around me from behind. He kisses my shoulder gently. "I've missed you, baby. I'm so glad I'm home. Everything smells so good."

I close my eyes and lean my back into his bare chest as I inhale his scent. He smells of soap, so fresh and so clean. "I've missed you too, babe. Now, have a seat and enjoy your dinner. I hope you like it."

As he spins me around, I notice he's only wearing a pair of semi loose fitting jeans that expose the perfect V in his lower abs. He kisses me once again, our lips and tongues dance in sync making my insides melt.

I abruptly stop Josh. "Hey, Mister! The apron reads, "KISS THE COOK" not "MAKE THE COOK SO HOT AND BOTHERED, HER PUSSY'S DRIPPING WET!"

"Sooooo...what you're saying is that you need me to lick you dry? Is that what you're saying? Because that's what I understood." Josh grabs my bottom lip with his teeth and begins to suck. "Spread 'em. I want your legs spread wide open."

I take a long sip of my wine and clear my throat. "You can fuck me and eat me like a crazy man after our meal. I'm your dessert, remember? Actually, we really are having strawberry cheesecake for dessert. So let's eat so you can tell me how I taste...I mean, how it tastes."

"Just so you know...I'm going to fuck you hard and senseless for making me wait. You need to be taught a lesson or five." He deviously grins as he pulls out my chair of the dining table to have a seat.

Being the brat that I am, I decide to continue with my tease. I untie my apron from the neck and back then place it neatly on the chair beside me allowing my breasts to be in full exposure. "The more lessons you teach me, the better." I reply sweetly.

He's at a standstill as I walk around him to go back to the kitchen for dessert. I figure we'll be getting to it much sooner rather than later.

When I return with the cheesecake and small dessert plates, I notice he still hasn't moved. I pretend not to notice. I cut the cheesecake and place the individual slices on the plates and place them away from the main meal. I have a seat and he does also.

"Do you honestly expect me to eat my dinner while you're sitting next to me wearing only 'Fuck Me Shoes' and a G-string? Your amazing tits are begging to be in my mouth! My dick is rock hard! And you want me to just sit here and have a normal conversation over our meal? What the fuck? I thought you missed me!" He's so in shock from me not following his commands that he ends up chuckling hard.

"Babe, you see...I have a few lessons of my own to teach you. I missed you...too much actually. So now, I have to remind you why you shouldn't be away from me for too long." I stick my finger into my slice of cheesecake and grab a bit. The texture is cool and soft. A wicked smile instantly plants itself on my face. I offer the cheesecake from my finger to my man.

In one smooth stroke, he licks my finger clean. A lascivious sneer takes over his expression. Josh gets on his knees before me, grabs a generous amount of cheesecake with a fresh strawberry and glaze using his two fingers, then spreads the sweet dessert across my chest. Immediately, he gives my breasts the attention they so desperately crave. He licks and sucks every inch of one breast. He then massages the other and expertly twists its harden nipple. "This is the best...fuckin' cheesecake I've ever had...in my life." He groans with a mouthful of my tit.

I remove my breast from his mouth. *I need his mouth on mine.* I urgently kiss him, blind with desire and hungry with need. Somehow, Josh brings me down with him and lays me on the floor. He grabs more cheesecake and spreads it on my chest, then smears the remaining amount in a straight line right in the center of my body. He licks every bit of it off as he lowers himself down to my sex. "Spread 'em and raise your legs high." He commands. Without hesitation, I do as ordered.

He grabs a fresh strawberry covered in glaze and glides it along my entrance. He lifts his head from below, stares at me eagerly, and pops the fruit in his mouth then dives in to savor the cum and strawberry glaze creation. Yes, my man was hungry...no, he was starving. The sucking sensation on my clit is beyond mind-blowing, my breathing is hard, and the feeling has me in a frenzy. My moans get louder as he inserts his finger inside me and continues to caress me with his tongue. Too soon, I feel my body tighten right before a blissful orgasm explodes in my most sensitive area. Josh manages to catch every drop of my juice and ravenously searches for more. Unable to contain himself any longer, he lifts his body and inserts his hard, solid cock inside me. As he's above me, he lowers himself to kiss me while he forcefully thrusts his fat delicious dick inside me, too caught up in the moment to be gentle...or so I thought. "I love you, baby." He breathes into my mouth.

"I love you more." I eagerly respond and welcome his tongue in my mouth along with every forceful thrust from his swollen cock. His whole body consumes me, his aggression is a bit violent but I know it's from missing me. At this moment, there's nowhere else I'd rather be than pinned down on the floor being worshipped by my man. I feel loved. I feel safe. I feel wanted.

I'm in my own version of heaven.

After my second mind-blowing orgasm, Josh finishes inside me, but remains on top of me. We both feel overly satisfied and content. Vaguely, I hear the song, "For the Love of You" by the Isley Brothers playing in the background. My body and mind feel too sedated to register just how perfect this song is for this moment.

The next morning, the alarm on my phone goes off. Well, at least the first alarm of the six I have programmed. All are five minutes apart from each other. I don't trust myself to wake up since I'm not a morning person. Vaguely, I realize I'm alone in Josh's room. "Babe? Where are you?" I yell, too lazy to get up and search for him.

Moments later he shows up showered, dressed, and ready to start his day. *Seriously? Where does he get his energy from?*

"Baby, I woke up feeling great! Last night's dinner and dessert were mmm mmm good! How about we do it again for lunch? Or why don't you just call in sick? I'll go in late and leave early so that we can hang out." He raises his eyebrows twice suggestively.

"I wish. I can't. Today, I'm dealing with a special case at work." I pout. "In this case, the fifteen-year-old boy had a sexual relationship for years with both his eleven year old sister and twelve year old cousin against both their wills. The boy was sentenced to a rehabilitation facility. The families are torn. The cousin's family has moved out of the country. They don't want to deal with the issue. They fear their reputation and name would be tainted. The mother of the brother and sister is distraught. She feels horrible that her daughter was victimized by her son for so long, but at the same time...it's her son. She can't just stop loving him. The father on the other hand is cold as ice regarding the situation. He's a man of very few words. The mom does all the talking and crying. He just sits there completely heartless. The district attorney has decided to question the father more in depth. Something just doesn't seem right." Josh has a seat on the bed and places my legs over his lap to give me his undivided attention.

"The girl feels guilty that her family is now divided. She doesn't understand that the situation she's in isn't her fault. Despite the obvious, her relatives see and treat her differently. The sad part is the boy was only committed to a year sentence and now, he'll be getting out next month. I've been with this family since the beginning of the case. His family is pretty wealthy and paid for the best legal counsel. He'll be on probation until he turns eighteen, he'll have to attend counseling on a monthly basis not weekly like all other sex offenders, and he won't have to register as a sex offender. The sickening part is that he's never shown the slightest bit of remorse for his actions. This whole time while he was committed to the juvenile rehab facility, he never had to do group, peer, or individual counseling. His lawyer made it so that this kid could leave the facility weekly to see a private therapist. I have friends at the rehab facility, that shit's crazy and unheard of! What the fuck was that judge thinking? I swear, sometimes our justice system is a sorry ass joke. The victim got absolutely no justice! She was seven when he started molesting her then gradually made his way to raping her regularly. This kid is a lot bigger and looks a lot older for his age, so he used that to his advantage when threatening her. The girl knew the father always favored the son and that he wouldn't believe her if she told the truth. She was right. The father hasn't looked at her since the day her brother was arrested. Why do we live in such a fucked up world, babe? Some people can be so fucking disgusting! I feel so helpless. This girl has tried to commit suicide. The brother is returning to her home, a place that's supposed to be her sanctuary, but instead feels more like a prison to her. My heart breaks for her every time I see her."

Josh is focused on me intently. That's one of the many reasons I love him so much. He knows how to listen. Some people are only quite because they're busy thinking of what else they have to say, not him...he actually listens and comforts me. "Would you like my input?" He asks with warmth in his eyes, but in a serious tone.

"I'd love your feedback. You know I value your opinion, except when you side with Kade and talk all kinds of mumbo jumbo crap about eating healthy and being active." I giggle to lighten the mood.

"I think there's a lot you can do. Baby, you're a millionaire. You live in a tiny three bedroom house with one bath by choice. You have millions invested on your behalf. If you ever choose to leave your job and start some type of nonprofit organization, you can do it. You have the means, the smarts, the motivation, and the passion. Of course, your money won't last forever. You'll have to hustle by getting government grants and donations from big wigs, but you can definitely do it. You have this amazing drive to help others. It's astonishing. I'm not suggesting that you quit your job and try to start your own foundation tomorrow, but what I do suggest is that you start thinking about it. Do you want to work for someone else for the rest of your life where you feel more helpless than useful or do you truly want to make a change in our society? The choice is yours. I just hate knowing that you have the best intentions, but that your efforts aren't always appreciated. Don't get me wrong, in the line of work that you do, the rewards are few or rarely seen, but they're there and they're grand. You'll have the power and opportunity to help more people. Just think about it. Brainstorm. It doesn't mean you have to follow through. If you're happy being a victim advocate for the city and county, that's great. Do what you think will motivate you. Do what will give you peace of mind. But most important, do what will make you happy each day. If anyone's got this, it's you, baby. You're amazing."

I sigh heavily. "You make me melt, babe. I love that you help me see different avenues of my job. I'll consider your suggestions. I truly appreciate them." I give him a peck on the lips.

"Well, don't forget that your man is kind of a 'big deal' and has important connections." Josh laughs. "Oh, yeah...and don't forget that he's loaded too so I'm sure that if you were to rub him the right way, he would be more than happy to give you a lending hand with your entrepreneurial endeavors." He winks.

"My man is soooo loaded...in more ways than one, honey! Now, I have to get up and start my day. With your talk alone, I feel refreshed. Love you, babe!"

After a long day of work consisting of two hours of overtime, a belly dance workout class I had to attend due to my evil coworkers forcing me to, then visiting Celeste at the hospital, I arrive to Josh's house completely beat. We've been in contact throughout the day with quick texts since his return to work required all of his attention. He'll be home late, but that's fine by me, I'm too exhausted for anything tonight. After I shower, I immediately fall asleep in his extremely comfy Cal King bed.

In the middle of the night, I wake up to use the restroom. Josh's body is draped all over me as I try to get up without waking him. Once I'm in the master bath, I notice Josh's clothes on the floor, I pick them up and place them on the hamper. When I pick up his white shirt, I notice a lipstick stain by the collar. *I know this motherfucker isn't playing bitch ass games with me! What the fuck? I need to wake his ass up and see what the fuck he has to say about this shit!*

Once I return to the bedroom to confront Josh, I find him in deep sleep with his perfect features at peace. *Calm down, drama queen. Josh is so not cheating. There's a logical explanation for this. Just because it looks like lipstick, doesn't mean it is. Let the poor man sleep. Quit bugging and go to sleep also. You can bring up the lipstick issue first thing in the morning once you've calmed down.*

Wow. The new me sure is a lot more mature. I decide to listen to the new me and not jump to conclusions. I'll ask him about the lipstick and not make any assumptions. Once I return to bed, I immediately fall asleep again.

When I wake up in the morning, Josh has already gone to work. I receive a text five minutes after my alarm goes off telling me he has a busy day and wishing me to have a great one. I go downstairs to get some water and find a full breakfast feast waiting for me. The lipstick on his collar doesn't matter much anymore. I just miss him now. My heart tells me he's not cheating.

The weekend is finally here. Josh, Kade, and I head over to Market Street in the afternoon for the Chinese New Year Parade. Once we find a posting place, Kade tells us that Jacob is on his way to meet him. Apparently, he hasn't stopped calling and apologizing for his behavior.

"I can't stand people who feel entitled and expect things from everyone. Bitch, please...I don't owe anyone shit except my family." Kade states as he pours rum into his Big Gulp Coke. "I'm going to have to drink a lot to put up with his ass today."

What? This guy is crazy. "If you don't want to be around him, why did you agree to hang out with him today?" I ask.

"Hello? Isn't it obvious? I'm horny. I'm not going to fuck him or anything, but a good dick suck won't hurt. Shit, it's the only thing he has going for him right now. I told him how I felt, but he insisted on making things up to me. Another one who doesn't listen and thinks he'll change my mind. Umm...nope. But, I'll just go with the flow for today."

Jacob joins our group right as the elaborately decorated floats start passing by with school marching bands following behind. The parade is known to be the largest Chinese New Year celebration in the nation with its beautiful costumes, stilt walkers, Chinese acrobatics, exploding firecrackers, and the extremely long Golden Dragon that is always featured at the end of the parade. One thing I love about my vivacious city is its diversity in cultures; it always has an event or something to celebrate.

Once the parade ends, I decide to get to know Jacob. "So, Kade tells us you're a surgical intern, that's pretty awesome. Do you have a specialty?"

"Actually, I do. I plan on getting into plastics." He says smugly, but with a hint of a sexy Jamaican or English accent, it's so faint, it's hard to tell.

"A plastic surgeon? Wow. That's very impressive. Go, you! I'm sure you'll do well." I smile genuinely at him.

"Kade tells me you're a district attorney or something of that nature, I don't quite recall."

"Oh, no. I work for the district attorney's office, but as a victim advocate, not an attorney. They get paid the big bucks, I don't." I giggle.

Jacob's demeanor changes towards me as he analyzes me from head to toe with a condescending look. "Oh. So, you're just some type of secretary or something with a refined title?"

Oh, no this motherfucker didn't. I have a Master's degree from Berkeley, a job I'm very proud of, and he just wants to look down on me because he thinks he's superior to me...someone...hold me back. I'm about to go ham on his bitch ass.

Josh and I simultaneously stand to give this asshole a piece of our mind. Kade stops us and tells us to have a seat.

Kade first laughs then addresses Jacob. "You arrogant, narcissistic bitch. Who the fuck do you think you are to speak to my sister that way? She's an educated woman, with a career, and most important, has a heart of gold. You look down on her because you think you're better? Motherfucker, you've never had to struggle. You've been spoon fed your entire life. A bad day for you is when your maid messes up your laundry. Don't get me wrong, that's great that you've had such a wonderful fuckin' life, but when you look down on others because of their societal status or because of their position within an organization, that's when you become inferior to them. I've known people who were dirt poor who had more dignity and respect than you. You may have money, but you can't buy class. Now, be on your merry way before I make you my bitch. You're lucky I'm in a good mood and I'm letting you off easy."

"Bye, Jacob!" I wave as he walks away. "I hope you're able to surgically shut your mouth closed." I laugh.

Without wasting another thought on Jacob, we continue enjoying the festivities of the evening.

The weekend comes and goes. Throughout most of the week, I don't see any glimpses of Josh. With the development of his new projects, his free time has been scarce. He texts from time to time, but even the consistency of them has decreased. By Thursday, I find myself in a serious slump. I decide to leave work a few minutes early to bring Josh lunch and see how things have been with him lately.

Out of all days, today's rain is violent with forceful winds and hail. I decide to catch a cab to Josh's office instead of driving there. When I arrive to the sky rise building, I pay and tip the driver generously to wait for me. He reluctantly agrees.

Once I reach the fortieth floor soaking wet where his business, E-Con Solutions (ECS) is located, I immediately get struck by a bad case of anxiety. *Why am I anxious? What's with this bad feeling I have? Why am I so afraid of seeing him? We haven't argued, he's just been too busy at work to hang out. I'm being absurd. Fuckin' stop being such a "Paranoid Patty," Nina!*

As the elevator doors open, I recognize the pretty receptionist from the last time I went hunting for my man. She greets me with a warm smile. "Hi, I'm here to see Josh. I mean...Mr. Ryan." I stumble with my words.

From the right corner behind the receptionist, a tall brunette appears. "Mr. Ryan is unavailable at the moment, but I would be more than glad to relay a message to him."

I'm a bit awestruck when I see this girl. She's extremely thin with exotic features and full lips. She hardly has tits or an ass, but her poise is elegant, her confidence alluring, and her sensuality...evident. The worst part? The bitch looks like a freaking super model! She's absolutely breathtaking! Right away, I can't stand her. There's something about her that rubs me the wrong way. *Whoa...wait a minute. Take it easy, hater. Why the fuck do you have an issue with this broad? She hasn't done anything to you! You just met her! Are you thinking she's the reason Josh has been avoiding you lately? Stop it, Drama! He. Loves. You!*

I continue to scrutinize her in my mind. "I'm sorry and you are?" *Who the fuck are you, bitch? Answer me NOW!*

"I'm his new assistant." She smiles smugly. "Jelly."

"Jelly?" *Something your body lacks? Your name should be Sticks. But okay, if you say so.* "Well, it's a pleasure to meet you, I'm Valentina Moretti." *I have a nice name not a stripper name like you.* "His girlfriend. Well, I just stopped by to drop off some lunch. It's nothing much just some chicken parmigiana and penne alla vodka with a Mediterranean salad I made." I smile sweetly at her but my eyes have sliced her anorexic pretty ass in a hundred million ways already.

She triumphantly smirks. "Oh, your goodies won't be necessary. I already fed him."

Holy titty balls, batman! Does this bitch want a piece of Nina? Robin, my boy...I believe this skank whore sure does. Someone...hold me back. I'm ready to stomp on her boney ass! Don't do it, Nina! Don't cause a scene at your man's office. It's not cool. Walk away and talk to him later. Fuck you, conscience, or Batman, or Robin, or whoever the fuck is in my mind! No, fuck you, Nina Moretti! Take your jealous ass back to work and deal with your man later!

I laugh lightly without the slightest hint of humor. "MY Josh ALWAYS has an appetite for my goodies...just so you know." *Emphasis on MY...emphasis on ALWAYS, bitch!*

The receptionist must have felt the tension in the air because she interrupts the conversation between Jam, Jelly, whatever her fuckin' name is and me. *Where did this tension come from? I have no clue. No...scratch that...his new "no-assistant" wants him.* "Miss Moretti, I'd be more than happy to take it to his office and place the food in his mini fridge. I recently cleaned it out so I'm pretty sure there's plenty of space for the lunch you prepared him."

I'm too pissed to say anything. So I just force a smile, it's probably distorted and looks creepy as hell, but it's all I've got. I hand her the lunch bag, take a deep breath, and through clenched teeth say, "Thank you."

"Well, we don't want to keep you any longer than necessary, I'm sure you're a very busy person. I'll let *Joshua* know you stopped by." She gives me an exaggerated fake smile then walks away.

Bitch. Wait a minute...did she just refer to my man/her boss as "Joshua?" What the fuck? It's "Mr. Ryan" to you, Sticks!

I enter the elevator with my blood boiling. As it descends to ground level, I text Kade.

> **On my way home. PISSED!**
> **Getting shit faced. Join me?**

Kade immediately responds.

> **WTF? It's 11:56am! It's still**
> **MORNING! I have**
> **Standards. So, fuck no!**
> **UR drinking solo, my friend.**

I reply to his absurd text.

> **U SUCK! Fine. No Gossip**
> **for you then! Don't bother**
> **begging either. Had ur chance!**

He answers.

I'm a busy man. No time for gossip.

Womp, womp, womp.
A few minutes later as I'm getting in the cab, I receive another text from Kade.

It's noon! I can drink!
Those were the toughest minutes
of my life! Hurry ur ass up!
I'm thirsty for gossip & booze!

For several minutes, we're at a standstill. It appears there's a fender bender up ahead and spectators make it a point to drive by at a snail's pace to observe the scene in detail risking an accident of their own just to be nosey. *Either get out and help or keep it moving, people!*

Once the cars clear the road, my cab begins to move. Just as we're driving away, I see Josh coming out of the sky rise building with his arm wrapped around a woman in a protective manner. Her head is buried in his chest as he walks her to a cab in the rain. He gets in the cab also. I'm left speechless. Immediately, I call him. No response. I decide to text him. No reply. Despite the scene I just witnessed, I choose to trust him. But my heart chooses to shatter into a million pieces.

The cab driver drops me off at work. With a lump in my throat, I inform my supervisor I'm not feeling well. Since I rarely play hooky from work, she doesn't question me and allows me to go home early. I head over to the parking lot and catch a ride with Betty, my '66 sky blue Mustang GT convertible.

Poor baby, she's going to get man handled in this brute weather.

On my way home, I play "Don't Speak" by No Doubt on repeat and sing like a mad woman from the top of my lungs. It's a bit on the dramatic side, but I'm entitled to a meltdown.

"What. Are. You. Doing?" I ask as soon as I enter my house and see Kade completely spread out on the couch like a big lug.

"I'm in Barbados, bitch! Drinking a Long Island. Don't hate."

With a mixture of irritation and sadness, I dump my things by the front door, kick off my shoes, and throw myself on the couch next to Kade. "Watching *House Hunters International* doesn't constitute an actual vacation like the one you've conjured up in our living room."

Kade scrunches his face with an exaggerated pout. "Hey, 'Debbie Downer' how about you have a drink and tell me what's going on? Your aura is totally killing my buzz."

"Fine." I slowly get up and head to the kitchen. I return with a container filled with ice, a shaker, a bottle of Rose's Sour Apple drink mix, a large bottle of Grey Goose vodka, and a martini glass. I decide today's drunk fest will be sponsored by appletinis. *Yes!*

I station myself on the floor and place all my items on the coffee table in the center of the living room. While I begin my reenactment of today's crappy incidents, I have a sip of my appletini. *Sweet Jesus! This is delish! It tastes exactly like an apple flavored Jolly Rancher! Just what the doctor ordered.*

Kade interrupts my lust filled thoughts about my new favorite drink. "So what you're saying is that this skinny skank had the audacity to make sure Josh had eaten and didn't allow you to see him per your man/her boss's orders? The nerve of that bitch doing her job! And fuck her for calling him 'Joshua' like that's his name."

I finish my first drink in record time then give Kade the evil eye. "I don't need your fuckin' sarcasm! You weren't there! It's not what she said, it's HOW she said it that crawled under my skin! And then I saw Josh holding some girl and getting in a cab with her. I called him and sent him a text. He still hasn't called me back or responded! WHAT THE FUCK?"

"Don't start getting your panties in a bunch. Don't let your mind play tricks on you. You're confused as to Josh's distance lately and you're allowing your mind to conjure up the worst case scenarios. I'm sure things will get resolved once you speak with him. So chill, 'Desperate Debbie.'"

"Did I tell you that broad's name is 'Jelly?'"

"Hmmm...Is she a stripper or a porn star? That is the question." Kade states in deep thought. "What type of nickname is that? Why couldn't she have chosen a much more mature name like 'Cheesecake?' Come on! It's not like there's a story or meaning behind the name or anything. I'm embarrassed for her."

"You asshole! Stop with the sarcasm! You're making me feel stupid." I grumble.

He laughs uncontrollably. "Cheesecake, Cheesecake, Cheesecake, that's not my intention, but you need to see how you're coming across...like a total whiney brat. Don't start worrying about your relationship until you have something to worry about. Josh loves your ass. Jealousy and insecurity aren't very flattering on you. So stop. Talk to him tomorrow and enjoy your drinks in the meantime."

"Fine." I sigh. "I don't know how you made me go from drowning in a glass of water to feeling more at ease. I love you. You're the bestest bestie EVER! You wanna taste my appletini? It tastes like a fuckin' apple Jolly Rancher!"

"Oh, hell no! You suck dick. I don't wanna put my mouth anywhere your mouth has been!"

I start cackling at his crude comment. "Fucker! I wasn't going to give you any anyways! Besides, you should talk! I don't even want to think about all the body parts that have been in your mouth! Eww."

"Trust me...it's a lot!" Kade chuckles then suddenly becomes serious mid laugh. "You know what I don't get...when adults kiss babies and small kids on the lips. I'm sure those motherfuckers had a mouthful of pussy or a mouthful of dick hours earlier and later they kiss their poor babies on the lips. Nasty bastards! Kiss kids on their cheeks or forehead, bitches."

"Oh, yeah. I agree. You know what pisses me off? When I see some sorry ass parents completely covered up in cold weather, but their babies don't have a jacket or socks or a fuckin' blanket, yet the moms are nice and cozy in their warm clothes. Like...what the fuck?"

"I know, right? Hey, how come we're discussing kids? We don't know shit about them?" Kade's eyebrows crease with confusion.

"You brought up the kids topic, it's probably because your biological clock is ticking and deep down inside you want little monsters of your own." I tease even though he ignores my comment. "I'm sure it's the alcohol. Alcohol is a contradicting bitch, it makes people talk stupid and tell the truth."

"Not with me. It comes naturally. It's called keeping it real and being an ass. I embrace my qualities." Kade states smugly.

After several more drinks, we both pass out in the living room until the following morning. Surprisingly, I don't wake up hung over; I wake up refreshed and determined to get answers from my man tonight. As I'm leaving my house to head to work, Kade runs up the stairs.

"I hope you and Josh get shit cleared. I hate hearing you whine. You sound like such a girl. Yuck!"

"Ugh. I know. After work I'm going to work out, shower, then head to his house to talk. I'm not even going to call, I'm just showing up. How was your run?"

"I mostly walked. My gunshot wound still hurts. I'm trying to take it easy so that I can heal faster. I know everyone at the gym misses me. Hello? I'm their eye candy."

"Riiiiiiiight." I drag out the word.

Every hour and every minute of today went by at a snail's pace. Work wasn't enough of a distraction; I still managed to get anxious about my talk with Josh tonight and allowed the worst case scenarios to run through my mind.

The past half hour of waiting for my man to arrive was torturous until I decided to crank up the music in my car. I didn't feel comfortable going inside his house even though I know where he keeps a spare key, for some reason, things feel different and I no longer feel welcomed in his home. Instead, I choose comfort from the darkness surrounding my car and allow the mellow tunes of one of my favorite songs, "Wishing on a Star" by Rose Royce to put my mind at ease.

While hearing the song the third time, headlights that are too high for a car and even for a standard truck appear. *Josh. He's here.*

His wrought iron gate automatically opens as he steers into his driveway. His tinted windows don't allow me to see him, but I'm sure he sees me parked on the street. Before I exit my car, I take a deep breath and exhale slowly. *Ready? Yes, I'm ready.*

As I walk towards his truck, I see him getting out, looking handsome as ever. Even the night's dark sky can't deter his good looks. He makes his way to me. Seconds later, I notice a woman exiting his truck. My breathing, my heart, and steps come to a halt. Right when Josh gets within my arm's reach, I notice a little boy getting out of the truck's back passenger side and yell, "Dad!"

Josh's eyes widen, without saying a word to me, he turns around, and rapidly walks back to the small child and lifts him up in a protective hold. The lady immediately runs to their side. I turn around and walk back to my car with my heart shattering with every step that I take.

I refuse to shed any tears while being so close to that man's proximity. I can't even think his name without wanting to collapse into misery. I manage to maintain my cool and stay focused on the view ahead. I turn on my ignition and press forward on my CD player, I'm no longer wishing on a star. The next song to play, is "Tell Me This Is a Dream" by the Delfonics. I crank up the song and drive away slowly. Once I reach the bottom of the hill, I change the music and play an upbeat rockabilly song, "Pass That Bottle" by the Devil's Daughters is my companion during my miserable ride home and a much more appropriate song to play.

A sad truth? That man is now no one to me. There was no need for me to run off dramatically and cause a scene...it wasn't necessary. No one was behind me. No one chased me. No one felt I was worthy of an explanation or apology. Absolutely...no one.

Chapter 5 (Nina)

Magic Mike

Driving through the enigmatic, busy streets of the city in a heartbroken mood makes me want to get lost in the chaos of it all. I need to get away from my thoughts, from my recent memories, and most important...from my pain. As I'm down on Market Street, I stop by a liquor store. Not just any drink will do for tonight, I need something that takes me back...back to a more carefree time in my life. I purchase two Four Lokos along with a few more items. The memories of my "hood" drinks and drug usage days instantly flood my mind. I smile weakly.

When I arrive home, I remain parked in my car. I'm not ready to discuss the incident that just occurred, speaking about it will make it real. My heart needs a break even if it's just for a few minutes longer. I open my first tall can, fruit punch...I welcome the malt liquor in my mouth and wait for the numbness to take effect. "Higher" by Jhene Aiko begins to play when I turn on my radio. I allow the lyrics of the song to slice me and bring further agony upon me. After some thought, I realize I deserve the pain. My stupidity made me drop my guard and fall in love. What the fuck was I thinking? I hardly know him, yet he consumes me. Every bit of me. I felt like we connected, I wanted him to be the only man in my intimate life, but I learned the hard way that life doesn't always have a fucking happily ever after. The truth does hurt.

I grab my paper bag and pull out a lighter along with some cigarettes. I haven't smoked in years, but tonight...I'm smoking. I'd much rather smoke a fat blunt and really make my night of self-destruction something worth remembering, but for now...a cheap smoke will do.

Two Four Lokos and five cigarettes later, I finally decide I'm numb enough not to feel or care about the pain that refuses to dissolve. When I open Betty's door, a cool breeze crushes my senses. Instantly, my strong buzz escalates to drunkenness. When I enter the house, I find Kade in our retro inspired kitchen. *Aww...I have a pretty kitchen.* I notice.

Kade stops making his protein shake to analyze me. "Dude...you look hella fucked up." He scrutinizes me a bit longer then walks past me to look out of our living room's window. "What the fuck, Cheesecake? You drove drunk?" He yells.

"What?" I take a moment to consider his accusation. *Man...Kade looks pissed. That fucker sure is a cutie when he's pissed. How is it even possible for a guy to have such long lashes? He's definitely prettier than me. Asshole. But I love him because he's my bestie. Besties FOREVER! Woooooo!!!*

"Answer me! Did you drink and drive?" He yells then gets right in front of me.

OMG! Why is he yelling? He can be so fuckin' obnoxious sometimes.

"Curse not." I slur. "I'm sponsible adult." I remind him. "I got shitfaced..." I stop to think. "while I was purked. See...nuffing to worry bout." *What the fuck? I can't feel my mouth!*

"Why the fuck, do you reek of cigarettes? You smoked?

Without me? Spill the beans. Right now!" Kade commands as he grabs me by my arms.

His demanding tone makes me feel like a child being reprimanded. My emotional strength escapes me and chooses this moment to make me feel the hurt I've been so desperately trying to suppress. I begin to wail...loud.

"Aww shit, Cheesecake." Kade loosens his hold on my arms and wraps his arms around me rubbing my back for comfort. "Tell me what happened and I'll do my best to fix it."

His words make me recall the earlier situation with that man. I cry even harder burying my face into Kade's chest for solace.

"Please, calm down. You're making me freak out. Tell me what happened." He strokes my hair gently while I continue to sob onto his chest.

I take deep breaths and still whimper, but manage to calm down slightly. Once I feel my breathing has evened, I decide to talk to Kade. As soon as my first word escapes my lips, I continue to ugly cry uncontrollably. He holds me tight once again. When he feels me moving away from him, he loosens his hold. My tears and mucus are too overwhelming, so I grab the bottom of Kade's t-shirt and use it to wipe my eyes and blow my nose.

"No. You. Fuckin'. Didn't." I hear Kade whisper. "I so don't like you right now."

I hear his words, but don't comprehend their meaning. It doesn't matter...nothing matters at this moment. Exhaustion fiercely consumes me; I push Kade away and stagger to the living room. I throw myself on the couch where my mind finally shuts off.

Bacon. The delicious scent awakens me. The voices of Kade and my mom make me alert. With miniscule movements, I rise from the couch. I feel light headed and remain sitting up right with my eyes closed.

"WAKE UP! WAKE UP! WAKE UP! THIS IS NOT A DRILL, CADET! YOU WILL GET YOUR STINKY ASS AND SHOWER PRONTO, PRONTO, PRONTO! UNDER-STAND?" Kade screams into my right ear.

Ugh. I must be in hell.

"Kade! Leave your sister alone! Can't you see she's hurting?"

"But, Mama V! Yesterday she put snot all over me! On purpose! If you expect me to let that go...then you don't know me!" Kade whines. "Mom, Cheesecake came home reeking of cigarettes, she came home drunk off her ass...and to be hon-est, I still don't know if she was drinking and driving. The worst part, you ask? She didn't ask me to join her! What.The.—" Kade's rant is interrupted by my mom.

"Valentina Isabella Moretti! Were you drinking and driv-ing, little girl? It's one thing for you to go out partying and catch a cab because you've had one too many drinks, it's a completely different and unacceptable story if you were out drinking irresponsibly! I have put up with years of you and Kade's shenanigan's, but never have I feared either one of you being so stupid that you would get behind the wheel while drunk and put your lives at risk, let alone those of innocent people! Now answer me! Were you or were you not drinking and driving last night?" My mom demands an answer.

I open my eyes and notice the frustration, hurt, and worry in my mother's eyes. Immediately, I feel like a child again. A faint sob escapes me. "No." I answer simply but within se-conds, the waterworks are in full effect.

"Why are you crying?" My mom asks perplexed.

Her simple inquiry now has me in hysterics because I re-call the reason for my drinking last night. "JOSH IS A FATHER!" I yell out.

"YOU'RE PREGNANT?" Both Kade and my mom ask in unison with a similar urgency to my words.

"NO!" I scream and continue to wail. In between sobs, I explain last night's incident. "Josh has a son, he's small around three or four. I saw them together last night along with the little boy's mom. I left as soon as I saw them all together. Josh didn't try to stop me to explain himself. He just let me go. So I left." The disappointment in shedding tears for someone who is now no one to me is crushing. Kade has a seat next to me and hands me a box of tissues. Once I clean myself up, I'm resolute to end the pity party.

My mom has a seat on the floor and faces me. "So, do you think Josh has had a family this whole time and has been living a secret life or do you think the little boy was just as much of a surprise to Josh as it is to you?"

"I don't know what to think anymore. All that matters is that Josh has been avoiding me for several days and hasn't called to explain his son to me. At this point, I'm done with Josh." I state firmly. All tears no longer welcomed.

My mom shakes her head in frustration. "Talk.To.Him! Only he can give you answers. It's better than you speculating the worst scenarios."

I'm completely over this conversation. "I'm done! That fucker has my phone number, knows where I live, and has been to my job, there's no excuse for his avoidance and for not getting in touch with me. I'm done chasing after him. Done!"

Kade raises his hand and waits to be called upon.

"What, Kade?" Although I'm irritated, he makes me smile.

"Let me just give my two cents then we'll be done speaking about Josh. I think...the little boy was a surprise to Josh. I doubt he knows what to do. Josh is completely anti-marriage, let alone anti-kids. It's so not his thing. He might be avoiding you because you've been pretty vocal yourself about never

93

wanting rug rats. Now that he has one...if the kid is truly his...he's probably scared shitless that you'll leave him and is delaying the inevitable. That's just my opinion. Do with it as you please."

"I won't give your opinion a second thought for now, but thanks for putting up with me and allowing me to use you as my tissue." I laugh.

The next Sunday morning, I drive to Fort Baker in Sausalito for a photo shoot. One of the photographers I've worked with in the past, reached out and asked me to be the featured model along with a 1949 Chevy Fleetline for a vintage car magazine. His grandfather is the owner of the vehicle. We've worked together several times and since he's always really nice, I gladly do the favor for him. Most of the shots are taken from a position where the Golden Gate Bridge is the background.

The stylist on set opted for several ensembles including a polka dot pencil dress, a rockabilly swing Audrey dress, a Lauren top with capris, a classic coat dress, and paired the outfits with black and white wingtip or peek-a-boo pumps.

Initially, my hair was in perfectly smooth curled locks and later, it was styled into upswept rolls. Bright lips, cat-like eye makeup, and a light finishing powder along with various accessories complete my different looks.

Once the photo shoot ends, I change my clothes to sweats and a t-shirt, but leave my hair and makeup untouched. Being dolled up during a time when I feel so ugly inside was a great remedy to my melancholy mood. I decide to prolong my pretty look a bit longer. The distraction of the shoot was welcomed and served its purpose, but I'll have to admit I'm glad it's over. I quickly gather my belongings and say good bye to the crew.

I arrive home and find it empty. The house is clean, neat, extremely orderly, but I find myself lonely. Kade has such an ostentatious presence that at times the house feels too small. With his absence, the house feels too grand and cold. I realize I'm afraid to be alone with my thoughts. Yesterday, I worked out, cleaned, and reorganized my home without a single call or text since I turned off my phone. There's no point in turning it on again, I have no one I need to be in touch with.

A knock on the door pulls me out of my reverie. I answer it without a second thought.

Sexy, alluring eyes stare me down while my name escapes a lustful mouth. "Valentina?" A deep voice utters my name.

In awe with his handsome looks, I respond, "Yes?" In the form of a question, since I don't know the handsome stranger at my doorstep.

A subtle smirk plants itself on his face. "I'm Michael, a friend of your father's."

Almost as if someone dumped a bucket of ice water on me, I snap out of my blatant observance of this man. I attempt to slam the door, but he wedges his foot between the door and frame. Panic hits me instantly. One thing my father, Diego doesn't have is a friend. Past acquaintances want him dead to overtake his drug empire.

"Valentina. Hija, please calm down. I promise you that Michael is a good man and one of my very few trusted men. Please speak with him." I recognize my father's voice and distant accent.

It takes me a moment to process Diego's words, but eventually I relax and open the door. Right away, he hands me his phone. "I apologize, Michael. You caught me off guard. Please come in and have a seat."

"No need to apologize. It's understandable." He enters and follows me to my living room.

"Diego? What's going on?" I speak into Michael's phone and leave it on speaker.

"Hija, it's so nice to hear your voice. I've tried calling you with no luck reaching you."

"I turned off my phone this weekend. Is everything...okay?" I'm afraid to ask.

"Yes, I just want you to know that you can trust Michael and that if you need anything, please don't hesitate to ask. Also, if you ever plan on visiting me again, please do it as Michael's paralegal. He's one of the attorneys on my criminal defense team. For your safety, I'd rather not let anyone know you're my daughter. I'm a very powerful man...even behind bars. Certain people would do anything to take over my business. Although my name is feared by many, it would be simple to conclude that you are my only weakness, the one thing in this world that could cause me pain. I can't risk letting anyone hurt you to get to me. It's not a chance I'm willing to take."

Sadly, I allow his words to sink in. "Your business? I thought you were done and were going to accept your fate in prison? I assumed you were done..." I think about my next words. "Um...can I speak freely?"

"Yes, hija. Of course."

"I thought you were done with the drugs, with murdering innocent people, I thought you were done being a cartel. I thought you wanted to be a better person." A tear escapes me.

"Hija, I have been given the opportunity of a plea bargain consisting of less than five years in federal prison with certain clauses attached to my sentence. If I want to survive, my name still needs to demand respect and fear, otherwise...I won't survive. I want to be a better person for you. I want to live for you. I want to change for you. But right now, I need to take care of business to survive and to protect you. I promise you this...I will never shed INNOCENT blood again." He vows.

It doesn't escape me that guilty blood is still fair game in his eyes. He wants to be a part of my life. He wants to survive. When I last saw him, he was broken, defeated, and with no fight left in him. Now...he has a purpose to live...me. "Isn't this conversation being recorded?" I ask to distract my thoughts.

"No. I have my ways of getting what I want, hija. It's usually just a matter of price. Most people...have a price."

"Oh. Um...I don't want to know. The less I know, the better. I'll speak with Michael and coordinate with him to visit you. Okay?"

"Okay." Diego responds.

"In the meantime, please stay safe. Don't do anything...unnecessary...unless it's for your protection." *Am I condoning violence? No! But I don't want him to get hurt either! Defending himself and searching for trouble are two completely different things!* "Will our conversations be recorded when I visit you?"

"No. I will make sure of it." Diego affirms.

"Even as a prisoner, you still have power?" I ask with doubt in my voice.

"Yes, even as a prisoner. The power behind my name, my reputation, my fortune, and my knowledge follow me wherever I go."

"Oh. Okay. Well, hopefully I'll see you soon."

"I look forward to your visit, hija. Please be careful out there and don't trust anyone besides Michael who mentions my name for your own safety. I love you, hija. Good night."

His concern for me melts my heart. "Good night." I reply simply and hang up the phone.

I turn to Michael and apologize once again for slamming the door on his face. He's young for an attorney I notice. His

facial expression is serious. His mood makes him look myste-
rious, yet extremely handsome. His dark eyes match the small
patch of hair on the top of his head. His hair has a razor blade
fade all around except at the top. He reminds me of a tall, delicious marine in a high end civilian suit. He's absolutely
yummy. Just as I'm drooling over my father's attorney, Kade
walks in through the front door.

"No need to apologize, Valentina. I'm glad you're not too
trusting of strangers." Michael responds in a business tone.

Before I have a chance to introduce Michael to Kade, Kade
interrupts our conversation. "Hi, I'm Kade Daly, but please
call me K.D." Kade extends his hand to shake Michael's.

This motherfucker... I shake my head. *Has absolutely no
shame!*

"KADE," I emphasize his name. "Michael is Diego's attorney. He surprised me a few minutes ago and stopped by."

"Oh, when did you two meet?" Kade asks confused and
with a hint of irritation for not telling him of this delicious
man.

"We literally just met when he stopped by a few minutes
ago."

"Oh. Are you new in town, Michael? Because if you are, I'd
be more than glad to show you around." Kade brazenly offers.

"Actually, I am. I won't be doing much sightseeing though,
I'm staying in a hotel and will be here solely for Mr. Cruz."

"Who's Mr. Cruz?" Kade asks confused.

"Hello? My dad! Diego Cruz...duh! Come on, Kade...keep
up!" I tease.

"Okay...sorry, sorry...well if you change your mind, feel
free to stop by any time, Michael." Kade no longer tries to dis-
guise eye fucking Michael. He blatantly does it.

Michael stands to shake our hands. "I appreciate the gesture. Thanks. It was nice meeting you both." Then directs his

attention to me. "Valentina, I'll be in touch with you tomorrow to set up a visit with Mr. Cruz. Your dad gave me all your contact information."

"Sounds good. Just let me know when and where and I'll be there." As I'm speaking to Michael, I notice Kade stand behind him and pretend to lick Michael's shoulder. I try my best to maintain my composure by not focusing on the sexual advances Kade is making near Michael's back. "Thanks for stopping by, Michael. I'll walk you out."

When I return to the living room, Kade yells, "Mmm mmm...damn that man is F-WINE! Can you say, 'Magic Mike?' I wonder if he's magically delicious. I'd love to find out!"

"Can you stop? I can't believe you're still pushing K.D. aka Killer Dick! Have you no shame?"

"Nope! Absolutely none."

"Of course not! Why do I even bother with you?"

"Exactly! Stop wasting your time! Hey, so this guy just showed up out of the blue while you're completely heartbroken?"

"Yes. Isn't that weird?"

"Fuck you and your powerful pussy powers! Never in my whole entire life of living have I ever had a hard on, then thought how great it would be if someone rode me, AND had a stranger appear to make it happen within seconds. You're upset and a dick magically appears at the door? Must be fuckin' nice! Not even with pizza do I get such fast service!"

I chuckle loud. "I needed the distraction bad! I can't stop thinking of Josh. Everything reminds me of him!"

"I'll bet he didn't cross your mind while Magic Mike was here." Kade states with smugness all around his pretty features. He really is pretty for a man. Yes, he's handsome, but he's also...pretty.

Chapter 6 (Nina)

Alcatraz

Over a week has passed since I last saw Josh with his son. My cell phone has been turned off, but that's still no excuse for him not to be in touch. He is a stalker after all. I guess to him, I'm just not worthy of his attention anymore. I push all thoughts of that man out of my mind.

Murder.

This morning, Kade contemplated ending my life while he strangled me. "It's four in the morning and you want me to get ready for a photo shoot in Alcatraz? Are you fuckin' serious? Damn...you bug!" Luckily his irritability quickly drifted away when we arrived to Fisherman's Warf and he recognized the makeup artist for the set. The photo shoot is for an online pin up style clothing store that has merged with a company overseas to expand its brand. Both businesses thought it would be fun to make all backgrounds of their shoots iconic places.

It's before dawn and the weather is piercingly cold as we ride the ferry to Alcatraz Island. The salty sea air and strong winds surround us. On a beautiful day, Alcatraz feels menacing, so on a dark and dreary morning like today, the ominous mood is intoxicating. Everyone on the boat is half asleep, bundled up, and trying their best to remain warm. Except for Kade, he's happy as can be flirting shamelessly with two crew members.

Upon arrival to our destination, Alcatraz, the photo and glam squad quickly gather energy and begin moving at rapid speed. We were granted sole access along with a tour guide of the prison for a few hours this morning before the tours begin, so time is of the essence. The Rock's contour is steep and rugged; lugging everything around is an unwelcomed challenge, but we all rise to it including Kade. We finally post shop at one of the cell blocks right by the entrance. The photographer and his assistant set up their equipment and lighting deeper into the building.

My first ensemble is nautical-inspired and consists of a navy blue bengaline wiggle skirt with a sleeveless red and white striped bodice. My accessories include a white belt, a sailor's hat, and red Mary Jane pumps. Glamorous Hollywood waves compliment my outfit beautifully. Glossy red lips, winged eyeliner, and exaggerated flirty eyelashes finish off the look.

Immediately, we begin with the photo shoot indoors. Pictures are taken inside the confined and deteriorating cells. Once the photographer is satisfied, we move the photo shoot outdoors to the Recreation Yard just as the sun is rising. Once the images with the sunrise are taken, we quickly move back to the cellblock to prepare for the next set. Luckily, the prison allowed us use of their electric shuttles to move around rapidly and conveniently within its grounds.

My next ensemble entails a baby pink Heidi dress that has a contrasting black trim along the neckline and sleeves. A black matching belt centers the bodice and full swing skirt. My lipstick is changed to a hot pink color while my hair is styled with two victory rolls and polished waves.

As I'm bending down strapping on my shoes, I get a tap on my shoulder. The first things I notice are black steel toe boots. Slowly, I sit up right allowing my eyes to scrutinize every crease of the jeans before me. With more courage, I force myself to look up past his stomach, chest, and finally...to his sexy, handsome face. He looks more rugged than I've ever seen him, the stubble on his face is more prominent, and the right side of his face looks to be healing from severe bruising that is now days old. "Hey, baby. You look beautiful." Josh states with warmth and love in his honey colored eyes.

His presence makes me weak. I'm thankful I remained sitting. There's nothing more I'd like than to throw myself at him, jump into his arms, and remain there forever. I'm left speechless for a few moments while I anticipate his touch, hope for his lips to be on me, and pray that he'll never let go. Almost instantly after my last thought, I remember his lies, his distance, his silence, and his betrayal. "I don't know what you're doing here, but you need to leave. I don't have time to talk to you nor do I have the patience or desire to hear shit you have to say. So...BYE."

I stand up and turn to walk away. On reflex, he grabs me by the hand and drags me further in the hallway. To avoid a scene, I just move along with him. As we're headed to the opposite end of the cell block, we see Kade. "Kade, be on the lookout while Nina and I talk. I need a minute or two." Josh orders him.

"Yeah, yeah you horny fuckers. Don't go dropping the soap. A minute or two? Are you trying to beat my record?" Kade laughs.

We both ignore his comments. *That is so not happening today.*

Josh leads me into an open dingy cell. Once we're inside the confined space, Josh extends his arms touching both opposite walls standing as a barrier from the exit of the cell. I decide to speak first before he overtakes the conversation. "Josh, look...right now, isn't the time or the place to be speaking with you. I'm on work mode and you're an unnecessary distraction. Everyone on set is working within a time constraint. You need to leave. I don't want to cause a scene. I'm assuming that since you stalked me all the way in prison, you must finally have something to say." A lump in my throat forms. I blink away the treacherous tears that threaten to escape. "I'll hear you out to-night at my house, but not now. I can't risk getting too emotional." I confess sadly.

Josh doesn't say a word. His attentive stare turns licentious almost instantly. He stands before me, observing me as if I'm a glass of water to his quenching thirst. Without a second thought, he grabs me tightly and smothers his face onto my neck. Smelling me...inscribing my scent into his memory. Licking me...savoring my skin and taste. Caressing me...penetrating his touch into my reminiscence.

An inward battle within me instantly commences.

Nina! Stop this shit right now! He doesn't deserve to hold you, feel you, kiss you! Remember all the pain you've felt these past few days! Stop. Him. Now! Oh, damn...is he really sucking on my earlobe? Focus, bitch! FO-CUS! I can't! Yes, you can. You just don't want to! You're in a shitty cell. In prison. With people waiting for you. With a guy who has lied and avoided you for several days. Um...hello? Get your horny ass together and walk away now!

The feel of his tongue as it maneuvers its way from my neck to my collar bone intoxicates me. It's a high I've craved for too long. I can't stop now that it's finally here. Josh places his hand on the nape of my neck then slowly lifts his head to meet my lips. His force is hungry; indomitable...determined not to let me stop him. I don't. I can't stop him. The taste and feel of Josh are enthralling. I've missed him too much. So much my heart and body won't let go right now. His free hand explores my breasts, squeezing them, and twisting my nipples causing an engulfing sensation to electrically pierce all the way down between my legs. His eager kiss and anxious touch make my sex hot, wet, and desperate...desperate for him, his penetration, and his love.

Josh presses his body flush with mine. I smile secretly. I feel his need for me. I feel his lust. I feel his fat cock urged against me, frantic to be released, yet anxious be confined...inside me. He grabs the material of my dress and brings it up to my waist. With his free hand, he gives my bare ass cheek a hard squeeze reminding me it's still his. He works his hand to my front and massages my entrance over my panties. A traitorous moan escapes me.

Josh knows he has me.

Without another moment to spare, Josh moves my panties aside. His two fingers glide to and from my clit and entrance; taunting me...making me beg him to be his again...despite our surroundings...despite his absence in the recent past. At this moment, nothing matters, nothing hurts, nothing is worth turning him away. I add pressure to his bicep for support and with my other hand, I guide his fingers inside me. The dance with our tongues and the penetration with his fingers bring me to an oblivious bliss. Before I reach my peak, he removes his fingers from in me.

Nooooo! I'm afraid to open my eyes; a sense of being unwanted crushes me. Josh releases my nape, but remains flush against my body. He removes his lips from mine only to taste his fingers and undo his pants. This is my chance...the only chance I'll have to think with a clear mind and stop him from taking over me. He returns his mouth to mine, lifts me up, and presses my body against the wall. On instinct, I wrap my legs around his waist. I try to say no in between kisses, but my feeble attempt does nothing to stop him. Before I realize what's happening, I feel the tip of his dick at my entrance. Josh doesn't waste any time and immediately enters me...filling me completely.

Fuck me...he couldn't feel any better even if he tried.

With every thrust, my lips and tongue become more aggressive with his. My longing of him is much too powerful to compete against the hurt I felt previously. I allow his presence to overpower my being. I let him fuck me hard...and deep...and savagely in a rotting prison with several people within an ear shot away. Too soon, my body tenses up and a violent orgasm releases itself from in me. It was desperate to be free.

Shortly after several invigorating thrusts, my man finishes inside me. I'm panting and he's breathing hard, but manages to plant a sweet and final kiss on my lips.

"I need to get down and go. People are waiting for me." I whisper even though I'm sure all our moaning and grunting were much louder than intended.

He rubs his nose against mine. *Aww...an Eskimo kiss.* "Okay, we'll talk later then."

"Okay. Tonight." I agree.

As Josh lowers me, I simultaneously release my legs from his waist. I smooth out my dress to head out of the cell. As I take my first step, I instantly feel light headed, my equilibrium is completely off. I take a moment to gather myself.

What is it about Joshua Ryan that has me so weak in the knees? Everything, absolutely everything. I laugh out loud. *OMG, I'm delirious.*

"What's so funny, cuckoo lady?" Josh rewards me with his rugged smile that I love so much.

"Nothing. You just fucked me into oblivion...that's all." I wink coquettishly. Reason and disappointment soon floor me.

106

What the fuck are you doing? Why are you flirting with him? You couldn't seem more desperate even if you tried! What the fuck? This man has ignored you for several days, he has a son and possibly a family you weren't aware of, and now you're acting like all is well because you two fucked? That's not okay! You fucked. Fine. You're weak...that's definitely clear Miss-I'm-A-Bad-Ass-No-Man-Can-Ever-Play-Me! Okay, you keep telling yourself that.

Before I have a chance to say anything, Kade barges into the cell. "What the fuck, Cheesecake?" He whispers loudly, defeating the whole point of his attempted murmur. "You look like you've been fucked all kinds of sinful ways! Let's disregard the fact that I'm beyond jealous. I'd like to have sex in prison too under the right circumstances...don't judge me. But for you two horn dogs to be doing it in the middle of a photo shoot is completely improper! We could hear you guys all the way down the hall of the cellblock! Hello? It echoes in here! That is so unprofessional! I doubt this photographer will ever want to work with you again! What is wrong with you?"

My face instantly turns crimson from embarrassment. I was aware of a moan or two escaping us, but never thought we were loud enough for others to hear. One thing about me is that I take pride in my work and professional work ethics. Listening to Kade's words only makes the disappointment in me increase to an unbearable magnitude. "Are you serious, Kade? I want to crawl under a rock and die!"

I glare at Josh. This is his fault for being so damn irresistible. *Fucker!*

"Of course, I'm joking. Everyone's taking a coffee break outside. I didn't even know you two were fucking since it was so quiet! What'd you do, Josh? Light candles and make sweet love?" Kade chuckles loudly allowing his laughter to echo throughout the cellblock. "If your lipstick wasn't off and lips weren't so swollen from all the spit swapping, I wouldn't have known shit went down in here!"

I stare at Josh expecting him to say something to Kade. Nope. Instead, he's in a laughing frenzy. *Ugh. Men!* "Fuck you for worrying me, Kade Daly! And fuck you, Joshua Ryan for fucking me in the first place! All men suck balls. I'm through with men! Get out of my fuckin' way, Kade!" I push him to the side and push Josh as well even though there isn't a need, there's enough space for me to exit the cramped cell. As I'm walking away, I hear Kade's annoying voice. "Tree Hugger, you turned Cheesecake into a carpet muncher!"

"Don't be mad, baby! Do you want me to beat Kade's ass? He has a few good ass beatings calling him. I'll kiss your ass tonight. If you let me, I'll lick it too. Deal?" I hear Josh call after me as I continue to walk away.

I turn around but continue walking backwards. "Fuck you, Joshua Ryan. I may have had a moment of weakness a few minutes ago, but that ship has sailed. I'm giving you a good tongue lashing tonight!"

Josh does his best to contain his smile. "Sooo...what you're saying is that you wanna toss my salad? Because that's what I understood, baby. It's freaky, but I'm game. By the way, you look pretty when you're mad." He smiles sweetly.

He thinks I'm playing. The fact that he doesn't take me serious only makes my blood boil to a scorching hot temperature. "Well, I'm going to look fuckin' beautiful tonight when we talk! You're in for a fuckin' treat!" *Asshole. He has a lot of explaining to do.*

I should be angry with myself for giving into him so easily, but I find it's much easier to place blame on others for my stupid actions.

"Hey, Cheesecake, so now that we've established that

you're a carpet muncher, are you or aren't you going to make the lasagna you promised me for lunch? Last time I checked, lesbos like to cook too!" I hear Kade yell along with his thunderous, obnoxious laughter as I step outside. His inquiry doesn't deserve a response.

After a restless night of tossing and turning, I decide to start my day with a run on Lucifer, my treadmill. I hit a steady speed of six miles per hour. Throughout my run, I try not to focus on Josh and his absence. I have work along with other things more worthy of my time and energy than to waste them on him. Unfortunately, somehow, some way, he still manages to overpower my thoughts.

Why didn't he come over last night? Does he think I'm at his beckon call to fuck as he pleases wherever...whenever? Well, that's the impression I gave him. People only treat you wrong or take advantage of you if you let them. I let him. I allowed him to get away with fucking me without an explanation for his lies, absence, and betrayal. Why should I expect him to keep me on a pedestal when I've shown him I don't keep myself on one?

After my hour run, I still don't feel better but decide to push forward and focus on my day. Before I leave the house for work, I prepare a ham and cheese stuffed croissant. I pop it in the oven for a few minutes and fantasize of stuffing my face with the buttery pastry and melted cheese. *Mmmm...*

"Yum. What smells so good?" Kade walks into the kitchen half asleep. He checks the oven then gives me a disappointing look.

"What? You can't say anything. I ran six miles this morning so that means I can eat whatever I damn well please."

Kade sighs loudly. "You're defeating the whole purpose of

your workout. Hello? You're supposed to eat clean and be active to live a healthy life."

"Blah, blah, blah, blah, and some more blah. Yes, I probably shouldn't be nourishing my body with this breakfast loaded in calories, but the truth is I only workout to eat whatever I want. The words 'healthy' and 'active' are bad words as far as I'm concerned. Well, unless we're talking about being sexually active...then it's fine." I giggle.

"You're a lost cause, but I won't give up on you." He swears.

"I won't listen to you preaching about being healthy when you tend to chug bottles of liquor on the weekends. Josh works out daily but eats whatever he wants. That's bullshit. I want to live the good life too!" I proclaim.

"Men are programmed differently. It's easier for us to handle business. Speaking of your freaky man, are you still butt hurt that you gave up the chon chon so easily?"

I'm confused. "What the fuck is chon chon?"

"Oh, don't play the role with me...you're half beaner. All beaners have seen the movie, *Blood In, Blood Out.* Benjamin Bratt has never looked so good. Damn!"

"Oh, that's right! I love that movie. You can't go around saying racist comments, someone might get offended! But you're right...I sure did give up the chon chon super quick. Ugh! Don't remind me! "

Kade makes a face reflecting pure irritation. "I'm so sick of how society is full of 'Sensitive Sallys.' Hello? At least I have the balls to say whatever the fuck I want. I mean, these delicate flowers that get so easily offended are the biggest hypocrites always running their mouths about everything and everyone behind closed doors. Shit...I don't give a fuck, I keep it real wherever the fuck I'm at. Well, except around Mama V because sometimes she gets violent with me and checks me, but that's a different story. Besides, I'm your best friend! I can talk shit about Mexicans and Italians all day, every day because as your bestie, I have an all access pass...just like you can talk shit about us Irish men, bisexuals or gays...you're linked to me so it's all good. People need to understand that 'talking shit' has absolutely no validity...that's why it's referred to as 'talking SHIT.' Anyone who doesn't like me or doesn't respect me based on my honesty, choice of words, or values can just suck on my right nut and make my left one jealous."

"You're so vulgar! Stop it! Just once can you speak to me with a filter on? Dang! Did you forget that you're in the presence of a lady?" I try desperately to contain my laugh.

"Okay, okay. Hey, Beaner...remember when you got fucked in prison?"

I chuckle so hard, I accidentally snort. "You're such an ass."

"Yes, I am. That's one of the many reasons you love me."

Work is so hectic today I didn't have a chance to take my full lunch break. I decide to run across the parking lot to the roach coach for a quick bite before it takes off. As I'm standing in line, I get tapped on the shoulder. On reflex, I turn around. With pure disgust radiating off me, I stare at him.

"Remember me, pretty girl? I remember you." He says with a lewd sneer; a defendant from a previous caseload who I can't stand has the audacity to speak to me.

"I have nothing to say to you. Leave me alone." I turn around and thank God for allowing my order to be ready. I snatch my meal and walk away hastily.

"You people think you're so smart, you're not! I'm the smart one!" I can hear the dirty bastard yell.

Goosebumps instantly rise throughout my body. This man is an evil, conniving, narcissistic sex offender with no remorse for the pain and suffering he caused his seven-year-old niece due to his perverted and malicious actions upon her. I've kept in touch with the victim and her mother for the past two years. As I walk back to my office, my mind goes into overdrive. Once I reach my desk, I immediately call the victim's mom who is also the defendant's sister. No answer. I hang up and contact the probation officer handling his case. Luckily, he responds.

Our conversation lasts about half an hour. The P.O. informs me the defendant hasn't paid any restitution, was allowed by the Court to work as a truck driver that consists of him driving through various states, isn't attending his mandated weekly counseling sessions, and hasn't reported bi-weekly as ordered by the judge. To make matters worse, the defendant moved to southern California without the authorization from probation and is claiming to be transient. The violation submitted for all the offenses was denied. According to probation, the defendant may have either the judge or public defender in his pocket. Instances like this from our judicial system make me lose hope in its purpose.

Sex offenders supervised by parole or probation are supposed to get approval from the Interstate Compact Division. This division is supposed to inform any state that a known registered sex offender is requesting permission to enter their state. The Interstate Compact Division from that state is to decide if permission on their end is granted. Sex offenders under state or local supervision are not allowed to roam the nation freely...it's a violation of federal law. Yet, this sick bastard is allowed to do as he pleases? Where's the sense in that? And now, he's here, wanting to speak with me? Where's my security and protection as a law abiding citizen? Where's the justice to the victim and her family?

My supervisor advises me to write an informational incident report just to be on the safe side...to err on the side of caution is an unwritten rule within our office. Before I head home in the late afternoon, I leave a voicemail message to the defendant's sister. The victim is entitled to know everything regarding her sex offense case, especially the denied violation of probation and that the whereabouts of the defendant are unknown.

As I'm walking to my car from my office, I get an eerie feeling. I look around to see if anything or anyone out of the norm looks suspicious. No. Everything seems normal. Nonetheless, I decide to power walk a bit faster. For whatever reason, I feel like I'm being watched or followed, but I know it's just my paranoia kicking in after seeing that sick bastard earlier today during lunch. As soon as I reach Betty, I immediately turn on the ignition and take off with my heart beating a mile a minute.

When I arrive home, Kade is in our home office working on a new website. Since he's in the zone, I leave him alone to work. I shower and prepare to watch the shows on my DVR. Once I get situated on the couch with my *Breaking Dawn* fleece blanket, I hear a knock at the door. *Ugh. I'm so not in the mood to talk right now.*

Regardless, I get up to open the door. *He's here? Hmm...I wasn't expecting to see him, but I'll have to admit, it's a nice surprise.*

Michael.

"Hi, Michael. I wasn't expecting you." Panic quickly hits me. "Is everything okay? Is my da...Diego okay?"

"Yes, he's fine. He wanted me to check on you and see if there was anything you needed?"

Relief washes over me instantly. "Oh, okay. No, I don't need anything, but please come in. Are you hungry? I have

113

some left over lasagna I made yesterday, you're more than welcome to join me." I'm actually not that hungry, but I figure I can pick his brain and get insight on Diego while he eats.

"No, that's quite all right, I didn't mean to bother you during dinner."

"Oh, stop it. Come in. I don't want to toot my own horn, but my lasagna is kind of a big deal around here." I laugh.

Michael seems to relax a bit. I offer to take his coat. As he takes it off, I notice his broad shoulders. *Stop checking out your dad's attorney, bitch! You're still with Josh! Well, sort of, kind of, not really...oh, shut up! It's just dinner over a casual conversation. Lighten the fuck up!*

I heat up our meal in the microwave, add some salad then grab two beers. His tie is now loose and his sleeves are rolled up. Michael doesn't seem as tense as he did the first time we met. He analyzes me just as much if not more as I analyze him. He's handsome, in a bad ass Marine sort of way.

I decide to break our silence during dinner afraid he might catch me drooling. "How's Diego doing?" As an afterthought, I decide to ask, "Does he talk about me much?"

He takes a sip of his beer. "Your dad is a very strong man. He's a fighter. He's determined. Nothing can hold him down...but you. You're his reason for living and wanting to be a better man. You're the reason he's now fighting his case. Does he talk about you? Well, he mentions your name, but never says anything about you. It's as if it's his way of protecting you, by keeping you a secret...a secret he wants known to the world, but can't."

"Oh. I understand. Umm...Michael? I know we don't know each other, but would you mind talking to me about Diego from your perspective? How did you guys meet? How did you become part of his 'trusted' circle?" Oh, what the hell. It doesn't hurt to ask.

Michael goes from being semi-relaxed to being tense once again. His facial expression and posture don't change much, but something about his aura feels strained. Regardless of his inner battle, he decides to fill me in on his relationship with my dad. "Since your dad has indicated I can speak to you freely about him, I'll answer your questions."

"Thanks." I give him a hint of a smile, but inwardly I'm ecstatic to hear about Diego from someone else other than my mom.

"Your dad used to date my mom." Michael begins.

"Oh." I'm not sure what I was expecting, but that definitely wasn't something I was anticipating to hear.

He continues. "They dated years ago while I was in high school. He was in and out of her life even though they never actually broke up. He was just never a constant presence in her life, but regardless, she always welcomed him back."

"Hmm...that sounds familiar." I mumble. *He did the same thing to my mom! Ugh. Nina! Let the man continue with his story.*

"Excuse me?" He stops his conversation, but seems amused by me.

"Nothing, nothing...please, continue."

"Well, during his absence my mom found out she had a brain tumor and due to its size was now inoperable. She used to complain of severe migraines. Sometimes even the light caused her pain to increase. It had been sometime since my mom had heard from Diego, I could tell she missed him. I decided to go through her things and contact him. Once I was finally able to get ahold of him, I informed him of my mom's health crisis. The next day, he arrived to our house and that's when I met him for the first time." Michael takes a minute for himself.

After a moment of silence, he continues with his story. "My mom didn't have medical insurance at the time, so bills quickly started to overtake our lives. I quit school and worked two jobs just to make ends meet disregarding every single debt collector who contacted us on a daily basis. When your dad found out about our financial situation, he made me return back to school and paid off all our debt, our house, and put my mom's medical bills under his name. He was only in town for two days since he had pending business to take care of, but he made sure my mom was under the best medical care at the Memorial Sloan Kettering Cancer Center."

"Where's that hospital located?" I interrupt.

"In New York. That's where I'm from." He adds.

"Oh. Sorry for interrupting, please continue."

"No problem. Well, as the next few weeks passed, Diego would stop by to check in on my mom from time to time. He explained to me that he was a very busy man and couldn't stay. I understood. I was thankful for his help and never made an issue of his absence. A few short weeks after my mom's tumor diagnosis, her life came to an end. I was there during her last breath. She died peacefully knowing I would be okay. I called Diego to inform him of my mom's passing. Although my mom's family is small and extremely poor, they wanted to contribute financially whatever they could. Diego refused their money and paid for everything himself. After my mother's funeral, Diego asked me what my plans were after high school. I wanted to say my dream was to be a doctor in honor of my mom, but instead, I responded with...a criminal defense attorney."

I'm confused. "Why didn't you say you wanted to be a doctor?"

"I'm not dumb. I knew what business your dad was in, but I was also well aware of everything he had done for my mom and me. His financial support and his presence during my mom's last few weeks allowed her to die in peace. I will forever be grateful and indebted to your dad. I wanted him to understand my loyalty to him. He insisted on paying for my education. After high school, without a second thought I moved to Connecticut. After graduating from Yale Law, I immediately began working for him."

"Wow." Is all I can say. The array of emotions running through me is too much to handle. I try to gather my thoughts to better comprehend my feelings. I know my heart aches for Michael, the loss of a mother is an inconceivable pain no one should have to endure, yet too many of us do. Admiration...his devotion to my father is commendable. But, I also feel uneasy, sort of. If I didn't know any better I'd swear jealousy was also at the forefront of my thoughts.

Jealousy? No. Why?

"Michael?"

"Yes?"

"Did my father attend your high school and law school graduations?"

"Yeah. Why do you ask?"

Ouch. And there it is. My dad was there for Michael during special moments in his life. For me? Umm...not so much.

"No reason." I lie, but immediately shake the stupid feeling off.

I change the subject to a general one. We instantly become comfortable with one another once the topic of my dad is switched to a much more casual one. As he speaks, I unconsciously begin comparing him to Josh. Although they're very different, they're both extremely manly in their own right.

Once we finish our meal, Michael states it's time for him to leave, but first we agree to meet towards the end of the week to visit Diego.

"Well, thanks for stopping by. I appreciate you sharing your past with me. Since we'll be seeing each other often, I hope we can become good friends." I smile warmly at him. Now that I've gotten to know him a tiny bit, he's earned my respect.

As I walk Michael to the door, I give him a hug goodbye. Although my intention was for a brief hug, I notice Michael's hold on me remains a bit longer on my waist than expected. I look up at him and maintain my eyes fixated on his. Just then, the loud slam of my front door along with a deep voice yelling, "Get your fuckin' hands off my lady!" Immediately snaps me out of my reverie.

Shit.

Chapter 7 (Josh)

Breakfast

As I walk into the threshold of Nina's house, a barbaric rage overcomes me when I witness another man's arms embracing my woman. I don't feel my legs as I purposely stride forward toward this asshole.

"Josh! What are you doing here? You can't just barge into my house whenever you fuckin' please!" Nina yells.

I hear her words, but comprehension evades me. All I want is to punish this dick for touching what belongs to me. Vaguely I realize Nina is standing right before me. Without a second thought, I push Nina out of the way and land a right hook on this motherfucker's left eye. He falls back, but gets up and rushes me striking me hard on the side of my rib. Immediately, I manage to get him in a choke hold. Somehow, we end up on the ground with me having the advantage.

"Stop it! Fuckin' stop fighting! Josh, leave Michael alone! We weren't doing anything!" Nina gets on top of me to stop me from throwing punches at the motherfucker beneath me. Soon, I feel a much stronger body assist Nina in getting me off this guy.

I don't fight back afraid of accidentally hitting my lady. Instead, I give up willingly. The asshole on the ground gets up, but doesn't rush me even though he has the opportunity to do so.

Nina addresses her punk ass new friend. "Michael, I'm so sorry. I'll see you at the end of the week. We'll talk then." Then she does the unthinkable and gives him a hug.

"Nina! What the fuck?" I'm ready to pound on this guy again. I stare him down, but he doesn't back away. Nina gets in the middle of us and pushes him with the attempt to guide this Michael guy towards the front door.

"I look forward to seeing you again this Friday." The bastard tells Nina with a smug look.

On reflex, I rush him, but Kade is too quick and stops me before my fist makes contact with the motherfucker's face. Nina practically pushes Michael out of her house. Once he's out, she slams her door and directs her fury to me.

Good. Because I'm pissed as fuck too.

"Who the fuck do you think you are to be fighting in my house? Could you be any more disrespectful? You can't just barge into my house after being absent from my life without an explanation for over a week! No calls, no texts, no visits...nothing! What the fuck?" She takes a deep breath as an attempt to calm down. "You know what? Fuck you. I don't want to hear shit you have to say anymore! I'm done with you!"

I stare at her waiting for her to finish with her rant. She looks absolutely beautiful as she's ready to claw my eyes out.

Kade interrupts. "Oh, hell no! You're going to get an explanation. I'll be damned if I have to listen to you whine about him and wonder what the fuck is going on. Nope! You're gonna have to put your big girl panties on and listen to every word Josh has to say. I'll be by your side to give you support, to stop you from killing him, and well...because I'm dying to hear juicy gossip. It's been awhile. With that said, both of you need to sit your asses down in the living room and have a fuckin' adult conversation. Can you handle that? Yes, you can. As a bonus, I'll be here to act as a mediator."

After a long moment of thinking the situation through, Nina grudgingly makes her way over to the living room and has a seat on the couch. I do also, but sit on the other one since I'm positive she's still after my head.

Nina doesn't waste any time. "You like to preach about trust. How the fuck am I supposed to trust you when I find lipstick on your shirt and find out you have a new assistant who looks like a fuckin' super model with the name of a stripper? And then I see you hugging some lady as you're leaving your office? Did I cause a scene? Nope. But the worst part? You have a son or maybe a whole family! Why the fuck didn't you tell me? You can't expect me to trust you when you're not completely honest! It doesn't work that way!"

"Aww shit, Tree Hugger...you're in deep shit!" Kade adds as he makes himself comfortable on the couch.

I grab one of the many decorative pillows Nina has on the couch and throw it at Kade's face. "Kade, shut the fuck up! Don't make things worse!"

I then direct my attention to Nina. "Baby, I don't know of any lipstick stain you're referring to, I give half hugs to people all the time, so please let that one go. Now, as far as my new assistant is concerned, well, she came highly recommended. She was hired when I took time off to be with my mom at the hospital last month. I've been in Arkansas handling my company's new global account. I haven't had a chance to sit down and speak with her. I usually just give her orders to follow over the phone or by email. Her name is Jelly. So what? The director of my Human Resources department's legal name is

Sunshine and one of my superintendent's name is Happy. I can't help that their parents were a bunch of hippies. I didn't think anything of Jelly's name. Don't be so judgmental." I stare at my lady, but she's busy observing her nails. *No, she's not. I know she's hanging on my every word.*

"And as beautiful as you may think she looks, she will never be you. You're my type. You're the only woman I want to be with. No one compares to you, baby." I attempt to soften her foul mood. *I love you. How could you think I would do you wrong?*

Nina stops focusing on her nails to give me an evil glare. Then has the audacity to roll her eyes at me.

I guess my sweet talk didn't work.

"Nice touch, Tree Hugger. You're busting out the big guns." Kade gives his approval. I ignore him.

My attention is still fixated on my sexy, little spitfire. "Now, as for the lady I was hugging while leaving my office the day you brought me lunch, well, her name is Marisol. She's the ex-girlfriend of my best friend who was also one of my project managers, Daniel."

Kade interrupts...again. "Is Daniel the guy you were with when we caught you grinding some girl's ass over the pool table a while ago? I'm just trying to follow your story and have my facts straight."

"Yeah. Thanks for bringing that up."

"Oh, sure. No problem." Kade smiles genuinely at me.

I'm going to kill Kade.

"As I was saying before I was rudely interrupted. Marisol and Daniel have had serious issues lately. Daniel is back to doing drugs. Due to staff complaints about his aggressive behavior, I directed him to get drug tested, but he refused. I fired him on the spot and things spiraled down from there. Apparently, that day he locked his keys inside his car so he

122

called Marisol to bring his spare set. When she arrived, they got into a big argument. He ended up beating her profusely. I was on my way to your work when I saw him brutally attacking her. When he saw me, he rushed in his car and took off. Marisol laid on the ground unconscious, he left her there assuming she was dead. She was rushed to the hospital and luckily was released a few days later. When you saw her at my office, she was just thanking me for stopping him and rushing her to the emergency room." I stop to see if I get the slightest reaction from Nina. No. Not at all, so I continue with my explanations.

"Let me clarify a little more about Daniel. We were best friends in high school but after graduation, we went our separate paths. He chose drugs and prison. After his release from prison, I helped Daniel with rehab and gave him a job with my company. In time, he did so well, he was promoted to project manager. After the recent complaints of Daniel's aggression and hostility at work, I knew he was back to his old ways. When he beat Marisol that day in the parking lot, he didn't just beat her. Daniel also savagely beat Marisol's three-year-old son, Lorenzo. Daniel has never been fond of the kid because Daniel hates sharing Marisol's attention with him. Daniel's addiction and the resentment he has for the little boy brought on Daniel's abusive behavior.

Lorenzo's biological father passed away due to a coronary artery disease right after Lorenzo was born. Daniel became obsessed with Marisol the moment he first laid eyes on her. Eventually, she turned to Daniel for emotional support. She wanted a family for her new born son so she stayed with Daniel despite his flaws. Recently, he got her addicted to meth as a form of punishment and control.

Daniel has always been violent and jealous. I know he's aware I'm helping Marisol. I decided to keep my distance from you to protect you from his retaliation. The police still haven't found him. Both Marisol and Lorenzo have been staying with me."

Now, I have both Kade and Nina's undivided attention. I proceed with my explanations but focus entirely on Nina. "Baby, when you were parked in front of my house waiting for me, Lorenzo came out of the truck and yelled, 'Dan!' Not 'dad' as you had assumed. Daniel was standing by the gate inside my premises. Lorenzo doesn't speak most likely due to the trauma Daniel has caused him. When he yelled, 'Dan!' it was solely out of fear and desperation. Lorenzo must have known I hadn't seen Daniel yet. Immediately, Marisol grabbed Lorenzo from me and went inside the house to call the police.

Baby, when you took off, I was thankful. I didn't want you anywhere near Daniel. We fought, but once we heard the sirens, he picked up a large rock and hit the left side of my temple. He dazed me and took off running before the police could catch up with him. I'm still afraid he might come after you to spite me for protecting Marisol and Lorenzo. The only thing that gives me peace is the assurance that he doesn't know anything about you or just how much you truly mean to me."

"Well, that explains a shitload! So where are Marisol and Lorenzo now? Are they still at your house? By themselves?" Kade asks.

"Actually, no. I bought a place a block away from here that I'm renting out to them until Daniel is found and Marisol is able to get herself back together again. They're with one of my work crews at their new place. She's giving them direction to make the place more decent and more to her and her son's liking. Marisol has decided against rehab and plans on getting through her addiction on her own."

124

"Oh, okay." Both Nina and Kade state in unison.

"Now that I've said a mouthful, it's your turn to explain why the fuck this Michael guy had his arm wrapped around you."

Kade turns to Nina. "What the fuck? Magic Mike was getting 'touchy feely' with you? It's a good thing I copped a feel on his ass during the commotion. That'll teach him not to ignore me again!" Kade cackles at his own travesty.

Nina hits Kade's arm then directs her attention to me. "Michael is part of my father's defense counsel team. We're meeting on Friday to visit my dad. I spoke with Diego and he instructed me to pose as a paralegal working with Michael for my protection and to avoid suspicion of having close ties with Diego. I promise you there's nothing going on between Michael and me. Today, he stopped by unexpectedly per Diego's orders to see if there was anything I needed. I invited him to dinner just to get insight on my dad. That's all. I was just hugging him goodbye when you walked in on us. I apologize for doubting you, but you can't blame me. You can't keep me in the dark about things and not expect my mind to conjure up ludicrous assumptions. I'm a nut job...you should know that by now."

"You sure are! In more ways than one!" Kade chimes in.

Nina scowls at Kade as he's lying on the couch behind her; she gets up then plops herself right on his stomach. Instantly, Kade grunts loudly from being winded with the force of Nina's weight. Despite his lack of breath, he still speaks. "You know...you don't have...to eat...everything...on your plate."

If I didn't know any better, I'd swear an exorcist took over my lady's body. Her distorted expression looks sinister. "Fucker! Are you insinuating I'm fat?"

Kade just doesn't know when to stop. "No. Just very...heavy."

Nina's eyes come out of their sockets. It's my indication to get up and grab her before she kills Kade. It feels nice not being the target of her psychotic and rage. I take advantage that she gives in easily to me and place her on my lap.

Kade gives me a look of gratitude. "Thanks, man. I owe you one."

My demented lady takes off her slipper and throws it at Kade. "You! Be quiet! I don't want to hear the sound of your voice until further notice! Capisce?"

"Yeah, yeah...evil wench!" Kade gives Nina a disgruntle glower then turns his interest to me. "So, Josh, when are we going to meet Marisol and Lorenzo?"

Nina then focuses on me again. Clearly, she was wondering the same thing.

She stares at me with her beguiling brown eyes. Just one look, one smile from her can turn a bad day into a perfect one. "First, let me apologize to you, my beautiful lady for keeping you in the dark. I did it for your protection, but I probably should have communicated what my intentions were before I kept my distance. Call me crazy, but something told me that if you knew the situation I was in, you would have made your presence even more known. I know this may be hard for you to believe, baby...but...you tend to be tenacious and difficult during intense situations."

"Preach it, brother! Stubborn is her middle name...Cheesecake 'the stubborn mule' Moretti...mmm hmm...that's her name all right!"

Nina sighs. "I guess I have to mule slap you now." She gives my nose a light kiss.

"What's a mule slap?" I ask confused.

"The next time you go down on me as I'm lying down and I'm ready to cum, I'm going to slap my thighs together hard while your head is between my legs. That should make you clench up around my pussy and give me a little extra. It might make your ears ring, but oh, well!"

My eyes light up. "I'm just glad I get to tap that...ass...tonight!"

"Ba dum tss!" Kade makes the sound effect of a drum to my cheesy punchline.

We all laugh and I take that moment to text my foreman. I direct him to drive Marisol and Lorenzo to Nina's house. They're only a block away, but I don't feel comfortable with them walking here.

"Okay, Marisol and Lorenzo should be here any minute now." I announce.

"OMG...why did I just get nervous?" Nina states in a panic.

"Me too!" Kade yells.

"Huh?" I'm confused. "What are you both so worried about?"

"We've never really been around small kids. The kids I've dealt with at work are...different. We've never even had any kids in my mom's house or our home...ever." Nina explains.

Kade sighs. "I'm just going to be quiet, knowing me I'll choose this moment to have diarrhea of the mouth from nervousness."

"Are you two serious? You're both being ridiculous. I'm sure Marisol and Lorenzo are more nervous to meet you than you are to meet them."

Nina bites her bottom lip. "We don't even have baby food. Our house isn't kid proof with those weird latches on kitchen cabinets I once saw."

Kade adds to her complaints. "We don't even have those weird pouches kids drink from! Or any toys!"

Nina rolls her eyes at Kade. "You have your dolls, Kade! The ones you collect."

"What the fuck? They're not dolls! They're action figures! Get it straight!"

I can't help, but chuckle. Nina and Kade really are nervous of meeting Lorenzo. Marisol...not at all, but Lorenzo...definitely.

Within a few minutes, there's a knock on the door. I get up to answer it and leave both worry warts in the living room. Just as I suspected...I notice the anxiousness radiating off Marisol. I know she's craving a fix to calm her nervous, so she's definitely struggling to remain strong. All she can do for now is take things one step at a time.

Marisol gives me a forced smile which comes across as sad. Her brown eyes look tired, her brown hair is picked up in a ponytail, and she's wearing a black sweats outfit that covers her skinny physique. Marisol may be thin, but it's not in a healthy sort of way and her face now has small red blotches over her once perfectly smooth olive tone skin. Marisol was beautiful in her own right when she first met Daniel, but in the last three years, their relationship, his abuse, and her drug usage have taken a toll on her.

Lorenzo on the other hand, is perfect. The bruising he had has completely faded away since he moved in with me. He's been eating a lot more causing him to gain weight and look much healthier than before. His brown hair is slightly on the long side and a bit shaggy, but he won't allow me to give his hair a trim which is fine by me. He has the biggest, round brown eyes I've ever seen with the sweetest smile to make even the baddest bad ass melt. My heart aches knowing how cruel and malicious Daniel treated him. How could Daniel look into Lorenzo's sweet face and still have the nerve to beat him like he did? I decide not to ponder on the issue any longer and begin with my introductions.

Nina surprises me by rushing Marisol with a genuine hug. "Anything you need...please...don't hesitate to ask." Nina smiles warmly at Marisol. *Oh...that's right, my lady is really big on saving the world. I don't think I could love her anymore even if I tried. My heart is hers.*

Then Lorenzo catches Nina's eyes. She squats down to his eye level. "Aren't you the cutest thing EVER? I could eat you up, you're just so darn cute!" Lorenzo smiles shyly at Nina then hides half of his body behind his mom.

"Hey." Is all Kade says.

Oh, Shit! Kade was serious about being nervous! And to think...all it took was a three-year-old boy to shut him up!

The remainder of the evening we spend getting to know each other without asking intrusive questions. It's a very fine line that we all do our best not to cross. Lorenzo is kept entertained by watching *Team Umizoomi* on Nick Jr. Towards the end of the night, everyone is much more at ease, including Kade although he didn't say much. For once, he listened without interruptions.

"Lorenzo, sweetie..." Nina taps him on the shoulder to get his attention. "It's getting late, honey. Would you mind if I went with you and your mommy back to Josh's house? Is that okay with you?"

Lorenzo immediately nods his head enthusiastically for approval.

My lady then stares me down willing me to go against her and Lorenzo's wishes. Since I don't have a death wish, I remain silent.

Lorenzo quickly gets up, puts on his coat, and grabs Nina's hand leading her to the front door. "Okay, let's go, Lorenzo's ready." Nina snatches a fleece blanket from the couch and heads out the door. "Don't forget to lock up!" She yells at Kade. It doesn't go unnoticed that Nina's still wearing her slippers and didn't stop to grab a jacket. Now that Lorenzo reached out to her, she's not letting go.

When we arrive to my house, Lorenzo is asleep. The busy day finally caught up with him. I carry him inside and put him in my guest room. "Thanks, Josh. I don't know how I'll ever be able to repay you for everything you've done for us." Marisol tells me with tear filled eyes.

"Stop. Please. You have nothing to thank me for. Just focus on getting your life back on track without Daniel. You're a good woman. You deserve better than the life you've endured these past few years. He'll get caught soon then you'll be able to live your life in peace. In the meantime, go to sleep and rest up. Tomorrow, I'm giving you my credit card to buy the furniture you need for your new place. You need to make that place feel like home...for Lorenzo's sake. I don't want you going out by yourself just yet. I've added a high tech security system so you should be safe. Call me or the police immediately if you hear something out of the norm. I'll call to tell you when I'm on my way home so you don't get caught off guard." I hug her and kiss the top of her head. "Good night."

This situation has been draining, I'm just thankful Nina is aware of everything and that I no longer have to keep my distance from her. I'm tired of my loved ones having to live in hiding due to vengeful assholes.

I walk into my bedroom and see nothing. "Baby...where are you?" I hear music playing, but don't see her. I step inside my master bath to find my lady in my tub covered in bubbles with the song, "One in a Million" by Aaliyah playing in the background and the lights dimmed low.

Nina smiles at me as she bites her bottom lip. "Hey, stranger." She looks relaxed. "I've missed you. Care to join me?"

I take my time undressing. I want to savor the picture of my lady in the tub anxiously awaiting me. She's one hell of a sight. "Do you even have to ask? Isn't it obvious?" As soon as I remove my boxers, my stiff shaft comes to full view.

"Come here." My lady commands. She positions herself on her knees, but remains in the tub. As I stand before her, she places both hands on my ass and pulls me towards her even more. She then licks my cock from its base to the top and twirls her tongue around the tip.

Fuck me.

"I've missed you so much, babe." Nina dabs my dick with gentle kisses.

There's nothing more empowering, yet humbling than seeing my woman on her knees for me. "I've missed you too, baby."

"Get in. The water's perfect." She makes room for me to sit upright then lies on my chest with her back facing me.

"Babe..."

"Yesss?" I drag out the word in the form of a question.

"Tonight...I just want you to hold me." Instantly my arms wrap around her wet, silky chest. "Actually, no. I need you to hold me."

"Whatever you want. What's bothering you?"

"I thought I had really lost you this time. I assumed you had lied to me. My mind ran wild while you were away from me." She pauses for a long time wondering how to explain what is truly eating at her. "The worst part for me was thinking that you had a son by somebody else. I guess the moment Lorenzo ran up to you is when I realized that although I know neither one of us wants kids, I had assumed you would be the father of mine and I would be the only mother of yours if we changed our minds in the future. I don't want you to ever have that bond with anyone, but me."

I kiss her shoulder gently. "You don't have to worry about me having kids with anyone other than you. I don't want kids...ever. If I change my mind, you'll be the first to know. Deal?"

"Deal. So now, tell me...what did you miss about me exactly?"

"I missed how you always place your cold feet in between mine and expect me to warm them up for you. I missed waking up and finding you completely bundled up with the exception of one bare foot that always tends to hang out. I missed seeing you in the morning with crust between your eyes." I laugh.

"I never have crust between my eyes, liar!" Nina elbows me right in the gut.

"So violent. Okay, okay...honestly? I missed feeling your kisses in the middle of the night. Even when you're sleeping, you kiss my chest...or my back...or my arm...sometimes, even just my hand. I love it. It makes me feel loved even when I know you're not completely conscious, I know I'm still in your heart."

"You are...always." She whispers.

We continue with our light conversation and once we're finished with our bath, we get ready for bed. She puts her hair in a bun then gets under the covers stark-naked. Right away, I join her. Nina turns her back to me giving me a flirtatious smirk. I take advantage and glide my dick on the crack of her ass leaving a trail of precum behind. I caress the flawless, delicate skin of her stomach and work my way up to her large, perfect breasts.

"Umm...not so fast, Tree Hugger. We're not having sex tonight. You're going to hold me, spoon me, caress me, and kiss me, but that's it. No hanky panky tonight, Mister!"

I laugh. "No hanky panky? Deprive me from anything, but that! Why can't we have the best of both worlds...cuddling AND hanky panky?"

"If you think I'm just going to let you get away with fucking me in prison then not calling me, texting me, or coming over like you said you were without any consequences...you have another thing coming! Hmph." She exaggeratedly turns around for dramatic purposes.

"So, this is payback? Come on, baby." I kiss her shoulder and beg with no shame. "My dick is as hard as a rock. Let me pet your kitty...let me taste your meow, meow...let me pound the punanni." I look at the clock, it's almost midnight. "Come on, baby, let me fuck the old day out of you and fuck you into tomorrow."

"You're not funny or clever, you know." She's trying her best to remain serious, but I know it's just a matter of time before she caves.

As I remain behind her, I kiss her shoulder and work my way to her collarbone and neck. Then I massage her breasts and alternate by twisting her erect nipples. I get the effect I want and hear her moan. "Come on, baby, tell me some bow chicka wow wow doesn't sound good right now. You know it does. How about we do the nasty? Don't you want to be a cowgirl and ride this stallion? Or perhaps a little whoopie is more to your liking?" Now, I'm the one trying my best to keep a grave face.

"Oh, no...no...no, sir. No sucky fucky for you."

"Baby! I want to screw you! I want to smash you! I want to ram you! I want to plow you! I want to bone you! Name it...that's what I want to do to you! You're giving me blue balls for fucks sake!"

"Good. I hope you learn your lesson. There will be no relations jumping off tonight. No horizontal mambo. No rocking the boat. No knockin' the boots. Nothing. Zero. Zilch. Nada. Capisce?

"Fine. But I know you'll be going to bed craving the 'Dirty Dirty.'"

"Hmph." She can't deny the truth. The whole night she remains wrapped around me with a silly grin on her face.

The next morning, I wake up ravenous and kiss my lady's sweet lips. "Baby, I'm hungry for your peach." She smiles as she's still asleep. I work my way down until I get between her legs, then...I dig in. It's so good...I could eat her peach for hours.

"Baby, I'm hungry too." She whines. "I want a FAT sausage with eggs. I hear they're full of protein. Please, papi...give it to me." My little sex kitten begs. "You know I'm all about being healthy." She adds with devious happiness radiating off her beautiful face.

I raise my body above her and ram myself into her over and over and over again.

"Oh!" She yells. "This is...the best fuckin' breakfast...EVER!"

I couldn't agree with her more.

CHAPTER 8 (KADE)

ROTTEN KIDS

"**K**ade! Are you up?" Cheesecake yells as she barges into the house with a ridiculous grin.

"I'm in the kitchen. Can you tone it down a bit? I'm still half asleep." I complain.

She dismisses my request and continues to speak with a high tone. "I called you, but I got your voicemail. You have a doctor's appointment today I'm sure you forgot about. I took the morning off work to accompany you. Hurry up and get ready. I call dibs on the shower first!"

"That doctor's so boring though. He has no personality or people skills. He just has a miserable face. My wound is healing just fine. I'm not going."

"I'm sure you'll think of a way to fuck with him. Besides, I left my man to attend this appointment with you, so now...you're going!" She just loves barking orders.

I give Cheesecake a long and dramatic sigh. "You. Suck."

Once we arrive at the medical center, Nina heads to the cafeteria to grab a drink while I check in for my appointment. Shortly after I've registered, a nurse calls my name. I follow her to a private room and allow her to take my vital signs. A few minutes later, the doctor enters with his sour puss face. Right after he's done examining my wound, there's a light knock on the door and Cheesecake enters.

"May I come in?"

"Are you his wife?" The doctor asks.

"Ha! She wishes she could get with someone as hot as me!" I chuckle. "Nah. She's just my sis."

"Please come in." The doctor moves aside to let Cheesecake have a seat.

"You're both brother and sister?" With a doubt, he turns his statement into a question.

"Yeah, we have different dads though. My dad is the milk man and Nina's is the mail man." I explain.

"Our mom used to get around. Total whore." Nina chimes in.

"Our mom used to be one of Hugh Heffner's girlfriends and lived at the Playboy Mansion, but then she got old so he gave her the boot." I add.

The doctor clears his throat. Clearly, we've made him feel uncomfortable. *Mission accomplished.*

It takes all my will power to refrain from bursting into laughter, but I manage to contain myself. "Back in her day, our mom was also a disco bunny at Studio 54...dancing and grooving to the jive music of the Bee Gees while snorting lines of cocaine with celebrities." I manage to say with a straight face.

"Okay, Mr. Daly, since your wound is healing accordingly, you're good to go unless you have any further questions.

"Nope. No questions. Thanks! Oh, and my mom owns a bakery in Little Italy. If you're ever in the area, be sure to stop by and say hello." I shake the doctor's hand on my way out.

Nina smiles at him. "Oh, and if you do run into our mom, tell her I said it's okay for you to taste her biscuits. Bye!" Nina smiles sweetly at the old man whose eyes just popped out.

We decide after our appointment to stop by Mama V's bakery for brunch. When we arrive, she's thrilled to see us. She stops assisting a customer and lets one of her staff to take over the order.

She rushes us with open arms. "Aww...my brats! I'm so happy to see you!"

"Us too, mom. We brought food!" Nina states excitedly.

"Awesome! Have a seat while I bring some drinks and dessert."

We sit by the window overlooking the park across the street. Mama V returns with a tray consisting of two cannoli, a large slice of fedora, and three drinks then has a seat with us. "So tell me. How was your doctor's appointment?"

Screw my meal. Dessert comes first when it comes to Mama V's amazing cannoli. "My wound is healing fine. I thought the appointment was a total waste, but I'm glad I went. We talked about you to the doctor." I take a bite of my favorite Italian pastry.

"Ugh. Don't tell me you're still telling people I'm in the process of a sex change." Mama V says as she prepares to dig into her salad.

"Nope. That got old after the twentieth random person we told. Today, we just said you're a whore." Nina states nonchalantly.

"And that you snort lines of cocaine." I add.

Mama V shakes her head. "You kids are rotten."

Oh, no she didn't. "Hey, we said you snort cocaine with CELEBRITIES. So...you're welcome." *Some people can be so ungrateful.*

"Gee...thanks. You're stories just keep getting more and more elaborate. At least you're not telling people I had sex with a priest in a confessional anymore or that I only have threesomes with midgets." She tries to sound appalled and contain a smile from being revealed, but fails miserably. "There's never a dull moment with you two."

Nina suddenly becomes overtly excited. "OMG...it just hit me! Kade! We can finally brag about mom! Hello? She's a cougar dating a young stud muffin! Finally! Something interesting!"

"Fuckin' shit! Oops...sorry, mom." I try not to curse too much around her. "I can't believe I haven't told anyone! I'll get on that asap!"

During the remainder of our visit, Nina and Mama V discuss Diego, I add my two cents about Michael, Josh's situation is mentioned, and mom opens up about her new relationship with our friend, Dillon. Then Mama V informs us that Celeste and her male friend, Michael are no longer together. She directs us not to mention him to Celeste. Overall, it's a great time spent with my two favorite ladies. As Cheesecake and I are about to leave, Mama V hands us to two pink boxes from her bakery to take to Josh's since we're headed there to check up on Marisol and Lorenzo. One box has various pastries and the other is filled with different Italian cookies...Taralli, Anisette, Chocolate Toto, and Cucidati.

I look at Mama V crazy. "Mom! That's a lot of food for only three people."

She laughs. "Obviously, you've never seen Josh in action. He can eat! That boy has a mean appetite."

"He sure does." Cheesecake says with a smirk.

"Eww. Did you see that mom?" I point at Cheesecake. "Your daughter is being inappropriate."

"What? Me? Noooo."

"We all know what you meant by 'he sure does,' perv! No one wants to know about your freaky shenanigans with the Tree Hugger. Well, I do, but not in front of mom!" I give Mama V a sly wink.

"Okay, you two. Drive safely." She hugs us goodbye. "I'll be leaving in a few minutes to visit Celeste at the hospital."

In route to Josh's house, I pull over in front of a store and direct Cheesecake to buy a car window marker. She doesn't ask questions and gets out to buy it. I remain in the car since I'm illegally parked at a bus stop. Once she returns, I check to see if any buses are coming, none are so I get out and head to the back of my car. Cheesecake hands me the marker. On the back of my X5's tinted window, I write, "OUR MOM'S A COUGAR DATING A YOUNG STUD! FINALLY! WE'RE SO PROUD!"

Cheesecake snatches the marker from me then adds, "#OurMomIsCoolerThanYours" with a smiley face. "There. Much better!" She gets her phone and takes a picture. As I'm driving, she sends the picture to Mama V and posts it on Instagram, Facebook, and Twitter.

Instantly, Mama V replies. "What did she say?" I ask.

"That she's going to choke us, but added tons of laughing emojis with her text. She's so silly. She's lucky to have us. Her life would be so boring otherwise!" Cheesecake jokes.

When we arrive at the Josh's house, Nina sends Marisol a text warning her we're outside and are coming in so that she won't get startled. Marisol is glad to have us as company, but appears a bit nervous. I can only guess she's struggling with her addiction, but does her best to remain strong and avoid temptation. Lorenzo immediately rushes Cheesecake and me to show us his new coloring books with a genuine smile.

Cheesecake bends down to his level and crushes him with a big hug. He rewards her with an even greater smile than before. "How are you, cutie? We couldn't wait to see you so we brought you some special treats." Cheesecake turns to Marisol and asks if it's okay for him to have a cookie. Marisol lightly nods her head. "Yaaaay! Your mom said you can have one!"

"Hey, what's up little man? How about you give me a high five?" When he reaches over to slap my hand I instantly remove my hand not allowing him to slap it. I notice he gets a kick out of being tricked so I do it a few more times. His posture changes to a determined one so I finally cave and let him slap my hand. He's so excited he grabs my hand and pulls me into the living room. "Hey, Cheesecake...how bout you ladies bring us men some milk and cookies? Right, little man?" He nods his head enthusiastically.

"Okay!" Cheesecake smiles at Lorenzo lovingly. "Marisol, can you give me a hand please?" That's code for girl talk.

"Of course." Marisol replies.

Lorenzo and I spend our time coloring and watching a cartoon of kid pirates. He loves it. I ask him questions and he either nods or shakes his head as a response. Although Lorenzo doesn't speak, he can be very animated and I find myself truly enjoying his company as we eat our snack in front of the TV.

My heart breaks for Lorenzo when I imagine everything Daniel put him through. To think of how he beat Lorenzo and Marisol so savagely makes me recall my own tortured childhood. Unfortunately, I didn't have anyone who came to my rescue. I did have neighbors who took pity on me from time to time and fed me. I'll never forget their graciousness because they gave me food during a time when they had nothing to give. The woman who gave me life, also made it hell for me. She hated me. She told me every single day how worthless I was and how much she regretted having me. She brought various men in and out of my life all worse than the previous one. Too many nights I would get beat for crying...crying from stomach pains due to starvation. My mother never had money for food, but she always managed to buy new things for herself. After all, she had to look good to get attention from men who usually only used her for a night or two. I'm glad Lorenzo now has us and no matter what happens, I will never allow anyone to put him through the abuse I suffered at his age. His mom better get her shit together sooner rather than later. I try to block Marisol from my mind since all I tend to do is judge her. I don't know her story and I'm no one to judge, but it kills me to see her little boy be so traumatized that he doesn't speak.

After an hour of hanging out, it's time for me to drop Cheesecake off at work. We say our goodbyes, but before leaving she promises Lorenzo she'll be back in the evening with a little surprise just for him. Lorenzo's eyes get bigger with enthusiasm, I didn't think that was possible since he already has the biggest, most adorable eyes I've ever seen.

A week has passed since Cheesecake and Josh got back together. All is great in their world. Marisol and Lorenzo will get to move into their new place in a few days. Lorenzo has become somewhat of a celebrity within our small family, both Mama V and Celeste fell in love with him the instant they met him. I've progressed from walking to lightly jogging. The pain from my wound decreases daily as I become stronger. I'm back to my whorish ways and loving every minute of it. Normalcy is finally back in our lives.

"Cheesecake! Hurry up, already! What's taking you so long?"

"Sheesh! I'm ready, I'm ready. The alcohol isn't going anywhere! So, what do you think?" Cheesecake spins around to show off her outfit. Today, she's wearing black capri pants and a black v-neck fitted t-shirt that reads, "Drink up, Bitches!" in white lettering over a green shamrock. She has her hair in a neat sock bun with very subtle makeup.

"You're so hot, you're on fire even with that turd on your head. Now here...drink this." I hand Cheesecake an Irish coffee.

"Hater. It's too early to be drinking." She looks at me crazy.

"You can't drink all day if you don't start in the morning."

"You're so right, I'm game!" She sees Josh and instantly lights up. "Hey there, sexy beast!" Cheesecake kisses Josh then makes her way over to Dillon and gives him a hug. "What's up, MILF lover or should I say mother...fucker?" She giggles. "Long time no see! So glad you're hanging out with us today. Ever since you got with my mom, you've been M.I.A."

Dillon smiles and blushes slightly. He's always been the reserved one in our group. "Let me guess, you and mom are still in the stage where your farts smell like roses." Cheesecake teases and we all laugh. "I'm glad she chose to stay with Marisol and Lorenzo, they'll have a good time together while we get shitfaced."

Just then, we hear a honk. "The cab's here!"

We head over to Market Street to post for the St. Paddy's Day Parade showcasing the Irish community and culture in various forms. Afterwards, we make our way to a block party on Green Street in the North Beach district sponsored by an Irish Pub. The whole day consists of live music, bagpipers, Irish dancers, and of course food from the motherland. At one point, my neck was so full of green beads, I made two cougars work their magical lap dancing skills to get my beads. We drank green beer, Irish Whiskey Sours, and Car Bombs throughout the day.

As we're enjoying an 80s tribute band, I see her. Cheesecake rushes to me and pinches my arm, "That's her! The Jelly chick. Ugh. She just rubs me the wrong way."

"You mean...that tall glass of water in this dry desert heat walking towards us."

142

Cheesecake looks at me as if I'm speaking in tongues. "Are you fucking kidding me right now?" She walks over to Josh and wraps her arm around his as he's talking to Dillon. Shortly after, the Jelly girl approaches our group.

"Hey, there boss. I'm surprised to see you out here." She directs her gaze solely at Josh. *What the fuck are we? Chopped liver?*

"Jelly. Hey. Let me introduce you. To my right is Dillon, the beautiful lady wrapped around my arm is my girlfriend, Nina, and that handsome guy who's blatantly staring at you is Kade." *Handsome guy...I always knew you wanted me, Tree Hugger, but not now. Right now, I need to get a piece of this Jelly chick.*

I extend my hand for a handshake, she takes it, but I use that moment to pull her closer to me and kiss the back of her hand. "People who like me call me K.D...the choice is yours."

Jelly gives me a knowing look with a wicked grin as she runs her tongue over her perfectly white teeth. "It's nice to meet you, K.D."

Aww...shit. Sookie sookie, now. My horns immediately come about.

"Everyone, this is my new assistant, Jelly. She recently moved to the Bay Area. She's originally from Spain." Josh states matter-of-factly.

"Jelly, would you like to join us? I was just about to order another round of drinks."

Josh interrupts. "Kade, I'm sure Jelly needs to get back to her friends. The last thing anyone wants to do is hang out with their boss on their day off."

Jelly only focuses on Josh and me. Dillon and Cheesecake might as well be invisible. "Maybe some other time, I just wanted to say hi to my boss, that's all. You guys have a great night. I'll see you around, K.D."

As she walks away, I can sense the drool forming. "Fuck. I'd give up my right nut just to get a taste of her. She's fine and sexy as shit! Damn!"

Nina looks at me with a pout. "Whatever. I guess...assuming you're into the supermodel looking type. Lucky for you, she looked like she was ready to pounce on you."

"Lucky for me? Shit...lucky for her! She's gonna find out what K.D. stands for!"

"What does K.D. stand for?" Josh asks curiously.

"Killer Dick, baby!" I announce proudly.

Josh makes a disgusted expression. "Fuckin' asshole! You told me to call you K.D. when we first met!"

I sigh. "Tree Hugger, get over yourself. That ship has sailed. You had your chance. You chose Cheesecake. Now, I've moved on. Your loss."

"I need another beer. I can't handle Kade when he's delusional and his alter ego is in full effect." Josh gives a dramatic sigh.

❧

Moving day for Marisol and Lorenzo is finally here. Their new home is ready. Josh's crew practically gutted the whole place then worked vigorously to renovate it with modern conveniences. The furniture that was ordered online has been arriving these past two days. Marisol and Lorenzo literally left their old life with only the clothes on their back. Moving day was fairly easy.

Later that evening, Marisol and Lorenzo stop by our house with goodies in hand. "Lorenzo wanted to make you guys a special treat for being so kind..." Marisol stops speaking and instantly gets choked up. "So kind and generous with us. May

God repay you with countless blessings because right now, I have nothing to give." A tear escapes Marisol. Cheesecake instantly embraces her with a loving hug. Josh picks up Lorenzo and takes him to the kitchen to give the girls a private moment. Cheesecake hands me the cupcake filled tray.

"Aww, little man! You made us chocolate cupcakes." I ask. He shakes his head.

"No? So you're mom made them? That's still cool!" Lorenzo continues to shake his head.

"Did your mom buy them then?" Again, he shakes his head.

"They're not just chocolate cupcakes, they're S'mores cupcakes." Marisol states from the living room.

"Whaaaaaat? Those are my favorite! You made them with your mommy, little man?" Lorenzo finally nods his head proudly.

Cheesecake then yells. "Hey guys, we're going downstairs. I'm going to get Marisol some items to stock her house with."

"If you're leaving, I'm coming with you." Josh responds.

"No, silly. We're just going to my garage." Cheesecake clarifies.

Josh appears confused.

"Hey, Josh. Have you ever been to our garage?" I ask amused.

"No. Why?"

"So, you don't know about Cheesecake's hobby or obsession like I prefer to call it?"

"No. Spill it, Kade." Josh demands.

I chuckle hard.

Cheesecake walks in. "What's so funny? I forgot to grab some bags."

"You! You haven't told Josh you're a hoarder and have a serious shopping addiction!"

Cheesecake looks at me appalled. "Hoarders are messy and unclean! I'm not a hoarder! I'm a couponer, punk! Don't get it twisted. My stock pile is pretty and well organized so don't go around painting an ugly picture of me! I am not a hoarder!"

Josh stands. "Come on, baby. Let's go see what Kade is yapping his trap about."

I grab Lorenzo's hand. "Come on, little man. Bring your cupcake."

We all head downstairs to witness Cheesecake's well organized madness. She's the only person I know who had a garage modernized to accommodate her shopping habits. She has shelving and cabinets on every wall from top to bottom and a small corner for her treadmill, Lucifer. She changed the lighting and even had an epoxy shield added to the garage's floor so that it could look "pretty." Needless to say, our cars have never been inside our garage.

Women.

Every cabinet and shelf is completely stocked with hygiene products, cleaning supplies, and food. I used to get irritated with her when she would come home with sixty bottles of Downy or fifty bottles of shampoo. In time, I realized it was a battle with her I was never going to win. Once her stockpile increased in size, she began donating to several needy families, homeless shelters, and churches. It's one of the many good deeds she contributes to society with a hope of making it a better place.

She's fuckin' awesome.

"Nina, why so much?" Marisol asks.

"I'm glad you asked, Marisol! Because sometimes the stores practically pay me to take the items from them and other times I spend pennies per item instead of retail price. It hurts my heart and soul to have to pay full price on anything. I love coupons. They're like free money! You definitely have to come shopping with me one day!"

Marisol smiles at Nina's passion.

"Okay, okay...it's a little scary that you have so much of everything, but if it floats your boat. I'm cool with it." Josh winks at her. She returns the gesture.

"Oh, before I forget, I have some clothes I've never worn with tags still on them. If you're interested, you're welcome to them. Every time I see you, Marisol, you're always wearing black. Girl, I've been there. It might be time to embrace colors."

Marisol's expression immediately saddens. "Umm...I wear black because I'm in mourning."

An awkward silence instantly fills the room.

"I'm so sorry, Marisol. Sometimes I just have a big mouth. I apologize. Who passed away?" Cheesecake instantly regrets prying.

"I'd rather not discuss. The whole situation is very upsetting to me."

Cheesecake desperately tries to change the subject. "I completely understand. How about we get the items we came here for?"

"Sounds good." Marisol gives a hint of a smile to put Cheesecake at ease.

"Come, men! Let's leave the ladies and get some milk with cupcakes. How does that sound?"

Lorenzo excitedly nods his head.

The following evening, I go out on a date mostly to pick up the merchandise I ordered. The girl works at the gift shop in Alcatraz. I met her the morning of Cheesecake's photo shoot.

Since I was so busy flirting and keeping guard while Josh and Cheesecake got their freak on in one of the prison's cells, I failed to buy any cheesy memorabilia. Tonight she brought me the t-shirts I purchased over the phone that read, "Psycho Ward."

The girl was nice enough, but for some reason after we fucked, I had no interest to remain by her side. As I'm headed home past midnight, right by the corner of my block, I notice a small gathering of people in a panic. My curiosity gets the best of me, so I pull over to find out what the issue is. As I walk around them to see what they're hovering over, my heart instantly stops when I see a small lifeless body on the ground by the sidewalk.

Lorenzo.

"What the fuck happened?" I yell to no one in particular or to everyone standing witness. At this point, I'm not sure and it really doesn't matter. I push a lady to the side who's holding Lorenzo's tiny limp hand. "Someone call 911! What the fuck happened? Answer me!" Afraid to move him, I kneel before Lorenzo and bring his little hand to my chest, praying and begging God to save his life. I notice blood in Lorenzo's mouth running down his cheek. I instantly shut my eyes tighter and pray harder.

A young guy steps forward and states the paramedics are on their way. He informs me the little boy caught his attention because he was crossing the street so late at night by himself, but before he made it to the sidewalk, a black car drove by and hit him. The car never stopped.

Chapter 9 (Kade)

Muscles

The sirens of the ambulance shatter the hope of this situation being just a nightmare. It's a coldhearted reality. I stand to make room for the paramedics as they rush to Lorenzo's side. Having to speak with them and acknowledge Lorenzo's unresponsive tiny body pulls brashly at my heart. Tears I seldom shed are flowing freely as I see the emergency response team working desperately to save this little boy's life.

"We have a pulse!" I hear a paramedic say.

Everything after that statement becomes difficult to comprehend. I drop to my knees and beg God once again not to let Lorenzo die on his way to the hospital. "Please Lord, let him live. He doesn't deserve to die. Protect him. Have mercy on him and spare his life." I whisper as I pray intensely with my soul. I have never been a religious person, but I have always believed in God.

Numbly, I get up and join Lorenzo in the ambulance. I text Cheesecake directing her to meet me at the hospital closest to our house.

She responds immediately.

OMG! What happened?

I don't have the energy or the clear mind to text.

Lorenzo was hit by a car. Explain later.

She understands.

On our way.

Less than half an hour after finally arriving at the hospital, Cheesecake and Josh arrive. Cheesecake rushes me crying hysterically. "What happened?"

I do my best to reiterate the only facts given to me by a witness. Every other critical detail is unknown at this time. Josh excuses himself and makes his way to four police officers huddled up in a corner. A nurse then directs us to have a seat in the waiting room. She promises to inform us of Lorenzo's status as soon as she's aware of his situation. Josh remains in the emergency room speaking with the cops.

"Have you spoken with Marisol?" Cheesecake asks once we're in the waiting room.

"No. She didn't even cross my mind. All of this is probably her fuckin' fault!"

Cheesecake becomes livid. "We don't know that! I've called and sent her three text messages with no response. I hate not knowing what's going on! My thoughts have my mind in turmoil. I need to know something...anything! I'm starting to freak out!"

Three long hours later without any word from medical staff or Josh causes Cheesecake and I to be at our wit's end.

Eventually, Cheesecake and I fall asleep on the stiff chairs of the emergency room's waiting room. It's not until the wonderful aroma of freshly brewed coffee awakens my senses that I become fully alert once again. Josh pulls up a chair to sit right in front of us.

Cheesecake yawns with an exaggerated stretch. "Baby, what happened? How's Lorenzo? Have you spoken with Marisol? Does she know we're here? What's going on?"

Josh hands us our coffees.

"Just what I need...thanks, man."

Cheesecake blows him a kiss as gratitude. I do the same.

Josh looks so emotionally beat, he doesn't bother to look up. "The past hours have been hectic. Lorenzo was in a coma for several hours, but although he sustained spinal fractures and head gashes, none of his extensive injuries are life threatening."

Thank you, Lord.

"Oh, thank God!" Cheesecake yells forgetting about her surroundings.

"I know, I know. Trust me...I was praying also." Josh confesses as he pulls Cheesecake closer to him and kisses her forehead. "As for the whole situation, apparently the cops received notice from dispatch that the silent alarm I had installed at Marisol's house had been triggered and minutes later an emergency call from Marisol's neighbor was received stating they heard a lot of yelling and things being destroyed. Once the police arrived, the neighbor came out and informed the cops they had just seen a man leave the house through the back and saw him getting into a black Charger. The neighbor also informed the cops that she had seen a little boy leave through the front door while all the commotion was going on. The neighbor stated she was on her way to chase after the child when the police arrived. The cops called for backup as they entered Marisol's house. When they found her, she was on the ground, severely beaten, and with a needle on her arm. Her speech was slurred, her lips blue, and breathing was slow. They found her overdosing on heroin. She's here." Josh takes a moment to gather his thoughts. "She's been injected with naloxone to counter the effects of the heroin. She's been spewing vomit like crazy. Marisol isn't a heroin addict. She smokes meth. That motherfucker, Daniel broke into her house and did this to her. I went back to her house and saw a footage of the surveillance video before I handed it to the police, it was definitely him. I also saw Lorenzo try to push Daniel off Marisol. Daniel struck Lorenzo so hard, Lorenzo nearly flew to the other side of the house. That's when Marisol yelled at Lorenzo and told him to go to Kade's house...all while Daniel was on top of her beating her like a fuckin' dog."

"Fuck." Is all I can say. Then it hits me, "Did you say Daniel was driving a black Charger? One of the witnesses indicated Lorenzo was hit by a black car."

"I have no doubt Daniel was responsible for the hit-and-run incident. Another witness informed the police that it appeared as if the driver purposely went out of his way to hit Lorenzo. Lorenzo was just a few feet away from stepping on the sidewalk. The driver shifted to the right to hit Lorenzo then geared left to continue driving straight ahead. That motherfucker has reached a new level of psychotic evil. We need to watch our backs and be on high alert. I'm sure I'm on his hit list for helping Marisol and Lorenzo. He's always been extremely jealous regarding her even though he's cheated on her countless times. His mind is even more distorted when he's high. I got into it with one of the cops when he asked why there wasn't a restraining order on file after I explained Marisol and Daniel's past. I had to remind his bitch ass that an emergency protective order couldn't be placed since we didn't know Daniel's whereabouts and in order for the order to be effective, Daniel first needs to be served with the papers. Besides, at the end of the day, that's all a restraining order is...a piece of paper. How was that supposed to protect Marisol from Daniel's intrusion and brutal attack? Thank God for the nosey neighbor and the house alarm."

I'm confused. "I don't understand why Marisol was found with the needle on her arm if she's a meth head."

Cheesecake looks at me appalled. "What the fuck, Kade? Judgmental much? This isn't the time for you to try to be funny. You're coming across as a total ass!"

"Because I referred to her as a meth head? That's her drug of choice! That's not my fault. Look...this isn't the time or place to argue about semantics. Josh, let me rephrase that...Why was Marisol found with a needle on her arm if her drug of choice is meth?

"I'm assuming Daniel stuck her with it either to kill her or to get her addicted. It's a form of control for him, that's why he initially introduced and forced her into smoking meth. If she's dependent on drugs, she becomes reliant on him and won't leave his side. At least that was his frame of mind until his own addiction made him spiral out of control."

"So now what?" I ask.

"Now...we wait for Marisol to wake up and for the doctor to allow us to see Lorenzo." Josh responds.

"Hey! Wipe the drool off your chin." I nudge Cheesecake to wake her.

"Ugh. I'm exhausted. It's been over a week since Lorenzo has been in the hospital. I haven't had a moment's rest. I hate that he's finally being released today and we won't be there."

"I'm tired too. We can take a quick nap once we arrive at the hotel. The fashion show isn't until later this afternoon. I know...tell me about it. Poor thing is being released from the hospital without his mom. I'm glad Marisol agreed to the ninety day residential drug rehab and dual diagnosis program in Napa Valley. She knew she couldn't beat her demons on her own, I'm just glad she kept an open mind when Josh suggested it even though he didn't really give her the opportunity to refuse. It's hard to go against his authority. He has that take-charge and do-as-I-say personality. I've never really seen him in action, but now that I have, I can understand why you're so dick whooped."

Cheesecake rolls her eyes at me. "Josh has become attached to Lorenzo, he wants what's best for him. When Marisol admitted to struggling with her meth addiction and depression, Josh knew he couldn't risk Marisol relapsing now that she's been clean on her own for a few weeks."

"Do you think he'll be able to handle Lorenzo living with him while Marisol's away? That's a huge responsibility for someone, especially for a person who isn't around kids much." I wonder.

"I'll be around, my mom will help, and so will you."

"Me?" *What the fuck? Since when did I turn into Mr. Rogers?*

"Don't give me that look. I know damn well you've become attached to Lorenzo and you love him just as much as we do if not more. The nurses told me that when Josh and I were working that you would bring him special treats, do puzzles, read, and color with him, you big ol' softie!"

"Those bitches! I told them not to say anything!" I laugh. "What was I supposed to do? Leave him alone?"

"Of course not, silly. I'm just glad you did."

Once we're situated at the hotel and rested for what seemed like a few short minutes, Cheesecake and I are ready to commence the festivities for the annual VIVA Las Vegas Rockabilly Weekend Convention. When it originally began sixteen years ago, it entailed vintage purists, but over the years it has morphed by adding the rockabilly and pinup cultures. The four days dedicated to everything and anything remotely vintage consist of live bands, DRINKING, dancing, Tiki pool parties, embracing the old Vegas culture, DRINK-ING, burlesque shows, record hops, and more DRINKING. I fuckin' love VIVA!

"Damn, girl! You look fly as fuck!" I whistle as I see Cheesecake in a skin tight leopard dress with red accessories and her long hair swept to the side.

Cheesecake spins around. "You like? It's my newest Monica dress. Oh, I like your pompadour hairstyle. It's not high, but it looks great on you with your shades."

"I love it and thanks. Now, let's go and make up for lost time. We already missed the first two days of VIVA and we won't be here tomorrow so after the fashion show you're in, we have a lot of drinking to do, old friends to catch up with, and new people to meet. Time is ticking! It's a miracle Josh didn't make a big stink about you coming, if he knew how much of a hot commodity you are at this event he would've thought twice. Luckily, he's too concerned with Lorenzo to play the jealous role. And to think...he made me come with you to ensure your safety. Doesn't he know this event is my biggest playground?"

"Whore." Cheesecake shakes her head at me with mock disappointment.

"You only wish you could be a whore right along with me. Your bad for being tied down. At least you had the decency not to bring sand to the beach."

She pouts. "I wanted him to come! Mom said she would watch over Lorenzo for today while I fulfilled my obligation with the clothing company, but Josh insisted on staying with him."

"Come on, let's make the best of the day." I lure her out of our room and into the transformed rockabilly world.

As we're walking towards the fashion show, we recognize several people we've met at past VIVA conventions. Cheesecake runs into fans who stop her to take pictures recognizing her from calendars, magazines, and several pinup style catalogs. Even some of the big wigs stop to admire her beauty. Cheesecake is definitely in her element, the women here look beautiful and rock their vintage looks, but Cheesecake...she's in a class all of her own. She's beyond amazing.

After spending a whole day partying, we surprisingly catch the last flight home...drunk off our asses, but nonetheless, we made it on the plane. *Yay, us!*

"Dude! I can't believe how many people were disappointed you didn't do the burlesque show you were planning on doing." I comment with a strong buzz.

"Ugh. I know! Josh would've been pissed as fuck if he found out I was stripping and dancing for others. My babe has been so upset, I didn't want to make him stress unnecessarily. Aww...my babe, I can't wait to sit on his face."

"Whore." I tease.

"Don't be jealous that I'm gonna get some tonight and you're not! Actually, I thought for a minute that you and that Jelly chick were going to fuck right at the car show! What a coincidence that the bitch was there! She doesn't look like she's into anything vintage." Cheesecake points out.

"She's a fuckin' dick tease. The more she taunts me with her looks, the more I want the little cunt and she knows it. Not much happened, just a lot of back and forth banter. Eventually, I got tired of her games and went about my business to mess with old acquaintances."

"I'm just thankful she's into you. She better not mess with my man the way she does with you. If you ask me, flirting is a form of cheating so if Josh entertains her touchy-feely ways, shit's gonna hit the fan. That's all I'm saying."

Exhaustion has taken its toll and I'm ready for some shut eye. "I'm going to sleep. I don't want to hear you talking about my future fuck."

"Good. Go to sleep, I'll sing to you." Cheesecake offers.

"Don't you fuckin' dare! There are innocent people on this plane who don't deserve to hear the ear-splitting sound of your voice!"

Cheesecake looks at me with a repelled expression. "Asshole!" Then bursts into laughter.

The following Saturday, I head over to Josh's house to help out with Lorenzo after first making a pit stop at Target. When I arrive, Cheesecake's preparing lunch while Lorenzo and Josh are building a train track on top of a large, but short table. There are over a hundred pieces gathered on the floor that complete the train set.

"What's up, guys? Aww...cool train, little man! Can I help you put it together?" I ask Lorenzo.

He smiles and nods his head excitedly then rushes me to give me a hug. My heart instantly melts. He cringes slightly forgetting to be more careful since his body continues to ache due to his accident.

"Can I help you finish setting up your cool new train set? I think Josh needs me to show him how it's done." I point out with Lorenzo nodding in agreement.

Josh gives a roaring laugh. "We just emptied the box, but the more hands on deck, the faster we'll be done."

"Cheesecake! I hope you're making enough lunch for everyone! I'm starving!"

"I am! Mom's on her way...she said she has a surprise."

Half an hour later, Mama V shows up. She drops her things on the couch and hurries to give Lorenzo a big hug and kiss. He takes a deep breath as if he's imprinting her scent into his memory. *Aww...he loves her.*

157

"Lunch is ready!" Cheesecake yells from the kitchen.

"Great! I'm starving!" We all say in unison...except for Lorenzo who only allows his eyes to pop out with eagerness.

For lunch, Cheesecake made beef enchiladas with red rice and Mexican-style corn on the cob. The corn is slathered with some type of butter/mayonnaise/sour cream spread and is topped with salt, chili powder, lime, and cheese. After the first bite, I'm in fat heaven and so is Lorenzo. It's the first thing he eats and manages to get all over his face and chest since he's not wearing a shirt, just sweats.

"Lorenzo, why is it every time I see you, you're never wearing a shirt indoors?" I ask curiously.

He shrugs his shoulder and gives me that beaming smile I love so much.

"He loves to show off his muscles. Right, little man?" Josh states as he devours his enchiladas.

Lorenzo raises his eyebrows twice in agreement. "Muscles? You like showing off your muscles?"

He puts his corn down on the plate and raises his arms to show off his "muscles."

"All right then, Muscles! You've made your point!"

Everyone yells in accord. "Muscles!"

The adorable little boy formerly known as Lorenzo and is now known as Muscles giggles as he continues to eat his corn.

"Hey, Muscles...I forgot to tell you, I bought you more coloring books, puzzles, and games. I hope you like them. Just remind me to give them to you later." His gives me an enormous smile as a sign of gratitude. I gladly accept it.

"The lady at Target enthusiastically helped me pick everything out for you while she was eye fucking me, so I decided to take her out tonight." I state nonchalantly.

"Kade! Watch your fuckin' mouth! Don't curse around Muscles!" Josh scolds me.

"Oh, shit. I'm sorry, Muscles. I don't even notice when I fuckin' cuss. It just comes out fuckin' naturally." I realize my foul vocabulary too late.

"Fuckin' Kade, you asshole! Stop! Shut the fuck up already!" Josh yells then scrunches his face when he notices he also has diarrhea of the mouth.

"Fuckin' shit! My damn mouth has a fuckin' mind of its own! It's like...I can't fuckin' stop! I can't handle the pressure of fuckin' behaving! Shit!" I burst into laughter.

"Your damn cursing is fuckin' contagious, I can't bite my tongue either! Shit!" Josh covers his mouth.

Cheesecake is laughing like a damn monkey in the background when Mama V yells, "I've had enough of both of you! I don't care that you're both grown men, I will shove a bar of soap so deep in your mouths you'll be burping bubbles for the rest of your lives! Capisce? My little Muscles doesn't need to witness such vulgarity! Have some respect!"

Muscles just smiles sweetly and shakes his head finding the whole situation amusing. *Silly kid.*

"Mom, how about you tell us what your surprise is while these two learn how to speak properly in the presence of a child?" Cheesecake asks with smugness.

Brown noser.

"Oh, yeah that...well..." Mama V appears slightly nervous. "I bought a car." I think I hear her mumble.

"Huh? You bought a car?" Cheesecake and I ask.

"Yes. It's no big deal. I just bought the first car I test drove, that's all." Mama V states nonchalantly.

"Did you drive it here?" Cheesecake gets up and rushes to the front window to check out Mama V's new car." I join her.

"Aww...man. Why didn't you drive it here?" I asked bummed out.

"I did." Mama V states. "It's parked right out front."

Nina's confused. "Umm...I don't think so, mom. All I see is this huge white SUV."

"Yeah, that's my car." Mama says matter-of-factly.

Cheesecake and I look at each other then immediately go into hysterics. It gets so bad, Cheesecake has a relentless time breathing from laughing so hard and falls on the ground. When she finally catches her breath, she snorts out loud making my eyes swell up with tears.

"What's so funny?" Josh asks.

After taking a few deep breaths I'm finally able to speak again. "Since I've known Mama V, she has never, and I mean EVER driven a car. Now, all of a sudden she's driving this honker truck! We took MUNI and BART everywhere. She always said she had no need for a car when everything was nearby." I turn to Mama V. "So what changed? I always assumed that if you bought a car it would be one of those clown looking smart cars."

Mama V gives a long sigh. "Now that Muscles is here, I want to have the freedom to take him places. I got the Denali so that we can all fit in one car and not have to take separate vehicles. And it's the XL edition so that he has plenty of room for his things."

Uh-oh. Mom thinks we're keeping him. She's deeply attached. Truth be told...we all are. What's going to happen when we have to give Muscles back to his mom?

On Monday morning, I'm surprised to see Cheesecake over at our house since she's been spending almost every day with Josh playing house.

"Morning, you!" She says a little too cheerful.

"Morning. Hey, do you have a minute? I'd like to speak with you regarding mom." My grave tone allows her to instantly pick up on my mood.

Cheesecake's facial expression changes to a serious one then grabs my hand and leads me to the living room to have a seat. She faces me providing her undivided attention. "Talk to me. What's going on?"

I sigh. "This is difficult to say and you have to promise not to repeat what I'm about to tell you, okay?"

"Kade! You're making me nervous! What's going on? Spit it out!"

"I spoke with mom yesterday, the real reason she bought the Denali is because she's pregnant."

Cheesecake gasps. She's stunned. "Not only is she pregnant, but she's expecting twins." Now, Cheesecake's jaw has dropped from the shock. "And to make matters crazier, Dillon broke up with her once she told him the news."

It's a miracle Cheesecake's eyes are still in their sockets. "You have to promise not to say anything to mom until she tells you. I was sworn to secrecy, but I just couldn't keep something this big from you." I confess.

Cheesecake is literally speechless for the first time in her life. She gets up and heads to her room. I'm surprised by her calm reaction. I prepare for my daily jog. As I'm about to leave my house, I hear, "Kade, you fuckin' asshole! I'm going to beat your ass!"

I take that as my cue to spurt out of the house. Once I reach the bottom of the stairs, I take off running. Cheesecake steps outside, but doesn't chase after me. "Your ass is mine, Daly! You're a bitch for that one!"

"April Fool's, sis! I love you! Have an awesome day at work and don't fall for anyone else's pranks!" I yell as I walk backwards laughing my ass off.

Almost two weeks have passed since Muscles has been living with Josh. Everyone takes turns watching over him and spoiling him like crazy. Celeste was finally released from the hospital and has also been spending time with the new addition to our family. It's hard to resist his adorable smile and what are now becoming chubby cheeks. He's gained weight since I first met him, his physique back then was boney and unhealthy, but now he's quickly filling up, showing great improvement. In the mornings, I usually spend time with him and later Mama V takes over, but today the sadness in Muscles' eyes makes me have a heart to heart conversation with him. I call Mama V and tell her I'll be staying with Muscles for the rest of the day.

"What's wrong, little man? Why do you look so sad? Are you not happy being here?"

Muscles maintains his eyes focused on the ground with a heartbreaking expression. He's usually in positive spirits throughout the day. Until it's time for bed and loneliness overtakes his thoughts, that's when his mother's absence affects him the most. Today, nothing seems to take his mother off his mind. "Do you miss your mommy?" I ask as gentle as possible.

Although we shower him with affection, nothing compares to a mother's kiss, a mother's embrace, and a mother's love. He looks at me with his sweet, chocolate eyes and sadly nods his head. I pull him close to me understanding too well the need for a mother's presence and hug him tightly. At that moment, he breaks down and begins to sob. My heart instantly breaks for him. He's too young to comprehend the demons that hold some adults hostage. Marisol needs to overcome her addiction to be a better mother and put her son as her priority once again. He's too small to understand that sometimes people need to commit sacrifices to be able to move forward in life without chains keeping them linked to the past. I don't know what to say to ease his pain, but I get an idea. I excuse myself from Muscles for a quick moment and call Josh. "Hey, can you do me a favor?"

Leave it to Josh to always come through. I decide not to inform Muscles of my plans for the day just in case something unexpected prevents things from going according to plan. "Hey, Muscles! I have to run an errand. Would you like to come with me? I'll bring your favorite snacks and you can bring some of your toys with you. How does that sound?"

He nods his head sorrowfully, instantly making me pray his sadness goes away by the end of the day.

We finally arrive to our destination, a modern structure surrounded by a serene ambiance enveloped in orchards of grapes. When we enter, the place inside has a minimalistic décor, but cozy feel from its neutral colors. I ask Muscles to have a seat while I approach the receptionist at the front desk.

Minutes later, we're directed to have a seat in a small lounge area that contains a couch against one of the walls. It's surrounded with positive quotes throughout the room. Muscles and I make ourselves comfortable while the receptionist brings us juice and water.

Muscles still isn't sure why we're here, but he patiently waits at the table playing with his toy cars. Moments later, he sees her, his mother, the reason for his tears, the reason for his past sadness, and the reason for his instant happiness, Marisol.

I guess the staff must have kept Muscles a surprise to her also since she was so ecstatic to embrace her son once again after what must have felt like an eternity. Marisol's cries transpire from joy and gratitude of being with her little man once again. I allow them some privacy and wait for their visit to end in the waiting room.

The visit concludes after an hour. Marisol requests a minute of my time before her group therapy session begins. I agree to speak with her briefly.

"I can't thank you enough for bringing him today. Seeing him is like seeing the sun after being trapped in the dark for an eternity. He's my sunshine, the only thing I have in this world who can brighten up my day. A million thanks, Kade to you and to everyone else. Considering the circumstances, my little boy seems happy."

"We all love him, Marisol. I didn't bring him here for you, I did it for him. I hope that you overcome your inner battles with your addiction. Think of him when you have that demonic urge to cause yourself harm. Think of the pain you bring him with your absence. His love for you is unconditional, don't take advantage of the purity in his heart. Instead, benefit from this time to get yourself together, come out stronger than ever, and never rely on just any man for love or drugs to fulfill an empty void. Don't worry about Muscles, he's in good hands." I assure her.

"Muscles?" She questions.

"He likes walking around shirtless so the nickname kind of stuck." I explain.

She gives me a hint of a smile. "I like it." She says quietly then walks us to the lobby. Letting go of her son becomes unbearable for her to manage. Her eyes instantly turn red and glassy. She's fights desperately to remain strong in front of Muscles. It takes every inch of strength to resist the urge to shed the tears that are relentlessly trying to be set free.

"Be a good boy for mommy, okay? I'll see you real soon." She struggles to say.

Muscles immediately looks at me for confirmation. "Yes, we'll come back to visit your mom. But you have to turn your frown upside down otherwise your mommy is going to be sad if she sees that you're sad."

He nods his head understanding my point then gives his mom the biggest smile and hug he can conjure up. After a long moment, I pull him away and head out the door with Muscles by my side. Curiosity gets the best of me so I decide to turn around. I witness Marisol's strong façade crumble to pieces as her sunshine leaves her in the dark once again.

Chapter 10 (Nina)

Sancho

"Shhhh! Lower your voice!" I whisper not so softly. "You're going to wake him!" I tell my man as we're leaving Muscles' room. The quieter we try to be, the more noise we seem to make.

As soon as we enter his room, Josh closes the door behind him and dims the lights. "What are you doing?" I ask confused.

"What do you mean? I'm getting ready to dick you down." Josh states with hunger in his eyes.

"You know Muscles wakes up in the middle of the night, we can't just close the door. What if he wakes up earlier than usual? Open the door. No one is bumpin' and grindin' tonight." I put my foot down.

Josh stands by the door considering my words then after some thought, opens it. The room is mostly dark, barely lit but I can easily sense his devious smile rising to the surface. He clenches his jaw and makes his way to me, picking me up, and throwing me over his shoulders. "Babe!" I shriek.

He slaps my ass. "Shhhh! You'll wake up Muscles!" He takes me into his closet and shuts the door. The closet is pitch black, our eyes fail to adjust to the darkness even after being there for a few moments. It doesn't matter. Once he glides my body against his as he places me on my feet, I can immediately recall every inch of the delicious man who stands before me. His clean scent of soap mixed with mint overpowers my senses. He pulls off his shirt rewarding me with the feel of his muscular, smooth chest. The texture of his stomach changes once I caress my hand past his navel. I can trace a hint of hair in the center of his lower abs. I stop myself from touching him further below. Instead, I search for his handsome face in the dark and bring it down near mine. Our lips instantly connect allowing our tongues to glide graciously and our taste to flow freely. Josh grabs ahold of my bottom lip and with it between his teeth he reprimands me with his deep voice. "Don't ever refuse me." He reaches down between my legs and cups my sensitive spot as demonstration. "This belongs to me. I will kiss it, lick it, finger it, make love to it, and fuck it wherever and whenever the fuck I please, understand?" He adds more pressure as he massages my clit over my shorts.

His husky voice and the simultaneous pressure on both my lips cause a fierce sensation to spread throughout my body. An anxious moan escapes me. "I understand." He releases my lip from the grip of his teeth then returns to sway his lips against mine.

Josh directs me to my knees. He releases his rock hard shaft from his sweats then places his hands behind my head. "Suck and make me forget." He commands with no room for discussion as he places the tip of his cock at the center of my lips.

I welcome his thickness into my mouth. Instead of me pleasuring him by guiding my tongue and lips over his shaft, he takes absolute control...he fucks my mouth. His strokes are determined and hit the back of my throat, but his hands behind my head maintain only the slightest hint of pressure. His long, fat dick is too much for my mouth, so I use one hand to cup and massage his sack while the other strokes the base of his erection as he continues to rhythmically glide in and out of my mouth. I hear a growl deep within him. "Fuck, baby...your mouth feels like heaven. I can't get enough of it."

I stop him in motion to lick his shaft and savor the precum that eagerly spurts out. I twirl my tongue over the tip and suck with just enough pressure to make him moan in ecstasy. "Mmm...you have the best flavor." I compliment as I feel my own juices making their way to my entrance.

Some women see oral sex as a chore, but I see it as empowerment to make my man weak with just the feel of my mouth. I love it and take pleasure from being absolutely raw with the man who holds my heart.

"Stand up." Josh commands.

Fervently, I do as directed, but lick my way up to his chest. He bends down to grab the hem of my shirt and slides it upward to pull it off me. His lips find my face, he grazes his teeth along my jawline working his way to my neck. The darkness heightens my awareness and intensifies every sensation. He expertly unhooks my bra to release my swollen, sensitive breasts craving the attention only my man knows how to give. As if hearing my thoughts, he reaches with his hands to massage and gently rub my erect nipples. He surprises me by lowering himself on his knees and meeting my chest at eye level. He caresses his face in between my breasts then lovingly kisses and worships my tits. He makes his way to the nipple and begins to suck, then tug at my pebble while massaging the other breast with his hand. He brings his free hand down to my waist and begins to take off my loose shorts right along with my panties. His hand then finds its way to my entrance. On instinct, I spread my legs wider hoping he'll invade my sensitive area. "You're so wet, baby. What is it you like best? When I fuck your mouth or when my mouth worships your amazing tits?" He massages my clit then enters me with his finger.

"I love it all. Your touch, your mouth, your demanding ways." I whimper. The friction of his gliding finger inside me while he sucks on my tit gives me a mind-blowing sensation. I want to scream, moan, tell the world of my blissful state, but I can't. I have to contain the exhilaration pent up inside me.

"I can't hold it any longer, I need to be in you." My man confesses. His words are a beautiful soliloquy to my ears.

"Fuck me then, babe. Show me how much you want my pussy." I wrap my arms around his neck as he lays me down on the floor of his walk in closet. Without waiting a second longer, he rams his swollen penis inside me. I gasp. His size, his depth, and his force take me by surprise. Although I've had him in me countless times, being fucked by my man in absolute darkness brings unfamiliar sensations that I hungrily welcome.

My moans treacherously escape. Josh brings his mouth to mine to keep my sounds restrained as he penetrates me deeper. Josh consumes me both physically and emotionally. His body engulfs mine as he's above me and his mouth overpowers mine. I love every thrust he gives me, I love how his body over mine makes me feel like an absolute woman, and I love how his touch makes me feel worshipped. We may be fucking in his closet, but his need, want, and love for me makes everything surrounding us feel just right. Until...we hear a knock on his closet's door.

OMG! Are you fucking kidding me? Let me just die now! "Muscles? I'm getting dressed, honey. Give me a second and I'll be right out, okay?" I hear him coughing near the door then hear his cough seem more distant. He left Josh's room.

"Get off me! I can't believe I allowed you to seduce me in the dark with your debonair and irresistible charm! Never again, Tree Hugger!"

"Wait. I'm almost finished." My relentless man says as he continues with his thrusts.

Men!

I laugh. "I cannot believe you're still fucking me! I want to die of humiliation and all you care about his busting a nut? You're too much!"

"Ahhh...there...I'm finished." He announces then rolls off me.

"You have a one track mind, Mister! Poor Muscles will need additional therapy to deal with such a traumatic experience!" I state completely mortified.

Josh chuckles, but I can sense him rolling his eyes. "It's not like he saw us."

"No, but he must have heard us! That's just as bad!" As I'm searching for my clothes in the dark, I ask, "Hey, where's the light switch?"

"Right outside the door."

"What? How am I supposed to get dressed if I can't see shit? What if he's still in your room? I don't want to open the door and risk having him see me!" I whisper in a panic.

"Are you done with your rant? Because I'm ready to open the door and check on him. I kept my sweats on and just finished putting on my shirt, cuckoo lady."

I sigh with relief. "Oh." Then giggle uncontrollably.

The following day as I'm walking to my office from the parking lot in the city's morning work rush, I get a perturbed feeling. Although I'm surrounded by several people all scurrying to get to work, I feel prying eyes focused solely on me. I discreetly look around to see anyone who I may recognize or someone worthy of suspicion, but no one catches my attention. I blame my paranoia on last night's dream featuring the ever so dead, kingpin, Mateo Blanco who continues to haunt me in my sleep. I try to brush off the presentiment, but the nagging feeling refuses to fritter away.

Once I step foot into my office, the sense of security I desperately yearn for fails to surface. As I walk to the printer, I scrutinize every coworker wondering and mistrusting their intentions. *Nina, stop! No one is after you! You're being silly.*

My first appointment arrives and is waiting in our lounge area along with her mother. Once I see her, all my personal issues escape my thoughts. I provide my client my undivided attention along with the empathy she distraughtly longs for. She's a twelve-year-old girl who has endured sexual abuse from her grandfather since the early age of six. No one likes to think about such disturbing cases, but they exist. In this situation what adds to this young girl's horrid circumstance is that the mother is more concerned about freeing her dying father despite the inhumane acts he committed upon her child. How can anything take precedence over her daughter's traumatic experience?

This particular case is sickening on countless levels. What kind of "man" and I say the term loosely, would look at his own flesh and blood and want to perpetrate heinous acts upon them? What kind of mother would overlook such an atrocious crime carried out on her own child...a child whom she brought into this world, a child whom she carried for months in her womb, a child whom she gave life to? Aren't mothers supposed to love and protect their children with all their might, heart, and soul?

This situation repulses me even more because despite the family bond they're supposed to have, this monstrous act was committed on a defenseless child! Anyone can sympathize for this young girl on a human level, right? So why is the mother more concerned for her dying father than her own child? Because the man is severely ill now, that grants him forgiveness? I don't think so. In the bible, it states that we're supposed to honor our mother and father...not in this case. This woman's father is a malevolent demon. She is too self-involved with all the wrong priorities to be a good parent. Even animals have the instinct to protect their own. Not this woman, she cares more about her father and her financial status than she does about the well-being of her daughter. What's even more revolting? The mother also endured the same sexual abuse from her father. Why would she allow the abuse to continue?

My heart breaks for this little girl who sits in front of me with an expression of misery, desolation, and emptiness. She's the same age I was when I went through my own violation. Unlike her, I had my mother's unconditional love. I don't know what would have become of me had things been otherwise. Because of my mother's support, I wasn't a victim, I was a survivor of rape. As far as I'm concerned, the mother is just as perverse as the grandfather in this case.

I spent the whole morning in the Court's chambers with the little girl trying to calm her nerves. The hearing is continued to a later date. Once lunchtime arrives, I'm famished and emotionally spent. When I return to my office, I realize I have a visitor.

Michael. Damn...he's some serious eye candy.

"Hey, you!" I embrace him immediately with a genuine smile. He reciprocates the gestures.

"I hope you're okay with my unexpected visit." He asks.

"Of course. How's Diego?"

"He's fine. Here I brought you lunch." Michael hands me a foam takeout container.

"Bless your heart. I'm starving!" I don't bother to keep my cool. "Did you bring some for yourself?"

"I did." She states simply.

"Great! We can have lunch together here at my desk. So tell me, what brings you by?"

"Just checking up on you. A routine visit...if you will." Michael gives me a hint of a smile.

"Let me guess...Diego? What's he so worried about? My whole life he never made himself known, now he's everywhere even though he's not really there. You know?"

"Maybe, he's just making up for lost time." Michael comes to Diego's defense.

"I'm not complaining. I appreciate his letters and phone calls. It's nice hearing from him so often. But truth be told...I slightly panic when I see you. I'm always afraid you'll come bearing bad news."

Michael looks at me with slight disappointment. "Don't think that way. He's going crazy not being able to protect you. Your dad is someone who is used to controlling all his surroundings, although he still holds power behind bars, it's still not the same."

I stop chewing my food mid bite. "Why would Diego need to protect me? I thought I was no longer in danger since Mateo Blanco is now six feet under." Remembering my environment, I get up and close my office door.

Michael acts nonchalant, but something tells me he's keeping something from me. "You know how fathers are with their daughters...overprotective."

"I think you're lying, Michael." The nagging feeling from this morning instantly returns. "Am I in danger? Tell me the truth. This morning I felt as if I were being followed. Don't lie to me. I need to know if someone is after me and the reason behind it."

Michael sighs. "Your dad has one of his men following you...for your protection."

For my protection? What the fuck?

"Only a handful of people are aware Diego is my father. Outside of my intimate circle, no one else knows. So what's the problem?"

"It's more complicated than that. Your name, Josh, Kade, Celeste, Victoria, and Emme's names were all included in the police reports as innocent bystanders or witnesses. Everyone else with the exception of your father is dead. Mateo Blanco's family isn't just going to leave his death unaccounted for. Evidence shows that Blanco wasn't killed by law enforcement. The weapon used to shoot Blanco to death still hasn't been recovered. Your dad's concern is that Blanco's son might come after everyone who was there the night of his father's murder in pursue of answers or to seek vengeance."

Slowly, I try to piece things together. "Wait a minute. Diego's men surrendered right along with him so how is Diego the only survivor left of the group?"

"Don't ask questions you're not prepared to hear the answers to. I've been directed to tell you nothing, but the truth."

"Tell me." I demand.

Michael sighs. "Diego's men knew too much. He couldn't risk putting your life in danger on his account. He did what he had to do...to protect you."

"Oh." I understand. *Diego promised not to shed innocent blood again. Those men he had killed were not innocent. He got rid of them to protect me. It's not right, but I won't reproach him for it.* "What about Emme? She was working for Diego. Is there a hit on her?" I'm afraid of Michael's response.

"Emme's life is being spared because of the friendship she holds with you and for no other reason. You have to understand that she holds a very serious threat to your father and you due to all the information she possesses."

I decide to keep quiet about ending all ties with Emme. Although we're no longer friends, I can't live with her death on my conscience. How did my life become so complicated? I shouldn't have the power to decide whether someone lives or dies. No one should.

"Can we visit Diego soon? He's due for a visit. I have questions I'd like him to explain."

"Of course. We'll go this week." Michael suggests.

"Thanks."

The remainder of our lunch is spent discussing lighter topics. The more Michael conducts his routine visits per Diego's request, the more he relaxes around me. I become fond of his company and have earned great respect for the loyalty he holds for my father.

When my mom babysits Muscles, they're usually at the bakery for the last half hour, so after work I head there to pick him up. When I enter, the delicious, warm aroma of baked goods feels inviting to my senses as opposed to today's piercingly, cold weather that has me on the defensive. It's the perfect contrast. My mom informs me that Muscles appeared to enjoy his first speech therapy session. Tomorrow, he'll begin occupational therapy to deal with some of the violent tantrums he's been displaying lately. Since he's not able to verbally communicate his feelings, he aggressively lashes out in frustration. Due to his past, we all made a group decision agreeing that the more therapy Muscles is involved in, the more beneficial it would be for him in the long run. We also elect on a hearing test and an EEG to measure his brain's activity as forms of precaution per his pediatrician's recommendations.

When Muscles sees me, he gives me such a softhearted smile, it instantly makes all the negativity of the day into a forgotten memory.

I've been spending nearly every day at Josh's house, it's now beginning to feel like my second home. I cook for him and Muscles, yet I find myself cooking extra food since we always have unexpected visitors. Each and every one of them always providing a lame excuse as to their visit, but I know better, I know we have all become so attached to Muscles it's difficult to part from him. My mom and Celeste haven't had a small child to care for in years, Muscles' presence was a welcomed surprise.

As soon as we arrive to my man's house, Muscles and I change into more comfortable clothes. My hair goes into a bun, I put on a white tank top, some grey shorts, and decide to remain barefoot. Muscles wears his usual...sweats...and that's it. *Aww...he's so cute.*

While I'm preparing dinner, courtesy of Delia who doesn't mind me picking her brain and getting the recipes to some of Josh's favorite meals, Muscles is coloring at the dining table. Lately, Delia and I have been on the phone quite a bit. She's absolutely one of the sweetest women I have ever met in my life and her accent always has me beaming with joy.

"Always play music when you cook, it's the best therapy. It relaxes you and allows you to cook with love. A man can taste the love in a meal. If you do it right, he'll do you right." Her advice every time she provides me with one of her delicious recipes.

I decide to play salsa music while I attempt my first try at chiles rellenos. So far, the house smells amazing. I've made rice, a red salsa for the stuffed peppers, and fresh pico de gallo, which is a chunky salsa to compliment my meal. Although I know my way around the kitchen fairly well, my comfort is with Italian cooking since that's what I grew up on. Now that I cook for my man, I'm trying to incorporate some of his favorites which include everything his caregiver, who is more like family used to cook for him.

As I'm trying to sing along to the lyrics, I'm swaying to the sultry beat, and finishing up with the chiles rellenos. Once I'm done, I feel strong hands at the sides of my waist. He starts moving along with me to the rhythm of the music. I slowly turn around not skipping a beat. My fingertips have flour on them so I manage to lightly hug my man without getting his dark shirt dirty. His face has that light stubble that I love so much, he gives me a smoldering look that instantly makes me want to jump him and devour him alive. I've become better at remembering my environment and notice Muscles who seems highly amused at seeing Josh and me dancing. We both smile at him and decide to give him a show. As the song, "Vuelvo a Nacer" by Frankie Ruiz plays in the background, we get down in the middle of the kitchen with a three-year-old as our audience. Once we're done, we realize we have more spectators than before. Our moms are at the dining table getting a kick out of our dance fest.

"Oh, to be young and in love!" Celeste cheers in her delicate body, but with a much stronger spirit. "I can almost hear wedding bells."

We all freeze and stare at Celeste, but Josh breaks the silence. "You probably need to fix your hearing aid, mom because there are no bells ringing."

"Son, please bite your tongue. My hearing is perfectly fine. Will everyone please stop looking at me as if I'm being delusional? So help me...I will announce the names I have picked out for my grandkids."

Everyone instantly looks away. Celeste grins triumphantly.

Moments later, my mom asks, "Do you really want to be a grandmother that bad?"

"As if you don't. You're ready to load babies into that honker bus you bought! You want them just as bad as I do, there's no denying that." Celeste slyly winks at my mom.

176

My mom laughs guiltily. *That traitor.*

Changing the subject seems best. I inform everyone I'll be meeting with Diego later this week. Celeste surprises me by asking if she can attend the visit with me. I tell her I'll have to double check with Michael first. My mom isn't ready to meet with Diego just yet. She doesn't speak ill of him, but she also doesn't feel comfortable with the mention of his name.

Once our moms leave after dinner and Muscles is put to bed, I decide to bring up the issues discussed earlier with Michael.

Josh is in bed anxiously waiting for me to join him. With no hesitation, I wrap myself on top of him. "Babe, did you know that our lives are still in danger?" I try to sound nonchalant. "Your half-brother may be after me, you, and everyone else from that horrid night." Just the thought of the madness, confusion, and gun battle from that evening brings a chill down my spine.

"My what? Baby, please don't refer to him as anything of mine. He's Mateo Blanco's son...that's it. Just because we have the same sperm donor in common doesn't make us family. I've been doing my research on him, he's evil as shit. Fuck him and fuck Blanco. Anyone who tries to hurt my loved ones is an enemy. To me...there is no such thing as a blood bond."

I know, babe. I will never forget you tainting your hands with your father's bloodshed...and feeling no remorse.

"So did you know this nightmare still isn't over?"

"Yes." He states simply.

"Why didn't you tell me? You know I don't like being kept in the dark about these things. Is that why we rarely go out anymore? Are you doing it to protect me and keep me safe?" I need answers.

Josh gives me a brief peck on the lips. "Of course not. We haven't gone out because I'm cheap and you come at a hefty price."

I catch him off guard and punch him in the stomach. He drags out his groan dramatically.

"You're not funny. Tell me the truth." I insist.

"I don't take you out because I'm cheating on you and don't want my hoes to find out." Josh replies sarcastically.

I don't bother to entertain his comment. "Babe, I'm being serious. Please tell me what's going on."

Josh gives me a long sigh. "Knowing that your life is in danger has me stressed with a tremendous amount of pressure to keep you safe. When we're home and I'm with you, I don't want to consider any threats or negativity, I just want to enjoy you. Let your father and I handle this situation. We've been in contact. You're being watched over, you'll be safe."

"Are you communicating with my father through Michael? How's that working out?"

"Michael and I have moved on from our altercation. That's a thing of the past. We have too much on our plates to worry about insignificant things."

"Glad to hear you're not jealous anymore and acting like a crazed lunatic." I tease.

Josh tilts my chin upward to ensure we're making eye contact. "I was never jealous of HIM. What enraged me was seeing another man touching you...and you returning the gesture. If you're mine...then you're MINE, for my touch only. I have you on a pedestal in a flawless condition. If someone else comes along with their filthy hands and thoughts, they're ruining what belongs to me, my most prized possession."

His words catch me off guard. I swallow hard. "You know I'm not perfect. You know I'm tainted."

He keeps his entrancing hazel eyes fixated on mine. "To me...you're perfect. Your past experiences have molded you to be a strong, intellectual woman with a heart of gold; your present shows a sense of humor like no other with an empathetic virtue that is so rare, it's priceless; and your future's perspective on life is aspiring...always wanting to give and make society a better place. I know I don't deserve you, but every day you make me want to be a better man and for whatever profound intention...you chose me. I won't let anyone threaten our bond. I'll fight for what belongs to me. No one touches you...absolutely no one. Understand?"

I stare at my possessive, unreasonable man lovingly. "I understand."

"Good. Now give me some sugar." He exaggeratedly puckers up his lips waiting for a kiss.

"How about some crazy kisses instead?" I don't wait for his response. Instead, I contort my face, cross my eyes, and smother his entire face with smooches.

He closes his eyes with a smile and enjoys the attack on his face.

Despite being here several times with Michael, I'm still not used to entering this dark, grey building surrounded by barb wire. Today, my meeting with Diego is different. Celeste was granted permission by both the federal detention facility and Diego to visit. When we enter, Celeste and I provide our fake IDs to the correctional officer behind the informational desk. We pass through a metal detector then a female officer pats us down to ensure we're not bringing in any contraband such as weapons, drugs, or cellphones. The lady officer leads us further into the facility and into a different room than usual. The room consists of six metal tables with matching stools bolted down to the ground. An officer remains at the far end of the room then turns on a small radio loud enough for him to block the conversation within our group.

While Diego is a man without freedom and detained within the brick walls of maximum security, he still walks with confidence and purpose even though his limbs are restrained with metal. Now standing in front of me, I see he lacks any fear of being confined. Seeing him without a glass wall between us feels surreal. My first urge is to greet him with a hug, but something in me stops me from doing so, instead I grab his hand to shake it and cover my free hand over both of ours smiling warmly at him. "Hi."

"Hija, it feels so good to see you." *Daughter.* Although initially I felt uncomfortable about the term, I quickly grew fond of it. Diego's hardcore prison attitude escapes him as soon as he sees me. He nods to Celeste and Michael as a form of acknowledgement then we all have a seat. Diego is on one side of the table with us adjacent to him just like a panel has one person under scrutiny.

An awkward silence rapidly unfolds. Celeste is staring at my father while he does his best to look everywhere else, but her. I get a kick out of their behavior, but decide to move our visit along since time is limited. "Celeste, you wanted to visit with Diego. Is there anything you'd like to say? Would you like some privacy? Michael and I can step outside the room if you'd like."

Diego finally chooses to make eye contact with Celeste. Before she speaks, Celeste inhales then exhales deeply. "I know what you did. I wanted to come today to thank you for saving my life and my son's. The murder of my parents is a pain that will remain in my heart for the rest of my life. I don't condone your actions, but I understand why you did what you had to. All these years I've been in hiding, I always knew it was you who called to warn my father that my whereabouts were known. I wasn't aware the agent who relocated me the second time was under your command. All this time you've known where I've been, yet you always kept me a secret from Mateo. Words cannot express my gratitude. I think back to when I dated Mateo and he would get in his tirade moods, he would become hostile with me and many times came so close to beating me. You always managed to turn his focus elsewhere during our explosive arguments. I haven't forgotten. You're my hero and the executioner of my parents' lives, the turmoil within my heart couldn't be greater. Nonetheless, I wanted to thank you in person for everything you've done for my son and me."

"Kaitlyn." Diego refers to Celeste by her legal name, not the new identity she was forced to take in order to remain alive. "I don't deserve your gratitude. I murdered your parents in their sleep, I won't minimize my actions. But I'd like to thank you for welcoming and loving my daughter as your own. She speaks very highly of you."

Celeste smiles and reaches out to grab Diego's hand. She squeezes it giving him a hint of a smile. "Let's move on and never speak of our past."

Diego doesn't move his hands, but he nods his head in agreement.

"Diego." I interrupt before another moment of awkwardness arises. "Can you please tell me why you have a man following me around? Why didn't you tell me? I've been paranoid with the feeling that someone was stalking me. Who is he? Can I meet him so that I won't mistake him for a bad guy? What's the situation with Mateo Blanco's son? What about his daughter? Didn't you say Mateo Blanco had twins, a girl and boy? Why is your concern solely for Mateo's son?" I feel myself getting in a panic.

"Hija. Calm down. I'll answer your questions. I didn't want you to meet Sancho, that's just his nickname by the way, because he can be a bit intimidating. He's not much of a people person. The top right of his face was burned leaving severely thick scar tissue. If you see a man with a burned face, you'll know it's him. Just know that he's good at maintaining a low profile. He drives a new silver Impala. If he switches cars, I'll notify you immediately so you won't be caught off guard. He's been my top lieutenant for over five years after proving his loyalty to me. As for Mateo's son, AX Blanco, he's someone to fear. Even as a child he was rotten as hell. The tougher he became, the prouder Mateo felt. AX was raised with a heavy hand, getting daily beatings for his mischievous ways. His first murder was at the age of thirteen per his father's command. Mateo had AX execute a man who had stolen from Mateo's cocaine supply. After that, AX became more ruthless...pouring acid over people, dismembering their bodies, and countless other acts of torcher and slaughter. He has his hands dipped in everything...drug trade, weapons, human trafficking, extortion, racketeering, money laundering, you name it, he's involved one way or another. Before when Mateo and I were alliances, there was nothing more AX wanted than to take over Mateo's drug empire. I know he's not completely heartbroken over the loss of his father, but regardless he has to show everyone his devotion to his family and go after whoever was responsible for his father's death. As for the twin girl, once the mother died she was sent to a boarding school here in the U.S. at a very young age. Mateo rarely spoke of her in an attempt to keep her safe. I don't even remember her name or AX's legal name. I've tried locating that information, but haven't found anything. When they were registered in the hospital, it must have been done under their mother's maiden name for their protection. I've had Mateo's financial reports checked and nothing indicates a consistent allowance to anyone. I can't imagine Mateo not providing monetary security for his daughter throughout her life. AX is so self-involved and heartless I doubt he has a relationship with his own twin."

"I hope I never run into this AX guy, he sounds like a total brute." I slump on the stool completely overwhelmed with my new found information.

Once our visit ends, Michael drops off Celeste at her home then takes me to work. I'm only there for the second half of my shift, but I feel like I've worked all day plus overtime. The visit with Diego along with my disturbing cases have me mentally spent.

After work, I rush over to my mom's bakery shop to pick Muscles up. I find him in the back past the kitchen in my mom's office playing with what appears to be homemade play dough. He gives me a welcoming smile that instantly makes all my troubles from my day disappear.

As Muscles and I are headed back to Josh's house, a black car driving several feet behind me catches my attention. I can't really make out the man's face due to the darkness of his vehicle and because the evening is quickly approaching considering I stayed with my mom longer than expected. I don't give the car a second thought and continue to drive on the busy streets of my overpopulated city. Before I arrive to Josh's house, I decide to grab dinner. I'm just too tired to cook up a feast tonight.

I'm driving in the inner lane of a four way intersection, a quesadilla with all the works sounds bomb right now. I realize I've missed the right turn to my favorite Mexican restaurant so I immediately squeeze into the congested right lane to make my turn and avoid going further into the opposite direction. As I'm turning, I notice the black car suddenly switch lanes almost causing a collision. He turns right and is now driving behind me, but keeps his distance.

Okay, that was a coincidence. Not a big deal. I tell myself.

I make another right then another until I reach Mission Street once again. I notice the black car continues behind me. I turn left on Mission then a right after the first block. Now I'm positive this car is following me, I know it's not Sancho because he drives a silver Impala. I try to remain calm even though my heart is racing. I look back to see Muscles, he's asleep in his booster seat. I need to keep us safe. My windows are rolled up, I lock the doors, and I return to Mission Street since it's busy with plenty of witnesses. I decide my best option is to drive to the police station and avoid Josh's house or my home. I call 911 to state I'm being followed. I indicate my location along with a description of Betty and license plate. I can't provide the license plate of the car that's in pursuit of me since he's savvy enough to maintain some distance. The 911 dispatcher informs me that an officer will get to me as soon as possible, but that in the meantime to continue heading to the police station.

Once I arrive to the new police station on Valencia Street, my stalker hits the pedal to the metal not allowing me the opportunity to get his number plate. Moments later, I notice a silver Impala floor it in order to catch up with the black vehicle that's rapidly evading.

Sancho.

I wonder for a brief moment if my stalker is Daniel wanting to get Marisol back or attempting to utilize me to hurt Josh. Then AX comes to mind, what if it's him or one of his men demanding answers regarding his father's death by any means? Being followed along with the uncertainty of my stalker has my nerves in shambles. Before I speak with an officer to file a report, I call Josh to inform him of the situation.

Josh and Kade soon arrive to pick Muscles and me up. Apparently, they must have concocted a plan prior to their arrival since both men appear serious and focused on their tasks with minimal words. Kade drives my car to Josh's house and parks it inside the garage. Josh gathers some of his and Muscles' belongings to spend the night at my place. Both conduct a perimeter check of Josh's home before activating the alarm. Josh returns to the truck carrying a duffle bag along with a silver case while Kade drives off in Josh's Range Rover.

"Why is Kade driving your date car?"

"He's taking it back to your house. That's your car from now on. Betty will remain in my garage until further notice. She stands out too much and draws unnecessary attention to you. You need a more inconspicuous car."

"Oh." Is all I can say. Josh is in his boss mode; when his mind is set, there's no arguing with him. As we drive down the hill from his house, already I miss my car and wish things could be simpler.

"Hey...smile for me, beautiful." He lifts my chin to get a better look at my face. I smile. He compliments me as if his opinion were a fact. "Everything will be fine. I promise you...I..."

I interrupt him. "Shhh. I believe you. Things will turn out for the best." I wink at him. "I'll have to admit, I'm concerned about the G-U-N." I spell it out so that Muscles won't completely understand our conversation. "I saw your silver case. I know that's where you carry it."

"Don't worry. Tomorrow I'm taking the day off to buy and install a safe in your bedroom's closet.

G-U-N-S need to be kept in a safe place, especially when kids are in the home."

My melancholy mood instantly brightens up. "Can I ask you for a favor? I know this is terrible timing, but if you get a chance, do you think you can add some shelves to my closet? It's so tiny I have a hard time finding my clothes since they're bunched up together."

185

"You want me to do something for you? Can Miss Independent actually be asking her man for help? Baby, if you'd let me, I'd build you a house just so I can show off my skills!" Josh turns to look at Muscles. "Besides the ones I show you in the S-A-C-K, that is." He laughs demonically.

"P-E-R-V! There is a child in the vehicle! We need to keep this convo rated G!" I scold him

"So, what you're saying is that on the late night, things will be rated triple X?"

"How did I go from being distraught about my life being in danger and someone chasing me to being hot and bothered?" I'm confused.

"I'm a man of several talents. Just know, once everyone goes to sleep, I'm smothering my face in your cream pie."

"Babe!" *Oh, I'm going to choke him!*

"Okay, I'm sorry! I'm definitely having BREAKFAST for dinner. There...better?" He emphasizes breakfast with a wink.

"Put the brakes on it, Tree Hugger! You can have all the BREAKFAST you want tonight, but you need to behave until then. Or else...you can forget about it."

"All right, all right. Just so you know...I'm having seconds, possibly even thirds."

I sigh loudly shaking my head at his inappropriateness, but deep inside I want to do flips due to my man's lust filled hunger. *Yeah, buddy!*

When we arrive to my house, my mom is waiting for us in her new Denali. Once she gets out, she looks ridiculously tiny standing next to the honker vehicle. "Mom!" I run to her and give her a hug. "What are you doing here? Come on, let's go inside."

"Kade vaguely told me what happened. I was worried, I needed to make sure you and Muscles were okay." Josh kisses my mom on the cheek while he carries Muscles inside the house. Then she puts her arm around my shoulder and tightens her grasp.

"Mom, I'm fine. Please don't make me discuss it, I just want to put it behind me and move on." I will myself to believe my words.

Despite my plea, my mom insists on knowing what's going on. After I explain my earlier conversation with Diego and later the incident with the black car, my mom goes into panic mode. "Mom, calm down. I have Sancho looking after me."

Just then, Kade walks in carrying two pizzas laughing hysterically. "You have SANCHO looking after you?" He directs the question at me then turns to Josh. "Tree Hugger, are you okay with SANCHO looking after your woman?"

Josh joins Kade in his fit of laughter.

My mom and I are confused with Kade's questions and his emphasis on Sancho's name. "I don't get it. What's so funny?"

Kade tries to stop laughing then inhales and exhales deeply. "Sancho is a term used to refer to a man that someone is having an affair with. Josh and I both met the man, trust me...he's definitely NOT easy on the eyes."

"Great." I roll my eyes. "Mom, I really don't want to talk about things with Muscles around, besides he needs to eat. Let's just change the subject."

"Fine." My mom agrees. "Kade, honey, how about you and Muscles spend the night, then you and I can have a LONG chat."

"Cheesecake, is there anything you don't want mom to know? Otherwise...I'm spilling the beans. You know how she likes to torcher me during her interrogations to get the truth out of me."

"Whatever...loose lips! No, I don't care what you say. Just do it after Muscles goes to sleep." I sigh then turn my direction to my man. "Is it okay if Muscles stays with my mom tonight?"

"Muscles, would you like to spend the night at Victoria's house?" As Muscles is happily eating his slice of pizza, he nods his head with approval.

"Great! We'll pick up a movie and popcorn on the way home!" My mom beams with joy. As Josh is grabbing two slices of pizza for himself, my mom stares at his plate slightly confused. "Josh, I know you can eat more than two slices, eat up, hun!"

"Oh, I can definitely eat, but I'm saving my appetite for later. I'm having breakfast for dinner." Josh states as I'm drinking a glass of juice. Instantly, I spit out my drink and start to choke. My mom rushes to me and pats my back.

Josh just laughs. I give him an evil sneer.

Asshole!

"Are you okay, Nina?"

"Yes, mom. I'm fine."

My mom returns her attention to Josh. "So, are you a big breakfast kind of guy?"

"Actually, breakfast has recently become my favorite meal. If it were up to me, I'd have it in the morning, for lunch, and dinner. There's nothing better in this world than having breakfast with my beautiful lady." The traitor who I once referred to as my man has the audacity to slyly wink at me.

You...fucking asshole! I'm going to eat you alive if you don't shut the fuck up and stop with this inappropriate conversation. I'm going to bury your dick six feet deep if you keep talking!

"Aww...you're so sweet." My mom gazes at him lovingly.

"Cheesecake, how come you're turning red? You actually look constipated." Kade adds his two cents.

Through gritted teeth, I respond. "I'm just not sure I'm feeling well anymore. Breakfast might have to be postponed."

Josh gives me a worried look. "Are you sure, baby? All day you've been begging me to have breakfast with you. I've been looking forward to it."

Motherfucker! That's it! I'm biting IT off!

My mom continues to chime in. "Josh, give her an hour or so, I'm sure her appetite will return and she'll be anxious to dig into her breakfast."

Ugh! You're killing me, mom, you're really killing me.

Josh gives my mom his handsome boyish smile that always makes me weak. "Victoria, you're so wise, I think you're absolutely right."

"Mama V! Stop! Don't you see what they're talking about?" Kade shouts with a cheesy grin.

"Umm...food? Breakfast? What?" My mom has no clue.

"Mom! They're talking about sausage and eggs! That's the breakfast these two are referring to! Sheesh, woman! Wake up and smell the innuendos!" Kade looks at my mom completely flabbergasted then turns his attention toward us. "You. Are. Sickos. Oh...you're so lucky Muscles is around, otherwise I'd let you both have it, you bunch of horn dogs!" Kade cackles boisterously.

My mom walks up to Kade and Josh. She stands between them then yanks both men by their ears. "You listen and you listen good. Josh! So help me, little boy, I will call your mother on the spot and tell her of your deviant shenanigans if you pull a stunt like that again. Kade! You never make fun of your mom! You should have told me as soon as you caught on, little boy! I will not tolerate your unsuitable conversations in front of my little man. Do I make myself clear?" My mom releases their ears and waits for a response.

"Yes, ma'am." Both men say in unison trying to show remorse, but failing pathetically.

My mom turns her attention to me. I quickly run to Muscles and place him on my lap.

"Chicken! Bwok bwok bwok! Hiding behind a child...that's a new low for you, Cheesecake!" Kade mocks.

"So." I stick out my tongue unabashed.

Chapter 11 (Josh)

Liar, Liar

The scent of her hair, the feel of her skin, and taste of her lips drive my need for her to a desperate state. I have to be in her.

"Baby, I'm starving. Feed me. Only you can satisfy my appetite." I say as I bury my face onto her neck and trail kisses down to her bare chest. "You can't expect me not to want to go another round while you're lying naked beside me. Your presence alone makes my cock hard." I grab her big milky breast and suck hard.

"Oh, I don't think so Mr. Inappropriate. No breakfast for you." She moans and squirms beneath my touch. "I said no, babe."

"You said no earlier also, but helped me slip your panties off, baby. You know you want me deep inside you, making you wet, and feel good all over. We have the house to ourselves. You can scream as loud as you want without having to bury your face in the pillow." I remind her.

"Mmm...no." She sighs trying to contain another moan. "I have to teach you a lesson. Your behavior was inappropriate today."

"Lesson learned." I grab her nipple with my teeth adding enough pressure to make her gasp. She does. I bring her body closer to mine and grab her ass as I continue to suck on her creamy tit. I allow her to feel my shaft and the precum that spurts out between us the harder I suck on her nipple's pebble. "Either you give in or I'm just going to take it."

She tilts my head to gently kiss me. Then bites my lip...hard. She deviously laughs as she quickly gets up and takes off running to the living room. "You're gonna have to catch me first, Tree Hugger!" She yells with a sardonic giggle.

So my lady wants to play.

"I love you, baby...with all my heart, but your ass...is mine. I'm having seconds on breakfast. You've been warned." I state calmly, but loud enough for her to hear. I take my time to put on my boxers. I slowly walk out to the living room with a scheming smirk. I look around and initially, I don't see her. After a closer look, I see her toes sticking out from behind the couch. I walk to the kitchen to pour myself a drink. There's nothing better than cognac during a game. I have a seat on the couch opposite of the one she's hiding behind. "Baby, when I get my hands on you, I'm going to finger fuck your ass hole. Slowly, I'm going to stretch you out and make room for my fat dick. As I fuck that tight little hole of yours, I'll be rubbing your clit making you beg me not to stop. When you feel like you can't take my cock in you anymore, I'm going to smack your ass so hard you'll be begging for more from delirium. Then I'm going to shove my finger deep in your tight pussy while I'm penetrating you from behind. You're going to scream my name so loud, your whole block is going to hear you. Do you understand?" I say with my don't-fuck-with-me-right-now tone.

Silence.

"This is the last time I'm going to ask you...Do. You. Understand?"

My lady peaks out from her hiding spot. "Yes." She responds meekly. As she's getting ready to stand up, I stop her.

"Stay in that position, baby. That's how I'll be fucking you." I take a sip of my cognac and savor its warmth as I admire my naked lady on her hands and knees. "Come." I command.

Nina's playfulness quickly evades. A tigress instantly overcomes her features as she bites down on her lip, breathes deeply, and seductively crawls to me. There's no denying the excitement in her eyes. She wants me. She wants this. She wants me to violate her from behind. She wants me to own her in every way possible. Her submission gives me an unexpected high, a feeling I eagerly want to return with my dominance.

Once my lady reaches me, I take another drink. I tilt her head to face mine and kiss her. As her lips welcome me, I allow the cognac from my mouth to flow into hers. She's taken by surprise from the complexity of the drink's flavor, but nonetheless, she swallows it.

After relishing over my lady's picturesque body, I decide it's time to follow through on my word. As Nina remains on her knees, I massage her chest from behind with one hand and with the free one, I glide her pussy's juice from her clit to her anus. On instinct, she tightens up her body from the unknown invasion.

"Relax, baby. Relax." I comfort her. I continue circling more cum on her forbidden spot until I manage to slip my finger inside. She gasps. Her breathing has escalated and she's trying desperately to relax, but her anxiety prevents her from doing so. After several strokes, her body is more accepting of the penetration. I remove my finger then glide the tip of my cock to her wet entrance allowing my shaft to coat itself with my lady's nectar. Gently, the tip of my dick enters her ass.

"Oh! Fuck!" She yells with a combination of moans. The louder her voice, the more satisfied I feel from fulfilling my promises.

The next morning I wake up completely revived. I'm full of energy and I feel great. Nina's already gone to work, I realize I'm home alone in her house. It feels strangely odd. I head to the kitchen and find breakfast already made with a note that reads,

My dearest Tree Hugger,

Fuck me like that again and I'll be sure to give you breakfast daily for the rest of your life! I love you, babe. Have an awesome day and know that I'll be thinking of you every moment that passes by. Why? Because my ass is sore as fuck!

Ouch! Lol! You still make my heart melt.

With love, Your Dirty Whore, Nina

x x o o x o

translation:

kiss, kiss, hug, hug, kiss, hug

I can't help but smile. I love this girl. She makes me feel whole...complete. I count the day I met her as one of my biggest blessings. I can't imagine not having her in my life or a future that doesn't include her.

Before I leave Nina's house, I get measurements of her closet then realize the wall between her closet and the hallway bathroom consists of dead space with no studs. I write down the materials necessary to improve my lady's closet then head to my warehouse. As I'm in route, I call my assistant. "Jelly, I need 175 fire and ice roses delivered to my girlfriend's work within the next hour."

Jelly seems a bit bothered by my request. "Umm...Joshua,

that's a big order to fill in such a short time frame. Did she put you in the doghouse or something?" She asks a little too hopeful.

"Jelly, you're out of line. Either you follow through with my request or I'll find someone else who can. You decide."

"I apologize. I'll get on it right away." She says with absolutely no remorse and a hint of anger.

Is she jealous? I don't give it a second thought and disregard the ludicrous idea.

Once I return to Nina's house, I immediately empty out her closet and place everything on her bed. I demo part of the wall with dead space allowing for a much bigger closet. I reframe the opening, tape, mud, and texture the wall, and add several shelving units and different compartments for better organization. I'm in the zone with music playing in the background that I fail to realize the day has quickly passed me by.

"Fuck. Me." I recognize Nina's voice instantly as I'm finishing up installing the shelves of her extended closet.

I turn around and smile as I notice my lady sitting on her bed on top of her things admiring her closet. "Hey, baby. Do you like it? I hope you don't mind that I tore down part of your wall, it was dead space with no structural beams, I figured you could use the extra space."

Nina looks at me with hunger then licks her lips. I'm confused. "Ummm...what's up, baby? Why are you looking at me like that?" I honestly don't know what to think. She looks like she's ready to pounce on me, but that can't be so since I'm dirty from working all day.

"Babe. Babe! You look like sex on a fuckin' stick!" She leaves her bed and approaches me. "I just wanna eat you up. You look delicious in your tank top and jeans, all sweaty and manly working throughout the day...just for me." She jumps on me. I gladly lift her up. "Fuck me, babe. Right here. Right now. Let me show you how much I appreciate your hard work and those beautiful roses I received. Thank you." She crushes my lips with hers then gently maneuvers her tongue into my mouth.

Heaven. I could get used to this.

Nina stops mid kiss. "Why 175 roses? I counted them."

"For every day since I met you." I quickly respond and return my mouth to hers.

She gasps and smiles.

After two servings of breakfast, we head over to Victoria's house to check on Muscles. Both Kade and Muscles are asleep by the time we get there. It seems they had a busy day at the zoo and the Exploratorium. We return back to Nina's house and fall asleep on the couch watching my favorite show, *Archer.*

The next morning, while Nina's at work, I spray paint the interior of the closet then touch up the exterior wall. I run a few errands allowing the paint to dry, once it's dry I add steel rods. Later, I place all her clothes and items in an order that I feel will work for her. If she doesn't like it, she can always change it. Once I'm done, I notice a box on the floor by her bed. I open it and notice several old journals. My curiosity gets the best of me and I open one up. It's Nina's. I skim through a few. They're all hers. In the past, my lady has reprimanded me several times about going through her things. Now, I'm well aware she feels it's a violation of her privacy. I decide to put the journals back in their box without reading any of them. I place the box on top of her closet then clean up my work area. Once I'm finished, that bitch, curiosity gets the best of me once again. I grab the box with Nina's journals and begin to go through them. A few pages mention some of her sexual encounters, it takes all my will to close the journal and not ready her private thoughts any further, then one journal with stars all over it catches my attention. I open it and after a few pages, my heart shatters, my blood boils with rage, and my fist loses control. I hit her wall punching a hole through it. My adrenaline is pumping so hard I don't feel pain. My thoughts are all in shambles as I try to comprehend what I've just read. I pick up the damn journal again and read the pages in detail. Each word, each feeling, each page causing a deeper wound in my heart. Once I can't bare the agony any longer, I grab my keys and head over to Nina's work.

I try to remain calm, but every cell in my body radiates with fury. I turn on the radio to calm my nerves. The song, "Liar, liar" by Cris Cab begins to play. I don't think another song could be more appropriate at this time. I crank up the song hoping the bass overpowers my grief.

Once the song is over, I pull over to take a deep breath. I get out and buy a 40oz beer. Before I open it, I call Nina. She answers immediately. "Go to my house right now."

"Babe, is everything okay? I'm busy at work, but if it's an emergency I'll go."

I feel like choking her over the phone. "It's an emergency. If you're not at my house in twenty minutes, I'm going to your job and things will just get ugly."

"Babe! Talk to me now. Tell me what's going on. You have me worried."

"Get your fuckin' ass to my house now!" I hang up the phone disgusted with the sound of her voice.

I rush over to my house. I remain in my car unable to move afraid of destroying everything and anything in sight. Instead, I keep the music on, twist the cap of my 40, and begin to chug. Within less than five minutes, I finish my drink. Sadly, I realize the beer didn't numb my pain. I head inside my house and take out my bottle of Gran Patrón Platinum tequila. Three double shots later and I finally sense a buzz, but I can also feel my pain lingering, refusing to abscond.

"Babe? What's going on?" Nina asks looking perfect as ever with concern infiltrated in her beautiful features. "Talk to me."

"Fuck you, you lying whore!" I get in her face preparing myself to hear her worthless reasons for lying to me.

"Josh! What the fuck is your problem? Don't speak to me like that! You're acting like a complete asshole. Tell me what has you so angry!"

I back away from her slowly. I want to observe her body language, her facial expression, and her demeanor as she tries to come up with a reason for playing me for a fool this whole time. "Why the fuck didn't you tell me that you and Kade had fucked? I read your fuckin' journal! You were in a relationship with him! You lied to me and told me he was like your fuckin' brother, you lying conniving bitch! Why the fuck would you lie to me?"

Nina's face is completely shocked. "Josh, what Kade and I had was years ago. He is like my brother! We're family!"

Nina insisting Kade is like family pisses me off even more. "Since when is it okay to fuck your family?"

"You're judging me without knowing the whole story."

"Maybe if you were honest with me from the start, this wouldn't be happening. I wouldn't feel so betrayed. Kade has no loyalty to me, it wasn't on him to tell me. But you? You're always preaching about honesty, yet you kept this from me!"

"Josh, please calm down. I hate to see you this upset."

"Upset? I'm not upset. I'm pissed as fuck! My lady lives with someone who she's fucked and was in a relationship with! You get upset whenever girls look at me a certain way. You were jealous of my fuckin' assistant for no reason! Think about that! How the fuck would you feel if I had a roommate who I used to fuck back in the day? Even worse...I lied about it, pretending she's considered family then later you find out there was something between us. You wouldn't like it for shit!"

"Please...let me explain." Nina begs not just with her words, but with her distressing eyes as well.

"Start fuckin' talking! The longer you stand in front of me, the more repulsed I am by you!" I refuse to get sucked into her manipulation.

Her sadness turns into fury instantly. "Stop it! You're being cruel! I don't deserve this!"

"No! You don't get to play the poor me role. You lied to me. I'm the one who's hurt. I don't fuckin' deserve this bull-shit!"

"Kade was the first guy I was with after I was raped by those three bastards! There! I said it!" Nina tries to remain cool as her unwanted tears flow freely from her eyes. "It happened a few years after that horrible incident, but it happened. Back then, I couldn't tolerate the looks of other guys, but my curiosi-ty and sexuality began to fight an inner battle within me. Kade was the only person besides my mom who I trusted. During those days, Kade and I used to experiment with drugs and al-cohol. One day while I was drunk and high on ecstasy, I kissed him. He was surprised, but didn't react. Since the first day I met Kade, he never crossed that line. I initiated it. Eventually, he caved. Since then, we would have sex from time to time usually when we were drunk or high. At the time, Kade used to get a lot of attention. I knew he didn't want to hurt me, but I felt like I was holding him back from sexually experimenting with others. We both made a pack to just remain friends. As the years progressed, our friendship grew into a strong family bond. We've lived together for thirteen years because our friendship was more important than anything else. Kade made me feel worthy of love and helped me gain confidence in my-self when I couldn't even look at myself in the mirror."

Nina sighs. "I won't lie to you, Josh. At one point, I did feel that I was in love with him, but that's only because he's the only man I had known. He constantly proved his loyalty to me. In time, I realized that what I felt for Kade wasn't true love, it was respect and admiration. Don't get me wrong, I love Kade, but I've never been in love with him like I am with you."

"Why the fuck would you lie to me? All those times we've had intimate conversations, you could have brought it up! You could have told me! But no! I had to find out on my own. What if I never would have read your journal? Would you have told me?"

Nina remains quiet.

"Answer me! You owe me the fuckin' truth!" I yell.

Nina continues to silently sob. "No, I wouldn't have told you."

That last stab in my heart does me in. "Leave." I command her.

"Josh, please...listen."

"I'm done, Nina. I don't want to see you again. I hope you have a great fuckin' life." I grab my bottle of Patrón and head to my room. After several more shots of tequila, numbness overpowers my pain and darkness finally finds its way to me.

Chapter 12 (Nina)

Kamikazes & Long Islands

It's been over three months since Josh ended our relationship. This time without him has left my soul empty. People say that time heals all wounds; I'm still waiting for the truth to come from those words. Every day I wake up with a pain in my heart that doesn't fade. Every week I live my life in a numb state. I eat, but I don't taste the flavor of my food. I breathe, yet I can't recall a specific scent. I listen to music, but can't make out the lyrics or the rhythm of the tunes. I sleep and live without dreams.

What can't I do? I can't think, I can't concentrate, and worst of all...I can't forget. I want to forget more than anything all those hurtful things Josh said to me, I want to forget his touch, his lips, his warmth, his smell, I just want to forget him...all of him. I want him erased from my thoughts as if he never existed. Why hold on to someone who despises and thinks so poorly of me? How can I move on if his memory remains anchored in my heart?

As time passes by, my bitterness towards Josh seems to grow. I didn't want to explain a situation from my past that to me was private. I've never had to answer to anyone before. I didn't feel it was a complete lie. I did omit a partial truth, but he saw it as a betrayal of our trust. It was a moment from my life that I simply wasn't prepared to discuss. Now, I find myself lying by omission to my mom. She constantly asks the reason behind Josh and my breakup, I always shrug it off and state it was due to stupid shit. How can I tell her that it was because Josh found out Kade and I fucked? I can't! Kade isn't just some guy. In my mom's eyes, Kade is her son just as much as I'm her daughter. The topic is simply too awkward and I want to avoid it all costs. I push those thoughts aside as I step inside my mom's bakery and see Muscles wearing an apron and playing with a toy cash register. Once he sees me, he drops his toy and rushes to me with his arms wide open along with his biggest smile. My heart instantly melts.

Muscles hasn't been around us much. Once Josh and I broke up, my mom informed me that Josh hired a nanny to assist Celeste while she took care of Muscles. Since Celeste's medical situation remains fragile, Josh didn't want his mom straining herself. Two weeks prior, Marisol was finally released from rehab after being there for three months. I haven't seen or spoken to her, but we text constantly. She's been busy participating in her NA meetings, attending individual counseling, and working part-time at the daycare Muscles was recently enrolled in. Today, Marisol had a doctor's appointment after work and asked my mom if she could look after Muscles for two hours. My mom instantly jumped at the opportunity and even invited her and Muscles over for dinner. Marisol was a bit apprehensive at first, but accepted her invitation.

"Muscles! You've gotten so big, honey! I can't believe how much you've grown and how handsome you've become!" Muscles shrugs his shoulders and grins simultaneously.

Just then, Kade walks in. "Muscles! I've missed you, bud! Rumor has it that you're staying over for dinner. Is that true?" Muscles nods his head enthusiastically.

"Well, I guess I'll be joining you!" He excitedly informs Muscles then yells to my mom who's in the back refilling her baked goods. "Mama V! I'm staying over for dinner, okay?"

"Okay! Sounds good!" She yells back.

Apparently, we're all joining mom for dinner even though we weren't invited.

"Count me in too, mom!" I laugh for the first time in weeks.

"Awesome! Will do!"

Within a few minutes later, we all leave the bakery shop. My mom allows one of her staff to reconcile the register and close the shop. As we walk to my mom's house together, I notice our energy is revamped from merely having Muscles with us once again.

When Marisol arrives to my mom's house after her appointment, I'm completely taken back when I see her. What once was a shell of a woman completely hollow inside is now a woman who's full of spirit with a positive energy radiating off her. She's no longer just bones. She's gained weight, her skin looks smooth, and her brown medium length hair now has bounce to it. Overall, she looks great, but most importantly she's healthy.

"Thank you so much, Victoria for watching over my son and inviting us to dinner. Here you go, I brought some fruit skewers with my own special blend of yogurt for dipping." My mom immediately embraces Marisol.

We greet each other then hang out in the living room as we wait for the food to come out of the oven. I notice Marisol is no longer wearing all black. "Marisol, you're wearing red and white! Finally! Some color in your life! It looks great on you."

She smiles shyly at me. "Thanks, Nina. I've finally come to terms with my father's death. He'll always remain in my heart."

"Oh. I wasn't aware your father had passed. When I mentioned it last time, all you said was that a family member had passed away. Well, regardless, I'm sorry for your loss, but I'm glad you're moving forward with your life. How did your father pass away, if you don't mind me asking?"

"Actually, my father and I hadn't seen each other in quite some time so when I heard about his death, it really hit me hard. We were close when I was younger, I was his little girl and he used to spoil me like crazy."

"Aww...so how did he pass away?"

Marisol sighs sadly. "I'd rather not say. I still can't comprehend his tragic story. I'm just not ready to elaborate on the series of events. I'm still having a hard time wrapping my head around everything."

"No worries, I completely understand. I apologize for my intrusive question. I tend to forget my filter sometimes." I giggle at my own awkwardness.

My mom changes the subject. "Marisol, I hope you allow Muscles to come over more often. We've missed him so much! I can only imagine how difficult it was for you to go weeks without seeing him."

"It was the most difficult time in my life, luckily my therapist made an exception and allowed me to see him weekly."

"When did you see him?" I ask.

"On Friday mornings. Kade used to take him."

My mom and I both stare at Kade. He simply shrugs his shoulders and tries to play off his thoughtfulness.

"My son's visits definitely made my motivation to improve much stronger than the first few days I went without seeing him. I will always remember and be thankful to Kade for his kind gesture of bringing my son to me during a time I didn't deserve to have him in my life."

Kade appears uncomfortable. "Okay, Marisol. You've thanked me enough. It truly wasn't a big deal. Let's just drop the topic once and for all."

The remainder of the evening is spent discussing much lighter subjects. When Marisol states she's ready to go home and catch a cab, both Kade and I intervene and offer to take her and Muscles home. Reluctantly, she agrees. She insisted on returning to her house once her rehab program ended. Josh offered to let her stay with him until Daniel was captured, but she refused to let Daniel dictate her life any longer. Now, that Marisol has support from several aspects, she has the strength and confidence to overcome her meth addiction despite the inner battle she faces with herself daily. Luckily, Daniel has been nowhere in sight, hopefully things will remain that way.

The following weekend, Michael stops by my house for lunch. We've been having a meal together at least twice a week since Josh and I broke up. The relationship between Michael and I has slowly turned into a friendship. He doesn't know about my past or the reason Josh and I ended things, but I still feel comfortable being myself around him. Today, we have leftovers from last night's dinner. While we're eating, he mentions Josh for the first time in weeks. "Hey, I went to Josh's office yesterday. That assistant of his is a piece of work. She acts like she runs the place. She has no boundaries; she was all over Josh when I got there."

The mention of Josh's name instantly pierces a sharp pain through my chest. I try to play it off by stuffing my face with lunch. It takes all my effort to swallow my food past the lump in my throat from the refusal of wanting to shed unwanted tears. I don't bother to ask Michael what he was doing at Josh's office, it's no longer any of my business.

Kade walks in just then. "Are you guys talking about Jelly? Man, every time I see them together, she's on the Tree Hugger like white on rice. She's a fuckin' leech on his ass. I'm not going to lie, I'm slightly jealous. I want a piece of her action! I just want to ram myself deep inside her conceited ass just to teach her a lesson about being a dick tease. I wanna fuck her so bad!"

Michael looks at Kade with a loss of words, but regardless manages to speak. "Kade, why don't you tell us how you really feel? Seriously, don't hold back. I really think it's time you stop being so shy and become more vocal about your desires." Michael states sarcastically.

"Look, Magic Mike...I no longer wonder if you're magically delicious, you're a bit too uptight for my taste, but given the right amount of alcohol, I may just reconsider giving you a ride on the K.D. train. The choice is yours." He winks and smirks at Michael.

Michael ignores him. Even he has learned to disregard Kade's sexual advances.

Two weeks later, Kade is absolutely fed up with my melancholy mood. "That's it! I've had it! I'm sick of seeing you look so glum! It's been over four months since you and the Tree Hugger broke up! Get the fuck over it! He's not the only man on this planet. All you've been doing the past few months is work, go to a photo shoot from time to time, run, hang out with Alex on a rare occasion, then throw yourself on the couch like a big lug watching *Scandal, New Girl, The Mindy Project,* and reruns of *Friends.* Enough is enough! No more girly shows! Get your ass up, put on something tight, let your twins hang out, and throw on some lipstick because tonight...we're going out!"

"But...but I don't want to. I'm comfortable here. This couple on TV is remodeling their kitchen on their own with hardly any experience. I need to see how it turns out."

"What the fuck? You don't NEED to watch anymore home renovation shows. They're so fuckin' boring! Our house is fine the way it is." Kade stops and analyzes me for a minute. "You don't watch those shows because they remind you of the Tree Hugger, right?"

I don't say anything. I simply bite down on my lip hoping he dismisses his ludicrous idea even though it's completely the truth.

"Fuckin' shit! Now I've seen it all. This is worse than I thought. Who the fuck watches *HGTV* because it reminds them of their ex-man? My best fuckin' friend, that's who! Girl, you need help. I should've intervened much sooner. I can't believe I didn't realize the night we were watching porn together you were admiring the kitchen cabinets and granite instead of checking out the couple getting down and dirty. That's just sad."

"The girl was boring! She was putting me to sleep with her sorry ass moaning. It's not my fault the décor of the kitchen was more appealing than the fuck fest we were watching!"

"Fair enough. Now hurry up and get ready. I'm cancelling my plans in order to be with you tonight."

The last thing I feel like doing is getting ready to go out, but I decide to put on my big girl panties and enjoy an evening with my bestie. "Fine...just know that I won't be much fun tonight."

Kade smirks. "Let's see if that's true after your fifth shot."

I grab the first thing I touch from my new spacious closet, a black skater dress with a white and red print of Marilyn Monroe in the front. I put my hair in a rockabilly inspired ponytail with a pump in the front then add a few coats of mascara and dab on some red lipstick. I put on high heels, but within seconds take them off. Wearing a dress is difficult as it is, being in heels simply isn't going to happen. Instead, I throw on my black and white chucks and call it a day. I'm ready in less than ten minutes.

When Kade and I arrive at the dance club, we make our way to the bar. The first level has the dance floor right at the center with a laser show and production that increases the energy of the crowd. The second level consists of an open space with a glass balcony surrounding the entire perimeter. It allows people at the two bars, opposite ends of each other and lounge areas to look down at the main dance stage. I gaze up and see everyone from the second tier admiring the view below them. I bring my attention back to Kade as he gives the bartender his credit card and directs him to leave an open tab for us. We begin our night of drunkenness with three back to back Kamikaze shots. Kade grabs my hand and leads me to the dance floor as soon as the DJ starts playing, "I Need Your Love" by Calvin Harris featuring Ellie Goulding.

We return to the bar after dancing for a bit then take two more consecutive shots each. Kade then orders us Long Islands. I usually try to refrain from mixing my drinks since it causes me a serious hangover the following day, tonight I'm living in the moment, not caring about tomorrow, and hoping the alcohol numbs my existing pain. Just as I'm about to reprimand myself for allowing Josh to cross my mind, I see him.

Josh is on the second level looking down at everyone. Beside him is his assistant, Jelly talking to several girls around her. *That bitch.*

What the fuck? What happened to you not hanging out with your staff, Mr. Ryan? What happened to you saying it would be inappropriate? Fucker.

As I'm staring at Josh from the main level, Kade rushes me

and puts his arm around me. He gets close to my ear to ensure I'm able to hear what he has to say since we're close to one of the speakers. "Cheesecake! I just ran into one of my old freaks from back in the day! She wants to hit a couple of rounds tonight! The funny part? I don't remember her name! Who gives a fuck...I'll be calling her sweet tits all night long!" He laughs in my ear just as Josh makes direct eye contact with me. His expression instantly turns sinister.

Josh turns around and grabs a hold of one of the waitresses with an empty tray. He takes the tray from her, tosses it aside, and forcefully pulls her towards him. The girl appears mesmerized by him so when he holds her face and kisses her, she doesn't pull away.

Bastard.

I try not to look. I don't need the added pain to my already open wound, but for whatever incomprehensible reason, I'm not able to stop staring. My stomach instantly turns, I feel light headed, and unable to stand on my own. Kade grabs me before I lose my balance then looks up. He sees Josh all over this girl.

What the fuck is up with him and waitresses?

"Come on. Let's get out of here. You don't need to see that bullshit." Kade tells me as gently as possible.

"No. Let me get some water. I need to clear my thoughts." Kade walks me over to the bar and gets me a bottle of water. Once I finish it, my aching heart gets covered up with rage. I'm determined not to let the Tree Hugger ruin my night or cause me more pain.

Fuck. Him.

I order two rounds of shots for Kade and me. Although he's confused by my sudden shift in mood, he doesn't question it and goes along with the flow. Once we're done pounding the Kamikazes, Kade's flavor of the night shows up.

She tries to pull him to the dance floor, but he stops her. "Kade, go! I'll meet up with you shortly. I'm just going to get another drink. Don't worry. I won't do anything stupid. I promise I'll go find you once I get my drink."

Hesitantly, he agrees.

Once the bartender hands me another Long Island, I feel a tap on my shoulder. I turn around and get taken completely by surprise. Holy shit! It's Channing Tatum. I take another sip of my drink to get myself together. Channing Tatum gets closer to me. "Hey, cutie. Do you wanna dance?" Now that I see him up close I realize...he's not Channing Tatum! Fuckin' shit! Damn, alcohol! I give him another glance. Mmm...he's cute and sexy though. He's no Channing Tatum, but he'll definitely do for the night.

"I'd love to dance." I smile at him coquettishly.

He grabs my hand and leads me to the dance floor. I search for Kade then lead the Channing Tatum look alike to Kade and his super freak of the night. With my drink in hand, the look alike and I begin to dance. Once I'm almost done with my Long Island, the buzz I feel soon starts to make my body tingle. The look alike and I start getting closer, bumping, grinding, and swaying to the beat of the music. He quickly becomes in sync with the movements of my hips and soon tries to be in harmony with my lips. I turn my face to the side not allowing him the chance to make contact, but taunt him by licking my lips. Just then, I feel strong arms push me to the side. It takes me a moment to register the tall build of a man pounding the face of the Channing Tatum look alike.

What the fuck?

I can't register the series of events. My mind is too hazed with liquor to think straight. All I focus on is Kade's voice. "Cheesecake! Let's go! Josh is going ape shit on that poor guy you were just dancing with."

"What? That was Josh who pushed me to the side?"

"Cheesecake, I'll explain later, let's go!" Kade commands allowing no room for further questions.

Just as we're walking out, I feel someone yank my arm from behind. "Ow!" I turn around to see Josh's menacingly face staring down at me.

Shit! Has he always been this tall? And intimidating? Fuck him. He's not running shit tonight. I've got plenty to say to this motherfucker.

I tug at Kade's arm and he immediately stops then notices Josh.

With minimal patience, I address Josh. "What the fuck? Let go of my damn arm!" *Oh...Say something...say something stupid so I can go off on your ass!*

Instead of doing the mature thing by walking away, I realize I actually want to fight. I want to go off on him and give him a piece of my mind. I want to say hurtful things so he can experience a hint of the pain I've felt these past few months. I want him to feel the stab in my heart I felt from seeing him kiss that skank. I want him to hurt, damn it!

"We need to talk." With the tone of his voice, he makes his statement sound more like a demand.

"Now you want to talk to me? After four fuckin' months? Fuck you! Go swap spit with that dirty whore you were making out with earlier. You've got some nerve to beat up a guy who I was only dancing with."

Josh jerks my arm and leads me to one of the exits. Kade comes chasing after us, but I signal him to go back. The last thing I need is for these two to go at it. "Just give me a few minutes! I'll be right back!" I yell at Kade praying he can hear me over the bass of the music.

Kade nods. Good, he heard me.

"Let go of my fuckin' arm!" I scream at Josh. "I'll talk to

you, but you can't fuckin' touch me!" He looks at me with disgust then lets go of my arm as if an electric shock just pierced through his hand.

Once we're outside, we walk in a deserted back alley towards his truck. When we get to it, he turns to me with fury radiating off him. "Do you think it's okay for you to be grinding some piece of shit you just met like some fuckin' slut?"

His question and insults take me by surprise, but only for a second. Immediately, I slap his face with all my might. "Fuck you, asshole! If I choose to suck every dick in this city, that's my fuckin' busy. You can keep your opinion to yourself because nobody gives a damn about it! You have some nerve pointing the finger at me when I saw you being your typical whore self, kissing some random skank. Don't you dare place judgment on me! I have every right to dance, date, grind, or fuck any man I damn well please. You broke up with me, remember?"

Josh opens the back door of his truck, then seizes my arm into his grasp. "I told you not to fuckin' touch me!" I yell.

He gets close to me, yanks my hair tightly with one hand, and grabs my face with the other. "You want to act like a fuckin' whore?" He growls as he ominously stares me down willing me to respond.

I don't dare reply.

"Then I'll treat you like one." Josh takes me by surprise and kisses me with force. I try to fight him off, but my attempt is futile. My bravado has treacherously disintegrated just when I need it the most.

His mouth is hard against mine while his tongue feels stiff as it seeks entry. Although I'm repulsed with the memory of him kissing another woman minutes prior, I sense my body traitorously welcoming his touch.

No! I want to scream.

Stop! I want to beg.

But, no words are said and no physical attempts are made to end his brute determination to make me his once again even if it's just for a final moment.

Josh lifts me up and sits me on the back seat of his truck. He slides me to the opposite end and closes the door behind him never losing contact with my lips. "You've hurt me...so fuckin' much these past months." Josh tells me as he continues with his determined kisses. He yanks my hips towards him, lays me down, then hovers over me as he undoes his pants and slides my G-string to the side. "I hate that I love you so much." And with that, he bites on my bottom lip then rams himself deep inside me making me scream from the shock of his thickness. His rhythm becomes slow and deep, filling me and expanding me beyond belief. "Why the fuck...would you lie...to me?" He asks as he strokes my insides with his unbelievable cock.

I hear his words, but I'm unable to comprehend their meaning. I attempt to speak, but I can't...only whimpers and moans escape me. "Answer me!" He yells then lowers my shirt and frees my breasts from my bra. Josh immediately latches onto a nipple and begins to suck mercilessly. The sharp pain from my breast and the overwhelming feeling from his dick inside me make my body tighten, anticipating the climax I know is ready to explode.

Without warning, Josh stops.

He remains inside me, but doesn't move. "Why the fuck did you lie to me? No matter how hard I try, I can't stop thinking about you. You're engraved in my fuckin' heart. I want to erase your memory forever. If there's something I can't tolerate, it's a liar."

I can't have this conversation now! This man has me completely filled. I have an orgasm anxious to be released. I just can't deal with this right now. I need to cum!

213

"Please...don't stop. We'll talk later. I need to feel you...I need you stroking me." I say with my eyes closed, frantically trying to move beneath him to gain the friction I urgently need.

"You wanna cum, Nina?" The question makes me open my eyes. "I don't think you deserve to cum, NI-NA." Josh states through gritted teeth.

The need for him to continue fucking me is unbearable. With tear filled eyes, I finally cave. "I'm sorry! I'm sorry for not telling you the complete truth about Kade and me. It was a thing of the past. I didn't want a reminder of that time in my present. I'm sorry for omitting the complete truth from you, but know that Kade is family to me. You're the only man I've ever loved and the only one who holds my heart. Please...believe me." I beg.

Josh doesn't speak again. He remains serious, but grants me mercy by relentlessly fucking me over and over again. I feel elated after remaining at my peak for what seems like an eternity. He joins me and finishes inside me. He remains on top refusing to let me go.

"I need to leave before Kade comes searching for me. He met an old friend and has plans to go back to her place, but he won't leave me. I don't want to ruin his night."

"Okay." He gently removes himself from within me. Instantly, I feel a great emptiness, both physically and emotionally. "I have a lot of issues to sort through. We'll talk later this week."

"Okay." I reply sadly. When I sit up, I feel an immediate head rush. I try to shake it off before I exit Josh's truck. The fresh air surprisingly makes me feel better. We walk back to the exit and bang on the door. Right away, Kade opens it.

Kade looks at Josh then looks at me. "Is everything okay?"

I'm at a loss for words. I simply nod my head as Josh walks away.

I excuse myself from Kade and his fuck buddy then head over to the restroom to freshen up. When I return, I insist on taking a few more shots. I need to numb the pain from the fresh wound in my heart, a wound I brought onto myself and has caused a darkness to seep throughout my veins. Luckily, I have Kade to join me in drinking away my sorrows.

Once we leave the club, Kade waves down a cab. Since he knows I'm pretty drunk, he insists on taking one cab to ensure I arrive home safely, then he and his partner in crime for the night will go back to her place. While we're heading home, I check my phone. I only have one text message. Sadly, it's from Michael and not from Josh. The message states he has a letter for me from my dad. Immediately, I call Michael.

He answers right away. "Nina? Are you okay?"

I'm confused. "Umm...yeah, why?"

"It's almost two in the morning. I just wasn't expecting your call that's all." He sounds caught off guard.

"Oh, my bad. Hey, you have a letter for me from Diego?"

"Yeah, I'll drop it off at your house tomorrow morning if you'd like."

"I'm near your hotel, is it okay if I pick it up now?" *Please say yes, please say yes.*

"Sure. I'll text you my info."

"Thanks. I'll see you in a bit. Bye."

I provide the cab driver my detour information.

"Cheesecake, why on earth are you going to Magic Mike's hotel room? Why not just get the letter tomorrow?" Kade asks frustrated.

I feel my eyes begin to swell with unshed tears. "Because...I feel sad. Diego's letters always make me feel better. I need positive thoughts before I go to sleep." I manage to say past my desire to cry like a helpless child. *Damn you, Josh! And damn you too, alcohol!*

215

"Ugh. All right! I don't want to see anymore crocodile tears. You've shed them enough already."

Once we arrive to Michael's fancy hotel, I quickly get out of the cab since everyone will be waiting for me.

"Cheesecake, Magic Mike's been living here all these months? Damn! How much does your dad pay him and can I get a job?"

"You're not funny, Kade!"

"Yes, I am! But, hurry up! Remember...you're only going to get the letter then you're coming right back. It's not time for you to be a Chatty Freaking Cathy!" I hear Kade yell once I've already entered the luxurious lobby.

When I reach Michael's room, he opens the door after the first knock. For the first time since I've met him, I see him in sweats and a t-shirt not his usual business suit attire. Although he's in his late twenties, seeing him in comfortable clothes makes him appear a few years younger. It's nice to see him in a different light.

"Hey, Michael. Sorry for waking you. I wasn't paying attention to the time." *Is it me or is it hot in here?*

"No worries. Hey, would you like a drink? I have wine."

"Oh, no. Not today, Kade is downstairs waiting for me. I just came to pick up the letter from Diego."

"Sounds good." Michael smiles at me kindly then heads to the desk area and pulls out his brief case. When he opens it, I notice a photo album.

"Do you have any pictures of your mom?" I ask curiously wanting to get a glance at Michael's private and past life.

"Of course. I have pictures of your dad also."

"What? I wanna see!"

"I don't want to hold you up any longer since Kade is waiting for you. But if you'd like, you can hang out with me for a bit and later I can drive you to your house. I'm a night owl, I have a difficult time sleeping. I could always use the company."

Without a second thought, I call Kade. "Hey, I'm going to hang out with Michael for a little while. He has pictures of Diego and his mom. I want to check them out. Kay?"

"No. Get your ass down here. You can see them tomorrow."

"Kade, I wasn't asking for permission. I'm telling you so you can be on your way. Michael's going to drive me home. Okay? Okay. Love you. Be safe. Bye." I hang up before Kade goes into one of his famous rants then I turn my phone on silent.

We spend the night drinking wine and going over Michael's few photo albums. As the night progresses, Michael's presence gets closer and closer to me. He sits beside me touching his leg with mine. He looks me in my eyes and takes my wine glass away, placing it on the end table next to him. He returns his gaze to my lips and leans in with a kiss. I don't push him away. Once I feel his tongue against mine, the reality of my actions sets in. I stop the kiss not allowing it to go any further and well aware the alcohol has taken a toll. I decide to switch over to drinking water. The remainder of the night Michael goes more in depth about his childhood and his past. It's nice hearing him open up and be more comfortable with me.

In the morning, I wake up with my spirit uplifted. I'm half asleep, but I quickly sense myself getting aroused. As I turn over, the texture of the sheets feels lavishly smooth against my skin. Slowly, I open my eyes to commence my day. A shocking discovery prevents me from speaking or moving. I see him lying next to me completely naked...just like I am. Before I have a chance to react, he turns to face me then gently kisses my bare breast.

Michael.

What have I done? What have I done? What have I done? My mind is in panic mode while my body feels paralyzed from the shock of the scenery before me.

217

"Good morning." Michael whispers as he sucks on my nipple.

Please...stop. "Michael." I push him away gently, cover myself with the sheet, then look at the time. "I have to go. I'm sorry. I'm already late." Like the coward that I am, I don't have the nerve to face my mistake.

"Okay. I'll drive you home." He offers.

"No, please just stay. I'll just catch a cab. It's no big deal."

He seems baffled at my suggestion. "Don't be silly. I'll drive you. Let me just jump in the shower real fast then I'll take you home."

I decide not to push the issue. "Okay. Where are my clothes?" I no longer want to look at anything. I simply want to close my eyes and wake up from this horrid nightmare.

Michael gets up in all his naked glory. "By the chair next to you."

I turn to my right and see my clothes neatly folded over the arm rest. My eyes then focus on the ground. My heart literally stops beating. "Michael, why is there a used EMPTY condom on the floor?"

"Don't you remember? You begged me to take it off. You wanted to feel me raw inside you." He affirms my biggest fear.

No! Nina, you stupid bitch! What the fuck have you done? If this is a dream...someone, please wake me up!

It takes all my strength not to shed any unwanted tears. "Michael, I really need to leave now. Can you please hurry?"

"Of course."

As Michael is in the shower, I quickly change and cowardly abandon his hotel room, leaving behind a trail full of tears and morals.

CHAPTER 13 (NINA)

REMORSE

Hiding from the world had to eventually come to an end. Leaving my suite at the quaint Bed & Breakfast in Napa Valley posed as a bigger challenge than expected this morning. After spending two relaxing days away from reality with my favorite books, delicious wine, and picturesque sceneries of vineyards galore, it's a wonder how I managed to leave my slow paced and tranquil oasis.

Unfortunately, I have responsibilities to attend. As I'm driving in traffic to work, the dark sky is fading away as dawn quickly approaches. I play mellow R&B music and allow myself to process the mistakes I've been avoiding since I left my house early Sunday morning. A wave of disappointment instantly crashes me with a mighty force. The reality and disgrace of my actions weighs heavily in my heart and on my shoulders. How could I have believed the ache in my soul would be numbed by alcohol? Why did I insist on drinking past my limit? Why didn't I value myself enough to set boundaries? What possessed me to give myself so freely to both men on the same night? Just the thought of that night disgusts me immensely. I behaved irresponsibly by drinking without considering the risks. To drink socially is one thing, but to consume alcohol to the point of unconsciousness is unacceptable. My poor decisions resulted in having unprotected sex with two men and putting my life at risk of STDs and AIDS. No broken heart can ever justify such reckless behavior. Sadly, I know better than to act so impulsively, in this case, my poor judgment overrode my intellect.

How I see things...I can either continue to dwell on my errors and shame or I can learn valuable insight from my poor choices to avoid making those same or similar mistakes once again. The choice is mine.

Once I arrive to my job just in time, I dive into my workload head first to evade personal thoughts. My clients deserve my undivided attention. All private matters need to remain at the front door. After a busy morning, I gladly welcome my lunch break. Just as I'm about to leave my office, Josh walks in with a long stem single red rose.

No. My already broken heart shatters into even tinier pieces.

I can't face him. I'm not ready to have this discussion. Even though we're not together and I'm entitled to do as I please, I know that what happened between Michael and me is something Josh has the right to know if we choose to move on together. Right now though, I just don't have it in me to inform him of my slut ways.

"Hey, pretty lady. May I come in?" Josh asks politely.

My chest instantly tightens. Josh's gentleman demeanor causes an abundance of guilt, betrayal, and shame to overpower me once again.

I try to act as if I'm on a time crunch. "Josh, I'm swamped. Right now is not a good time. Can we talk later?"

"Sure." He gazes at me warmly, tempted to reach out and hold me. "Here I brought you this. The simplicity and beauty of this single rose made me think of you."

I swallow hard then take it avoiding the most minimal contact with Josh. "Thank you. I'll walk you out." I come across as cold and dismissive, but if I remain near him much longer, I'm afraid I'll turn into a blubbering mess. This isn't the time or the place for my personal drama.

As we're heading out of the building, I keep quiet. Josh breaks the silence between us. "Where were you? I called you, text you, and went to your house...nothing."

"I needed to get away...to think. I was in Napa." I look up and bat my lashes fiercely determined to rid myself of the tears that threaten to escape.

Once we exit the building, we run into Michael.

No!

My heart palpitates a mile a minute. My hands become sweaty with anticipation. And my breathing accelerates at a ridiculous speed.

What is he doing here?

Michael greets me with a half hug and a lingering kiss that touches the edge of my lips.

"What the fuck are you doing?" Josh's mood sky rockets from mellow to enraged in seconds. His tight fists are at his sides ready to pounce on Michael if he dares say the wrong thing.

"Chill, Josh." Michael says with a smirk. "I'm just here dropping off Nina's panties. She left them at my hotel this weekend." He adds with smugness.

I stare at Michael shocked with disbelief at his bluntness. When I turn to look at Josh's reaction, it's too late to attempt to calm him. His fist is already in midair ready to do its damage. Josh swings a right hook making instant contact with Michael's face. Michael retaliates and swings back as he rushes Josh trying to restrict him against a wall. It doesn't work. Josh's visceral speed and strength allows him to block the punch and maneuver an uppercut to Michael's head. Michael gets dazed, but returns with a cross punch making direct contact.

"Stop! This is my job! Both of you, stop acting so fuckin' barbaric! Please...stop!" I try to pull one away from the other, but end up getting hit in the crossfire. I fall back landing on the ground. Two police officers call for backup then try to stop both men from their brutal attack. Josh and Michael tackle each other to the ground and neither man is willing to comply and stop the assault. Two more officers join the scene and manage to pull Josh and Michael away from each other. Each man is on the ground face down refusing to conform. They continue to struggle against the cops that are now threatening to use their stun guns. Josh and Michael disregard the threats and still make every effort to continue with their violent behavior. On cue, two officers back away and taser both men. Michael instantly stops his struggle, but Josh's rage seems to escalate and continues to put up a fight. Once Michael is secured in handcuffs, the third officer joins the two who are trying to steady Josh in an effort to restrain him.

"Josh, please...stop!" I beg.

Just like that, Josh ends his struggle and complies with the police. As they aid him in getting up from the ground, he looks straight ahead refusing to make eye contact with me. When the officers lead him to the back of the patrol car, Josh stops before me, but doesn't look at me. "I'm done with you, Valentina...done for good this time." Then allows the cops to take him away in the back of the police car as if he were some type of menace to society.

Once I'm ready to head back to my office, I notice several spectators nearby, all mostly my coworkers. I ask God to allow the Earth to suck me into the depth of its core, but even God knows I don't deserve such mercy. I return to my office and shut the door behind me refusing to cry any longer and determined to finish my day with the small amount of dignity I have left...if any.

When I arrive home, I feel like the walking dead, my thoughts are blurred, my spirit is crushed, and my soul is consumed with darkness.

"Cheesecake! What the fuck happened to your face?" Kade stands and hurries to observe me up close.

Actually, I didn't bother to look at my face. The pain and soreness was enough for me to know it wasn't pretty. The last thing I want to do right now is discuss the day's events. "Please, Kade...not now. I'll explain later. Right now, I just need to sleep."

He sighs. "Fine, but as soon as you wake up, you're going to tell me where the hell you've been these past few days and why you haven't been returning my calls and texts."

"Yeah. Okay." I agree just to get him off my back.

As I'm headed to my room, a knock on the door stops me in my tracks. Although I really don't want to see or speak to anyone, something tells me I need to answer the door.

I open it and immediately regret my decision. *What the fuck is she doing here?*

Jelly stands outside carrying a duffle bag with keys in hand. "Here you go, Nina." She hands me the items self-satisfied.

"What's this?" I ask.

"Joshua wanted me to drop off your things. Your car has been placed in storage, the business card with the location is in the duffle bag and the car's keys along with the storage's key are in your hand.

A blow to my gut.

"Oh, before I forget...I have something else for you. She goes downstairs and grabs something large from her trunk.

"Here you go. Joshua wanted you to have this." Jelly smugly hands me the black and white portrait of Josh and me, the

Valentine's Day gift I had given him. "He also said you can keep the Range Rover for as long as you'd like, just mail his keys once you're done using it. Is there anything you'd like me to give him?" The bitch deviously asks.

I can't speak. I simply shake my head. Kade joins me and takes the items from me.

"Okay, then. I guess my job here is done." Jelly's sneer and ill will is over the top.

Before she leaves she makes sure to stab me with insinuations. "Hey, Nina...you no longer have to worry about Joshua, I'll be sure to take good care of him. He'll be in the best hands with me." She winks at me sadistically.

Before I have the chance to respond, Kade intervenes. "You go ahead and have Nina's sloppy seconds, boo. Just know that when he's with you, he'll be thinking of her. But you go ahead and pretend like he's yours. Let the scraps he gives you be enough to satisfy you. Bye, you stupid bitch!" He slams the door and drops the items on the ground.

Kade reaches out and wraps me in his arms allowing me to drown myself in tears.

My phone rings early in the morning. I look at the caller ID and immediately answer the phone. "Good morning, Celeste."

"Good morning, Nina. I hope I didn't wake you."

"No, you didn't. Is everything all right?"

"Yes, I'm just calling to invite you to Delia's house tonight."

"Celeste, I would love to, but it's really not a good idea. Josh and I didn't end things on good terms. I haven't seen him in a month. I think it's best if it remains that way."

"This isn't about my son. This is about me and I want you and Kade there. I already spoke to your mom and Marisol, they'll be attending also. Just because things didn't work out between you and Josh, doesn't mean I've stopped considering you family. Please be at Delia's house promptly at six this evening."

How can I refuse Celeste after she's been so welcoming and loving with me? "We'll be there."

Kade drives my mom's Denali while Marisol, my mom, and I along with Muscles enjoy being driven around. To be honest, the drive to Delia's house has my nerves and thoughts in disarray. The possibility of seeing Josh once again after this long, torturous month has my stomach turning. I wonder what news Celeste has in stored for us.

When we arrive, Delia immediately rushes out to greet us. Kade and I introduce my mom, Marisol, and Muscles. She's thrilled to meet them. "Marisol...the ocean and the sun. What a beautiful name." Delia announces. Kade is caught off guard by the meaning of Marisol's name. He stares at her as if it were the first time seeing her. He's as quiet now as he was then. I notice warmth in his eyes, instead of the indifference he usually regards her with.

Delia then directs her attention to me. "Nina! Bella as always!"

I thank her for her compliment. "Muchas gracias, Delia. You look stunning also." Delia has on several bracelets that cover up her wrists. She's wearing half a dozen necklaces and is completely dolled up. She loves dressing up, even if it's just to cook.

"Muscles, you *hanson* little man, I have *son* treats in the house. Would you like *son*?" Muscles smiles and nods his head eagerly. Listening to Delia's accent always brings a smile to my face. I absolutely love her.

When we enter the house, Celeste rushes me with a loving embrace. She makes her rounds and thanks everyone for

225

coming on such short notice. Delia's family and Josh are also in attendance. Immediately, I make it a point to avoid eye contact with him at all costs. Instead, I direct my attention to the large spread of food Delia has neatly laid out. When she cooks, she makes enough to feed a whole city. As an appetizer, she made a shrimp cocktail with her own twist. She prepared two main courses for dinner, pupusas with a vinaigrette cabbage salad that compliments the meal and yucca with chicharrón along with a homemade red salsa to enrich the flavors of the vegetable and pork. Overall, her feast looks and smells amazing.

Before dinner, Delia gathers everyone around the table and says a prayer with each of us holding hands. She thanks the Lord for our blessings, asks for forgiveness of our sins, and asks for protection of her loved ones along with the protection of those who are in need of His aid. She then makes a special request begging God to grant Celeste a long and healthy life. Before she ends her prayer, Delia breaks down and gently sobs. Josh hands her a tissue then he and Celeste wrap their arms around Delia providing her the strength she needs to complete her prayer.

As we sit together after dinner, Celeste announces she has stage III ovarian cancer and has decided to travel to a cancer medical center in Arizona for her treatments. As an added shock, she states she's leaving to the airport in an hour. Just as we're wiping our tears, Celeste reprimands everyone. "You need to stop that. I need positive vibes not cries. If we believe, all will turn out for the best. I'm sure of it. My son will be taking me to the airport. Valentina, will you join us?"

"Of course." I don't bother to look at Josh's reaction, for the moment, this isn't about us.

"Please..." Celeste looks at everyone. "Don't make this more difficult than it has to be."

226

Once Celeste says goodbye to her friends and family, we leave. Celeste sits in the back seat of Josh's truck claiming she needs to elevate her legs. I can't argue with that so I sit in the front passenger seat next to Josh. We remain silent, things couldn't be more awkward. As we're headed south on Highway 101, Celeste breaks the silence. "I can't believe you two are behaving worse than stubborn mules! Neither one of you is perfect, so why do you expect perfection from the other? Everyone is entitled to make mistakes. Forgive your partner, learn from the error, and move on. Holding grudges is blinding. It doesn't allow you to catch the blessings that are directed at you. It's not healthy to be bitter and allow pain to consume your heart."

Then Celeste focuses her attention solely on me. "Nina, can you tell me what my son's favorite meal is?"

Her question takes me by surprise. "Umm...It used to be breakfast, now I can't tell you what it is." I sadly reply.

"Son! Can you tell me what your favorite meal is?"

Josh seems agitated. "Mom, I have more important things to think about than food. I don't see where you're getting at."

"Answer the question." Celeste insists.

"I still love breakfast." Josh confesses as he clenches his jaw and looks straight ahead determined not to look my way.

"See, Nina! My son still loves you!"

I turn around to face Celeste. "What? How did you come up with that?"

"Your mom told me that you're secretly linked to my son's obsession with breakfast."

I cover my face from embarrassment. "No, Celeste. This conversation didn't just get weird."

Despite himself, Josh bellows out a thunderous laugh. "Mom, you're lucky I love you so much. Otherwise, I would've made you walk by now for being such a Meddling Maddy!"

When we arrive to SFO, Josh and I agree to stay with his mom until her flight departs. Celeste insists that we leave, stating the airport concierge is waiting for her in the departure section of the airport. When we find the airline Celeste is flying through, the concierge is promptly awaiting Celeste's arrival with a wheelchair beside him.

Celeste hastily says her goodbyes making every attempt to avoid eye contact. "Son, I'll see you on Sunday. Nina, I'll see you real soon. I love you both. While I'm away, I'll be thinking of additional names for my grandbabies. Do me proud." Celeste smiles cunningly and winks at us.

"Celeste!" I yell.

"Mom, you're too much! I think it's time you go to an old folks home, woman!"

"Bite your tongue, son! Bite your tongue!" With that, Celeste enters the airport ready to face the medical obstacles that await her.

I haven't gone to visit Diego in several weeks. I've been avoiding Michael and mostly keeping to myself. Whenever Diego writes me a letter, Michael drops it off with Kade. I correspond to Diego in the same manner. Today, I decide to surprise Diego with a visit.

I go through the routine procedure before I'm escorted to the visiting area. Once again, I'm allowed a contact visit instead of meeting with Diego in that tiny room with half a glass wall separating us. As I sit on the cold steel stool, I realize I'm actually excited to see Diego again. Our past can't be erased, but our present is work in progress that is headed in a positive direction. The sound of a heavy door opening interrupts my thoughts. Diego along with a correctional officer walk in. As they stand by the door, the officer takes off Diego's handcuffs, he stands behind the small podium, and turns on the radio to allow Diego and me a private conversation.

Diego approaches me with a genuine smile. "Hija! What a surprise! I'm so glad to see you." For the first time since I've met him, Diego wraps his arms around me and gently holds me in his arms. I welcome his embrace, it's comforting and full of love.

"I wanted to see you and catch up in person." I explain with tear filled eyes from joy. "Here...I brought you something."

"You brought ME something?" Diego's taken by surprise once again.

"Yes!" I laugh. "Don't get too excited. It's only food." I place the medium sized lunch cooler on the steel table that's between us. "I made you chicken parmigiana, lemon orzo, and a Mediterranean salad. My mom sends you cannoli and cheesecake. I hope you're hungry."

It takes Diego a minute to respond. I notice he swallows hard before he thanks me.

"Can I ask you a question?" I decide to ask since the curiosity has been eating at me lately.

"Yes." He tries to remain serious, but a hint of a smile escapes him.

"Why are you so positive that you won't be doing a lifetime prison sentence? How do you know you'll only be incarcerated for a few years?"

"Because I've had an arrangement with the U.S. government for over ten years. I was allowed to smuggle drugs into the U.S. in exchange for information on rival drug trafficking cartels, including all pertinent facts on Mateo Blanco. Not only was he U.S. agents' most wanted due to his power in the drug and weapons industries, but his capture also became personal to many agencies. You see...Blanco was responsible for the kidnapping, torture, and murder of a DEA agent. Blanco ordered the hit because he was upset the DEA agent insisted that Mexican officials do a raid on one of Blanco's 200-acre marijuana plantations. The DEA agent's body was found in a shallow grave within Blanco's cartel territory. At the time, I was Blanco's second in command, he bragged about this particular murder, so I was able to easily provide the information to the U.S. government ensuring Blanco never raised suspicion on me.

As I became independent and established my own drug organization, the Enemiga Cartel; my power, alliances, and information to the U.S. became more valuable. I led agents to a 25-ton cocaine seizure along with several other large confiscations of drugs, weapons, and leaders of rival cartels. U.S. agents were refrained from interfering with my organization's illegal activities and weren't allowed to actively prosecute me. This arrangement was authorized by high ranking officials and federal prosecutors. Remember the night Blanco was killed? Well, I led agents to him even if it meant I would be detained for some time."

I'm shocked at his confession. "But why are you still here if you have an agreement with the government not to be prosecuted?"

"The government doesn't want to bring light to the deal they made with the devil...in this case, me. Although high ranking officials authorized the agreement, not everyone in government is aware or would be in conformity with the arrangement made. Initially, I did earn most of my money from drug trafficking, but the last few years, my wealth came from the investments I made on legitimate companies and real estate projects throughout the world. I've been trying to build my empire through valid means. I'm still connected to the Enemiga Cartel because technically, I'm still the leader and with that position comes an immense power that opens several avenues for me." As an afterthought, Diego adds, "I haven't killed innocent people in years and I've never done business that includes human trafficking. By no means am I trying to minimize my offenses, I'm simply stating facts."

I analyze him closely. "When we first spoke, you stated you were probably going to do a life sentence. Did you lie to me?"

"No, I didn't lie. If I didn't have this arrangement, then prison would be my destiny. At the time, I didn't think you wanted anything to do with me. I didn't care about fighting my way out. I had given up on myself, but once you came to visit, you gave me purpose to fight once again. Immediately, I contacted my attorneys. Right now, they're just looking for ways to get me out that won't raise too many eyebrows, one option is a violation of due process. We'll see how that goes."

"Any news on AX?"

"The little shit continues to be up to no good. The Blanco Cartel which is now under his command got a hold of three women from a rival organization, they took them out to a field, then made them get naked while pointing AK-47s to their heads with the intention of murdering them. Instead of killing them execution style, they pushed the women to the ground while they were still alive, chopped off their heads then dismembered the rest of their bodies. These sick bastards recorded the heinous murders. In the video, you can hear those men sadistically laughing as they were committing those horrific acts."

I can't believe what I'm hearing. "How do you know about this?"

"It's on the internet, but their faces and bodies are completely covered. It took a while to locate the video, but if you search it, eventually you'll find the gruesome act." Diego states completely appalled.

"AX is a danger now more than ever. He's on a power rush

with absolutely no regard for human life. He doesn't get satisfaction from just killing people, he requires torture beforehand to be completely gratified with someone's death. How are you and Sancho getting along?"

I sigh. "Well, sometimes when I see him from a distance in his car, I'll bring him coffee or food. He always thanks me, but he never smiles. He's really intimidating. Sometimes, I feel sorry for him because he follows me around when I don't do much. I've only had someone follow me once, Sancho went after him, but couldn't catch up to whomever was stalking me. Other than that, there's no news to tell."

"Tell me about you and Emme. How are you two getting along?" Diego asks with a straight face as he takes a bite of his meal.

"Huh?" *Oh, shit. I know he knows I'm no longer friends with her, why is he testing me? Why do I feel like a five year old child who was just caught writing on the walls?*

Diego then does the unthinkable. He gives me "the look." *What the fuck? He knows that look too? Why does he appear so intimidating? I thought only moms possessed that power! Ugh!*

I decide honesty is the best policy in this case. "We haven't really spoken lately. We had an argument and haven't been in touch since."

Diego puts his fork down and stares at me with a grave face. "I have to get rid of her. Emme poses as a big threat to you and me. She knows too much information about us."

"What? No!" I cry. "You can't do anything to her! I can't live with that on my conscience!"

"Hija, if Emme seeks revenge or if AX gets to her, she'll tell him everything. She's a high risk that needs to be eliminated. Her name was included in the police report, that report is public information. Just because AX hasn't gotten a hold of her yet, doesn't mean that he won't."

"Please! I'm begging you!" I'm in complete hysterics now that I realize Emme might actually be killed. I may not be friends with her, but at one point, I loved her like a sister. "Please, dad! Don't do this!" For the first time, I acknowledge Diego as my father. I understand his dilemma, but I won't accept his solution.

"Hija." Diego seems completely heartbroken from causing me so much pain. "What if I send Emme away until her baby is born? I'll spare her child's life." He tries to compromise.

I'm stunned by his words. "What? Emme's pregnant? How far along is she?"

"I thought you knew that's why you want her alive so badly. She almost had an abortion but she couldn't follow through with it. I believe she's due the first week of October. Hija, remember...she betrayed you once, she'll do it again."

I stop listening to my dad and immediately start doing the math. Emme became pregnant in the beginning of January. At that time, she was with us every single day and spent every night with Kade.

Kade! OH, MY GOD! Kade's going to be a dad!

My tears are now uncontrollable. I'm in a frenzy over everything my dad has just informed me. "Please, dad! Don't hurt Emme. Don't do anything to her or the baby. I'm begging you. Kade is the father of that baby. He doesn't deserve this loss. Kade has saved me in so many ways, please don't do this to him...to me. Please leave Emme alone!" I beg frantically, desperate for my pleas to be heard.

Reluctantly, he agrees. "Okay." He sighs. "I can't tolerate seeing you suffer. It breaks me. Just know that I'll still send my men to speak with her. It's necessary she understands the only reason she's alive is because of you. If she opens her mouth to anyone about what she knows, I'll be the one who kills her with my bare hands."

Despite my father's threat, I exhale with relief.

Once our visit comes to an end, Diego and I both stand. I approach and embrace him tightly. He wraps his arms around me and kisses the top of my head. "Thank you, dad."

"I love you, Hija." He whispers.

I leave the prison with my thoughts in utter chaos. It's the afternoon and realize I haven't eaten all day. I was too caught up with my conversation with Diego to take a bite of anything. As I'm driving, my head is pounding fiercely. The news I received and my failure to eat today has taken a severe toll on me. Once I exit and see the first corner store, I stop to buy water, a chocolate bar, and some aspirin for my migraine.

I pray the pills kick in fast. As I'm approaching my car to head home, I sudden rush of dizziness hits me. Before I know it, everything goes black.

An annoying beeping sound wakes me. Slowly, I open my eyes. There's a curtain surrounding my sterile bed area. I notice an IV has been inserted into my right hand. I'm not able to comprehend much else. Just as my heavy lids are ready to shut once again, a female doctor opens the curtains then closes them behind her. "Hey there, sleeping beauty. How do you feel?"

I consider her question. "The back of my head hurts and I'm thirsty."

"Your head hurts because you fainted and hit your head on the curb of the sidewalk. Luckily, you and the baby seem to be fine. Regardless, I want to keep you overnight for observation. I'll start you off with ice chips and see how you do from there. How does that sound?" The doctor asks.

"The baby?" I ask despite the dryness in my throat.

"Oh. You didn't know you were pregnant. Well, hun..you're about six weeks along. Congratulations! You're going to be a mommy!" The doctor says with a bit too much enthusiasm then hands me a black and white picture of what...I have no clue. "Here's your baby's first picture! See that white/greyish jelly bean looking thing? That's your baby! How exciting is that?"

After that...I tune her out.

I'm pregnant. I'm having a baby and I don't know who the father is.

My chest tightens at the thought and my eyes swell, but I refuse to cry.

To Be Continued...

PIN ME

THE PINNED UP TRILOGY, BOOK III

Author's Biography

C. Michelle loves a good laugh...you know, the type that accidentally makes you snort. Yeah, that kind. Her love of all things funny, romantic, and bad ass led to the writing of her debut novel, *Pinned Up*. C. Michelle resides in northern California with her husband and three children. She is currently working on the completion of the Pinned Up trilogy. Initially, *Pinned Up* was written as a stand-alone novel, but since the characters continue to harass her during the middle of the night, while she's driving, when she's eating, and while she's running against her will...she decided to continue with their stories.

C. Michelle earned a Bachelor of Science in Business Management and a Master of Business Administration degree while working as a probation officer and probation counselor. She also served her community as a Victim Awareness Program Instructor and an Aggression Replacement Training Facilitator.

Visit her blog – cmichelle.com

Follow her on Twitter – twitter.com/cmichellewrite

Like her on Facebook – www.facebook.com/cmichelle.write

Follow her on Goodreads – www.goodreads.com/author/show/7064906.C_Michelle

www.ingramcontent.com/pod-product-compliance
Lightning Source LLC
Chambersburg PA
CBHW070750280626
47162CB00018B/2821